The Shot from the Mountain:
An Appalachian Odyssey

by
Claude S. Phillips

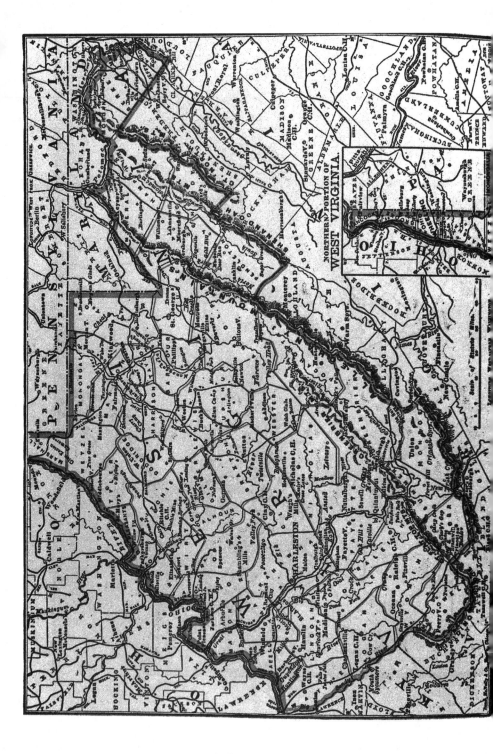

The Shot from the Mountain:
An Appalachian Odyssey

by
Claude S. Phillips

The Priscilla Press
Allegan Forest, Michigan
2004

To Nancy,
for her love and patience

and
to my good friends Harry and Delma Hatcher,
Roy and Priscilla Olton,
and Larry and Priscilla Massie who read various
drafts and offered encouragement.

PREFACE

I wrote this book because I felt that there was a moving story about the perils of coal mining during the 1920s and 1930s in West Virginia that would be of general interest. The protagonist of the story, Clyde Fuller, is a composite of coal miners I have known or who were described to me by my father, a coal miner. Clyde's personality and behavior, therefore, are fictional. But the work is more than fictional, in the sense that the environment of his actions was authentic and the struggles of his life occurred in historically significant settings.

I was raised in West Virginia and lived through my teen years in a number of coal mining towns, because my father was restless and always on the move. He worked in the mines for 38 years, having begun at age 13. Despite having black lung disease, he lived to age 83. He was a raconteur of some ability, and often around the supper table in the evening he regaled us with accounts of his youth and of people he knew. He told exciting, dreadful stories about tragedies in the mines leading to deaths. He especially described roof cave-ins, fires, explosions, runaway coal cars, electrocutions and every grisly experience he had seen as a miner. His objective was to discourage his sons from ever working in the mines and he succeeded quite well, since not one of the three of us ever thought of mine work.

Although I never worked in the mines, I remember well the experience of price gouging in company stores, the use of script instead of money, the company shacks that miners lived in during 1920s, the poverty of the Great Depression, and the appeal of fundamentalist religions to miners, which provided some meaning to their otherwise loathsome lives.

In the first third of the twentieth century, the coal mining areas of West Virginia were filled with turbulence due to the conflict between miners and mine operators over the question of unionization. At times, savagery was the only fit description of the relationship and many a miner paid the ultimate price for his drive to bargain over work conditions. Dramatic as these times were, I must say that my courses in West Virginia history in elementary and high school never alluded to them. I was only able to grasp the full significance of the times by extensive research, which undergirds the story told in the book.

Claude Phillips
South Haven, Michigan

Chapter One

Clyde Fuller, almost eighteen, a coal miner since he was thirteen, stood on a boulder on the New River in West Virginia. He looked at the clear blue water that flowed beneath him and wondered why it didn't look like the small black streams that flowed through the valleys of coal mining camps. He was pleased to get away from the pervasive sense of blackness that possessed him every workday. On Saturdays and Sundays he could escape his dreary workplace for a few hours. With his friend, Elmer, he'd loll on the banks of the beautiful river and fish. The giant rock from which they fished gave him a sense of stability in life that he did not find in the mines. The slight, warm breeze that gently rustled the tree leaves, which filled the mountains above him, merely added to his contentment.

Clyde acknowledged on many occasions that he didn't like working in the mines like a rat in a hole in the ground, but always followed this with the question of, "What else was a young man with only a fourth-grade education to do." Even so, almost five years in the pits had convinced him that he could make a living there, meager as it was, and possibly even get married some day. Marriage made him think of his one intimate encounter with Mary Ann, the only woman he had ever known in the biblical sense. If he was ever to get married, he was certain that he'd have to find a way to raise himself to a higher position in life than a mere menial laborer.

On this warm May Sunday of 1920, he was restless. Sitting on the edge of the boulder, then standing up, walking around and sitting again, he only perfunctorily watched his pole.

"What's ailing you?" Elmer asked. "You act like ants has crawled up your pants." He tossed his line with baited hook and watched it sink to the bottom in the clear water.

"I cain't rightly say," Clyde answered. "I wanna get away from here. . . . See some of the world. Do you know I ain't been no more than fifty miles from where I was born?" He casually watched the bob on his line for any sign of movement.

"Where would you like to go? Charleston? Or maybe Pittsburgh? I been to both of those places, 'bout 1910 or so, and they don't differ much from right here, 'cept they have large rivers runnin' through 'em, and lots of houses and stores and big buildings."

"Why not? I ain't never seen a large river or a big building. Can you get work there?"

"There ain't no coal mines right in the cities, but there are mines near by. I don't know if they're hirin' or not. If you just wanna get away, why I heard they're hirin' over in Mingo County. That ain't no improvement over here."

"What's wrong with it?"

"That whole county is owned by the Aggregated Coal Company, and they ain't got no concern for coal miners. The houses are shacks, and the company store sells everything at awful prices. But I heard they're offerin' higher wages to men who are willin' to work. That might mean strike breakin'."

"You mean they got a union?"

"No, not yet. What I heard was they was some men trying to organize a union and they all got fired. So the company is tryin' to hire more at better pay. As I heard it, there ain't no union yet. So I suppose if there ain't no union then it wouldn't be strike-breakin' to work there."

"Then I think I'll give it a try. How do you get to Mingo County?"

Clyde was thin and muscular with striking blue eyes that spoke of experiences belonging to much older people. His white teeth were set in a smiling face with a dimpled chin. Because his face was slightly

A glimpse of the New River Valley as seen in 2002.

rounded, he looked younger than he was. He combed his black hair straight back. Except for the elastic sock he wore on his right leg below the knee, he was in good health.

"What about your 'prenticeship as an electrician? That's good pay in the mines, you know," Elmer said.

"Yeah, I know, but that ain't the end of my desares. One of these days, I'm gonna know every position in the mines. I'm gonna be a fire boss some day, maybe even super. Right now, I just want to see the different mines."

From the boulder they were on, which overlooked a deep part of the river, they could see white water among the rocks upstream. "Did you know," Elmer said, "that this is one of the few rivers in the United States that flows north? This one starts in North Carolina, goes through Virginia, and comes by here on its way to the town of Gauley Bridge. There it joins the Gauley River to form the Kanawha River that flows into the Ohio. It's kinda queer how it starts up on the east side of the mountains and winds up on the west. Don't seem like it should be able to do that."

Elmer's left jaw protruded from the wad of Mail Pouch Tobacco he was chewing and he regularly spat a black hunk of the stuff into the river. He had high cheekbones, a face streaked with fine black lines from coal dust, and thin grey hair that he parted on the side. A missing front tooth exaggerated the other dingy teeth, which he exposed with an easy smile.

Each man had a line in the water, weighted to put the bait on the bottom to entice catfish. "Look at that one down there!" Elmer said. "He's going after your bait. There! He took it. Now reel him in gentle-like.

You've got it! Wow! That's got to weigh at least three pounds. Be careful and don't let those stingers get you."

Clyde pulled his catch out onto the rock, put his foot on the wriggling fish, removed the hook carefully, and then edged his trophy into a bucket. "This will shore make a nice meal," he said. "Where can we cook it?"

"Let's take it to my house. I'll fry it and heat up some corn bread I already have and we'll have a feast," Elmer said.

"Sounds good to me."

As they walked the five miles to Elmer's shack, the older man noted that it had already been four months since the Feds had closed his bar because of prohibition. "Right now, the only things I remember about that bar was it gave me a living and I got to meet you. The local police constantly tried to close me down, but a little money on the side kept them away . . . . Wonder what folks think about an old man like me running around with a young man like you?"

"Sixty-four ain't so old, an' you seem to be healthy."

"I guess I am at that, but these five-mile walks is beginning to tell on me."

"I don't care what people say. You're still my friend, and I don't care how old you are," Clyde said as they neared Elmer's two-room shack.

Elmer took some corn bread from the safe and then paused and looked at Clyde. "I like to see a young man with your kind of ambition, and darned if I don't believe you'll make it," he said, rubbing his hand across his thin hair. He lifted one of the lids on his cooking stove, dropped two lumps of coal onto the hot coals already there, and prepared the fish by spreading a little butter on the bottom of a skillet. He opened the heating oven above the stove and placed the corn bread in it. With a pan, he took some water from the heating tank at the right end of the stove and poured it into a basin, and allowed Clyde to to wash his hands. He then poured that water out the window.

"Excuse me, Clyde, but I gotta run out to the one-holer. Be right back," Elmer said as he dashed out of the house to the privy. Like many privies, Elmer's was rickety, leaning precariously to one side, with a five-point star cutout in the door, and an old Sears catalog on the floor. He returned shortly and got some clean water for himself.

When they were ready, he put large portions of the fish and hot corn bread on two plates and placed them on the small table, with cups of hot coffee. The leftovers he placed on the stove.

"Dig in, boy. This is a meal fit for a fire boss or even a super," Elmer said, smiling. He stared at his young friend. "You gotta lot of gumption to strike out to places you never been before. Reminds me of myself when I was your age."

"I gotta feelin' I gotta do somethin' different. So I'm gonna try to reach Mingo County."

Elmer remained silent for a few minutes. "I wonder," he said slowly, "if I could do somethin' like that again. It might be fun . . . . By golly, if you're really determined to go, I think maybe I'll go with you. Yes sir. That's what I'll do. I need a change, too. I been here for twenty years and it's time to move. Since I lost my bar, all I could find was a coal loadin' job, and that's too hard on me. Maybe, I'll find somethin' easier some-place else."

"Nothin' would please me more."

"Tomorra, we'll draw out the pay that's coming to us, and be ready to leave first thing Tuesday morning. Just pack your things in a pillowcase, 'cause a poke is too flimsy. We'll hop some freight trains and be there by afternoon."

"Thanks for remindin' me about the pay. I 'spect we'll need a few dollars before we find work .... You know, I never thought of it before, but are you married?"

"I was once, but my woman died in December of eighteen of the flu. It sure killed a lot of people. I seen wagons filled with bodies, and some of us simply dug graves as fast as we could to bury 'em. That's why I live here alone. I ain't got nothin' to hold me back."

"My folks was lucky. Not one of 'em died from the flu, but I know it was bad .... Boy, I'll say one thing, you sure know how to cook feesh. An' I like the thought that you'll go with me. Like I told you, I ain't been around this state much. I can learn a lot from you."

"Here in the south, it's just one mountain after another, and that's all we'll see on our way to Mingo County. Although each mountain has got its own name, all together, they're called the Appalachin Mountains or somethin' like that. C'mon now, finish the rest of this catfish. You're still growing and it'll do you some good."

"Thanks, Elmer, but I guess I'm about growed as much as I'm gonna. I'll eat the rest of that feesh, though."

"Good to see you do it. Go on home, now, and meet me here early on Tuesday."

"Okay, I'll see ya then. An' tomorra I'll stop by the payroll office," the young man said.

Clyde went to tell Uncle Charlie and Aunt Nell good-bye, and asked them to hold his rifles until he could return for them. They agreed, but Aunt Nell asked if he would also visit his father.

"No. I don't think I will. The Old Man Jack don't care much about me so I don't see no purpose in going over there." He had stopped referring to Jack Fuller as 'Dad' two years before. "Will you tell him good-bye for me?"

"Of course we will. I bet he'd like to see you even if he don't act like it."

"Me an' Elmer has to leave right away, so I don't have time now."

The following morning, Clyde and Elmer walked alongside the railroad tracks to the top of a long gradual grade, hoping the train would be slow enough there for them to grab a ladder.

"Listen," Elmer said. "That whistle tells us the train is probably coming around Polecat Bend. There ain't no sound as sweet as the whistle of a steam locomotive. By the sound of those drive wheels, I'll bet there's three engines pulling maybe a hundred cars loaded with coal. We'll be able to hop on this one, I'm sure, 'cause it'll be moving slow by the time it gets here. Why don't we get over there in the woods till the engines is past? No need to let 'em know we plan to hitch a ride."

They walked about twenty feet into the woods and disappeared into the new spring foliage. Leaning against a tree, they watched the three engines crawl by them. The engineer trickled sand on the rail to give the wheels more traction, the firemen shoveled coal into the huge furnaces, and great white clouds of smoke belched from the smokestacks.

Once the engines were further up the track, the two ran out of the woods and alongside a coal car. Elmer grabbed the ladder on the rear of one car, and Clyde grabbed the ladder on the front of the next car, and they maneuvered themselves into the triangular space at the end of each car. Elmer stepped gingerly across the coupling, into the same car Clyde was on. They had to sit on a narrow beam and put their feet, legs bent, on a piece of the framing, making sure they didn't dangle into the steel wheels. It wasn't comfortable, but it got them where they wanted to go. They hopped the train near Oak Hill, rode it to Crab Orchard, got another one to Mullins, and a third one that took them into Matewan, across the Tug River from Kentucky.

"Ya know," Clyde mused, staring at the steep, green, awesome mountains, and the rushing creeks that ran beside the tracks, "my Old Man Jack calls these valleys ditches. He said that people never could come together on anything, because the mountains kept them divided. Said there was no real sense of belonging together in this State, just a bunch of different little villages, each unconcerned with what's on the other side of the hill."

"Now that's interestin'," Elmer said. "But don't you think God made the mountains so people could avoid the big world. They's a lot of comfort bein' scrooched down here in the valleys where you're hard to find. I like it. Not many people around to bother you. I think of it as God's gift to a lot of lucky folks." He spat tobacco juice on the railroad ties beneath him.

"So you believe in God?," Clyde said. He changed positions often to relieve his elastic-bound right leg.

"Sure I believe in God, but I ain't sure he believes in me."

"I don't get ya."

"Well look, here we are ready and willing to work, and there's them good-fer-nothings like Rockefeller and Ford an' such people, who don't have to do a damn thing to live high like kings. If you ever get to White Sulphur Springs, you'll see how rich folks live. That's only about sixty or seventy miles from here. The people who go there don't ever worry about a thing. Now don't you think a good God would want to balance things a bit?"

"Didn't Jesus say there would always be poor people?"

"Sure he did, but don't that make you wonder about religion? Don't you think it's easier for Henry Ford to believe in God than for a miserable coal miner? After all, he's been blessed with more money than he knows how to spend, and we're lucky when we got a dollar that ain't already committed to somethin'."

"Ain't belief in God what gives poor folks hope? Even if they suffer now, someday they'll be in heaven and Ford will be in hell."

"That's what the preachers say, but what's the proof?"

"The Bible. Ain't the Bible true?"

"How do you know the Bible is true?"

"God says it's true right there in the Bible."

"Don't that bother you a little bit?" Elmer said, spitting his wad onto the ground. "The Bible is true 'cause God says it is. We know there is a God 'cause the Bible says so. That's like God is saying I exist 'cause I say so right there in the Bible that I wrote, and the Bible is true 'cause I said so. Seems to me we're going around in circles there. Seems to me there's got to be a way to show God exits without referrin' to the Bible, or that the Bible is true without referrin' to God. Now I don't know how to do that, do you?"

"Not when you put it that way. I just never thought of that before. Now that I think of it, there sure is a lot of sufferin' in this world, an' maybe God ain't the best way to explain it."

"That's a big subject, and I know I ain't gonna solve it. Maybe you can. You're still young and can figger things out."

"I got to think about that for a spell. Maybe talk to a preacher some time. It just ain't clear to me what religion is s'posed to do for a man."

"Well, religion supports preachers, so it's easy to see why they like it. It don't seem to make no difference how they act. Why, I seen preachers that could cuss and drink and raise hell, and I seen other people who don't believe in God who are kind and decent. 'Course, most of the men you see around coal mines ain't no preachers, although some of 'em are kind and decent. Wonder why coal towns is so full of fightin'? Why, last week over in Eccles, I seen two miners fightin' over a woman and one stabbed the other with a penknife. Can you believe it? Just a little penknife? Stuck him in the side and hardly bothered the man at all. People had to pull them apart. And just a year ago, in Sophia, one miner shot and killed another with his pistol, just because he bumped him as he entered the door of a cafe. Many miners carry a pistol right in the mines. Why, some of the fights between miners is like the Hatfields and McCoys."

"I know. I seen a lot of fights, too. My Old Man Jack says miners is hard drinkin' and hard fightin' 'cause they work like rats in a hole in the ground. He says it ain't fit work for a human."

"He may be right, but if minin' is all there is what else can a man do?"

An early novel about coal mining published in 1902,
Those Black Diamond Men, **by William F. Gibbons contained**
this photograph of miners hard at work.

"The way I see it, mine foremen and supers got it easier than a coal loader, and that's why I'm gonna try to better myself."

"Sometimes you ain't got no choice, 'specially if you're married and got children. If you get married soon, then I'm afraid it'll interfere with your ambition. You willing to put off marriage till you better yourself?"

"I shore ain't in no hurry, lessen I can find a woman as good as my mama. She worked as hard as any man. That's the kind of woman I want, one who will help me git ahead."

"Good luck! I 'speck most young men can't wait till they find the right woman. Soon as they find a pretty woman with nice tits, they look fer a preacher, and then discover marriage ain't made in heaven. I hope you do better."

"I'm gonna try, you wait an' see."

"You sure got spunk, so maybe you'll do it."

As they neared Matewan, Elmer said, "Let's hop off the train here and walk in. We'll get the layout of the place better. By the way, Matewan is an independent town. It don't belong to the company."

The village of Matewan was a nothing place. The valley spread out somewhat and allowed the makings of a small town. The houses were jammed together, along with a road, a creek, and the main railroad. A little further down the West Virginia side of the Tug River, lined up parallel to the railroad, were the post office, company store, company office, bank, and hardware store. Across the tracks from the hardware store was the depot. On the edge of town was a tipple, and feeder railroad lines that collected coal at the tipple and stored the loaded cars, until the engines could attach to them. As Clyde and Elmer approached the village, they came to the first shacks located on the edge of Matewan and under the control of the company. "That's odd," Elmer said. "Those places seem to be empty. There's nobody around. Look over there at those houses. Why, they're packed together tighter than coal dust and ain't even good imitations of places for humans to live. I don't see how they could crowd any more on the side of that mountain. Families practically live on top of each other. Some fronts of those places are resting on posts eight to ten feet high, while the backs is on the ground. I don't think they've ever been painted. That stink you smell comes from their privies, sunk so shallow they are allowed to overflow and run down the hill. Look, there's only a water pump for every four or five houses. I ain't sure we want to stay 'round here. Maybe we should try to get to Logan."

"Don't people complain about such housing?"

"'Course they do, but the super tells them to build their own houses. Then he tells them it won't be in this valley, cause the company owns everything from the top of one mountain to the top of the other mountain, except right in town. Then he tells 'em they can always move if they want to."

"Maybe we should go to Logan," Clyde said.

"Now that we're here," Elmer said, "let's go on in and see Matewan."

They walked another ten minutes when Elmer said, "Look up ahead. There's a bunch of men all dressed up not far from the hardware store, but there don't seem to be nobody else on the street. I guess we ought to go on and see what it's all about."

As they got nearer, Clyde said, "Look at that! Those men are all wearing coats, vests, and pants that match. They even have on neckties and black shoes that shine like the edge of a lump of coal. I never seen nobody that dressed up around a coal mine. They must be really important."

A large man separated himself from a small group and walked toward the two newcomers. "What do you want here?" he demanded.

"Who are you? Why should I talk to you?" Elmer said.

Without any warning, the big man hit Elmer square in the face with his fist, knocking him down.

"We jest come here lookin' for work," Clyde said, as he turned to help his friend.

The big man turned to his comrades and shouted, "They're looking for work. Should we give them a job?"

"Sure. Why not?" a man answered back and then added, "Watch out, Avery, he's got a club!"

As Elmer got up, he picked up a tree limb about three feet long lying between the tracks, and hit the big man on the head from behind.

The man stumbled and almost fell to the ground, but righted himself in the process, pulling a pistol from a shoulder holster. He shot Elmer three times, killing him instantly. He looked at Clyde and said, "Do you want the same thing, boy?"

"Why did you hafta shoot my friend, you bastard?" Clyde said as he knelt beside the lifeless body and almost cried. He had never seen a man lying dead anywhere, except in a casket, and certainly not between railroad tracks. The overpowering reality he was trying to capture, as he gazed at his friend, was that he had just been talking to Elmer only a few seconds ago. Now he was dead and gone forever. Was this when a person goes to heaven, he wondered? He touched Elmer's eyelids, closing them.

"Look out, men. I think this one's going to cry," the big man said, then he turned to Clyde. "I've killed men for calling me a bastard, but you're just a boy . . . and not a very bright one, if you're wearing long johns in this kind of weather. Pull up your pants legs and let me see what you're wearing."

Clyde stared at the man and made no move to obey.

"Hell, boy, you ain't got no sense," the man said as he shot between Clyde's legs. "Do you want me to kill you just because I want my friends here to see your long johns? Pull 'em up, or by God, I'll do it."

Clyde reached down and raised his pants' legs, revealing a pinkish elastic sock on his right leg.

"Well. Look at that! The boy's crippled. You're in luck, because today I don't feel like shooting no cripple, even one who called me a bastard. Get your friend's body out of here and bury him. Then leave town. Do you understand me?"

Clyde refused to answer. He took Elmer's arms and raised the body as high as he could. Then stooping, he quickly allowed it to fall across his right shoulder and raised up carrying the corpse and both pillow cases. He walked to the grocery store where he saw a man who was clearly not one of the well-dressed ones.

"Can you tell me if there's a cemetery here?"

The man looked to see if any of the well-dressed men were going to interfere. Then he said, "Yes. Just down the road there, beyond the tipple. I'll get a shovel and join you."

The man darted into the store and emerged with a shovel and caught up with Clyde. They continued until they came to a cemetery. Without saying a word, the man went to a spot and started digging. Generally, three inches under ground in southern West Virginia is rock. The man had chosen a spot he obviously knew, where water had washed topsoil down into a small crevasse. He was able to dig a trench that was two feet deep and helped Clyde bury Elmer. Before lowering the body, Clyde took Elmer's wallet out of his pocket.

"Do you want to say some words over him?" the man asked.

Clyde, without yet having spoken a word, arose, doffed his cap and said, "Elmer was good to me. I liked him."

Then with the quickness of a panther living in the surrounding mountains, Clyde grabbed the man's coat. "Who are you? Who are those men? What's going on here? Where is everybody?"

"Just turn me loose. I'll explain everything." Clyde released the man and waited.

"Those goons over there are so-called detectives from Bluefield, but their headquarters is in New York. The Company hired them to make sure nobody joins a union. When it was discovered that all the miners in Matewan had already met and were going to form a union, the Company fired them all and brought those goons here and drove everybody from their houses. Those thugs are waitin' around for the next train to get their orders on what to do next. That's why there ain't nobody else on the street. They're afraid to cross the

sons of bitches. I saw that big man kill your friend.
He's the chief of this bunch, named Avery Murphy. His
two brothers, Homer and Cedric, are with him and just
as mean. There are a few people right now in the stores
and bank, but they avoid those men as much as possible. I don't think there's a miner among them. Most of
the mining families left and are trying to find work
some place else. The rest are living in tents up on the
top of that mountain. Most of them have huntin' rifles
and shotguns, so I expect that maybe there'll be a
shootout of some kind."

"If you seen what happened, then we can get the
sheriff to arrest him. He'll go to prison, for that was out
and out murder."

"Oh, it was murder all right. All those goons have
been deputized by the sheriff, so they're all law
enforcement officers. The sheriff won't arrest his own
men. Besides, he's on the payroll of the Company. So's
the prosecutor and all the judges in this part of the state.
They all hate labor unions and will drive out or kill any
miner who even talks about a union."

"Do the owners want this to happen?"

"Actually, the owners sometimes don't even know
what's happenin'. They don't live in the coal towns, but
in Charleston, or Pittsburgh, or Baltimore, and such
places. All they do is hire the operators and tell them to
do whatever is necessary to get the coal mined. When
there's deadly violence, the owners always say that
they're sorry that the operators misunderstood their
wishes and hurt people."

"There are other people in that hardware store,"
Clyde observed. "They must've seen the murder.
Maybe they'll testify?"

"Don't count on it. People that ain't miners just try to avoid gettin' involved. Besides, they don't want to cross the mine operators who control all the land around here, except right here in town. What I've heard is that the chief of police, Sid Hatfield, is due to arrive here on the next train in about an hour. He's a miner himself and the only policeman I know who ain't owned by the mine operators. He don't like the goons and has said he intends to arrest 'em."

"Why are you telling me this? Why aren't you up there with those other people?"

"I'm John Kavalli, manager of the grocery store. The thugs make me stay here so they can have some place to buy things." He was a small man, slightly bent, with a bland-looking face, thin brown hair, a hooked nose, and eyes that seemed to search constantly in all directions.

"How can I get up there where those miners are?"

"Take that path right over there. You'll come to a couple of open spots, so go around them into the woods, 'cause they can be seen from the valley. It's better to let those thugs think you run away. Good luck."

"Much obliged for all your help. I'd better get going before it gets too late. Think I can make it up there in an hour?"

"Yeah, I think so. What's your hurry?"

"I got things to do. So long."

Chapter Two

Clyde took the path and started the steep climb. That, however, was one thing in which he was experienced. He was careful not to expose himself to the valley and soon approached the top. Once he stopped to rest and examined Elmer's wallet, which had eighteen dollars in it. That, added to his own thirty-one dollars, provided the only money he had. The clean clothes, shaving brush, and razor he transferred to his own pillowcase.

Twice, as he climbed, he thought he heard someone or something behind him but when he turned to listen saw nothing. Another time, he heard a train come into the valley tooting its mournful whistle, pause for a few minutes, and proceed onward. As he continued up the path, suddenly, from behind a large tree, a man with a rifle stepped in front of him.

"Where do you think you're going, young man?"

"I'm hopin' to find the miners that are camped up here."

"Why do you want to do that?"

"I'm a miner myself."

"You? You ain't old enough to be a miner."

"I been in the mines 'bout five years now. Started as a trapper boy when I was thirteen, then became a loader, an' even laid some track, and studied some electricity."

"Where?"

"In Fayette County, near Oak Hill, at the United Coal Company. We're in the New River seam."

"What do you want here?"

"My friend and I heerd there was work available

A trio of Juvenile coal miners as pictured in Gibbons' 1902 novel.

here, so we wanted a change and come here. We didn't know about the goons and all you people up here. One of those goons knocked my friend down when he refused to answer questions. Then my friend hit him with a piece of tree limb, and the goon shot him dead. I never seen nothing like it. He jest shot him like he was a rabbit." Clyde paused and looked away from the man.

"The son of a bitch shot him, just like that?"

"That's right. The storekeeper, John Kavalli, helped me bury him and told me you was up here. You got a place I could spend the night?"

"Yeah, I got a cot in my tent you can use. I sure hope Sid Hatfield learns about that killin'."

"Yeah. Kavalli told me he's expected. Maybe he was on the passenger train I heerd. Maybe he'll do something about the killer.

"Say," Clyde said, "have you got a extra high-powered rifle I could borrow for about an hour? I'd like to see if I can get a squirrel before dark. It'll help pay my keep."

"Sure, I got that rifle right here. Has a telescopic sight on it. Would you like someone to go with you?"

"No, I'd druther not. Look. Every thing I own is in this pillowcase. Ain't much, but I sure don't want to travel far without it. Hold it 'til I get back. Here, I can also leave twenty dollars with you. I'll return your rifle, I swear. If somebody goes with me, he might scare the squirrels, or maybe see somethin' he ort not see."

"I believe you," the miner said. He was thin all over including his face, and appeared to stare out of sunken eye sockets. He handed Clyde the rifle and three bullets. "We can't afford to waste bullets, you know, so I hope you get your squirrel on the first shot. 'Course, we need to practice now an' then, so when we hear your shot we'll do a little practice shootin' ourselves. That way, if anybody wants to know who was shootin', we'll tell them we was."

Clyde got the message and the rifle. He could see at least fifty tents scattered among the trees, and at least one hundred ragged women and children. Large trees were scattered randomly along the ridge, with heavy undergrowth beneath them, which the miners had to clear for the tents. Clyde wondered if any of them would try to survive through the winter in such a beautiful yet lethal place.

He headed out the ridge, walking fast for about fifteen minutes and figured he was straight up the mountain from the store. Once he stopped when he thought he heard some movement below him, but moved on when he didn't hear another sound. He was among virgin oaks, beeches, elms, pines, ironwood, hickory, and poplar trees. Some of them were eighty or more feet in height. He spied a magnificent oak with huge branches only a few feet off the ground, and was able to climb up twenty feet and out another twenty feet from the main trunk. From that position, by moving some foliage aside, he saw that the hardware store was below him. Some of the well-dressed men were milling around the store, and appeared to be looking at something out of Clyde's sight. There were other people at the front of the hardware store who clearly were not dressed as the detectives.

He laid the barrel of the rifle over a limb, and using the telescope on the gun, found the big man who had shot Elmer. He was standing near the door of the store with some other men. Clyde took careful aim and gently squeezed the trigger. He saw the man fall, as the sound of the shot reverberated through the hills. It was followed almost immediately by a volley of shots emanating from around the store and the depot. Hastily, he descended from the tree and listened. He felt certain that he heard at least one hundred rounds fired from pistols, shotguns, and rifles. Quickly, he retraced his steps through the woods. Before he reached the tent camp, he heard six rifle shots, apparently in front of him and not coming from the valley. He went to the tent of the man who loaned him the rifle and handed the gun back to him, with two bullets.

"I hate to say it, but I hit the squirrel and then let him get away. I didn't see no more. I 'preciate the chance to hunt. They sure was a lot of shootin' down in the valley. And I heerd you target practicin' too."

"Yeah, we did do a little target shooting, but before that we heard all that shootin' in the valley. No one's left our camp, and no one's come here, so we don't know what it means. Well, anyway, you got your chance to hunt. Now we better get you that cot ready for sleepin'."

"No, I've changed my mind. My being here might get you in trouble. Do you have maybe some bread I could take with me? I think I'll head over the ridge and see what's in the next valley."

"Sure, we got some bread you can have, and some jam too. Here, take them." He handed Clyde a generous chunk of bread wrapped in a newspaper, and a small glass jar, half filled with the precious fruit derivative. "Over in that next valley you ought to catch a freight train that'll take you into Logan. It'll be going to your right. There won't nobody know you was ever here. Here's your sack and your twenty back. Goodbye and good luck." No names were exchanged.

Dusk had set when Clyde, descending the other side of the mountain, emerged alongside a railroad track. He heard the sound of a train coming toward him, and hoped it would be going to his right, toward Logan. A heavily loaded coal train, seventy-five cars long with three engines, soon lumbered into sight, headed in the right direction. Clyde tossed his sack onto a beam in the triangle of a car and ran along-side for a number of steps before grabbing a handhold and swinging up. He miscalculated slightly, however, and his right leg hit a sharp corner of the car.

"Damn!" he exclaimed, as he positioned himself in the moving car and pulled up his pants leg to look at a tear in his elastic sock. It was surrounded by blood. He took a large red bandana from his bag and wrapped the leg, hoping to stop the flow. An hour and a half later, when he got off the train in Logan, he was limping. It was now almost nine at night and he wondered where he might find a doctor at that hour. He only had forty-nine dollars on him, and wanted to make it last as long as possible, yet he was certain that it was wise to have the leg looked at even if it cost money.

"Say, mister," he said to a stranger, "do you know if there's a doctor near by? I hurt my leg and need to find one."

"At this time of night, you'll have to go to the hospital, about ten blocks that way."

He found the hospital and, limping badly, tracked blood as he entered a frame construction that had once been an impressive home. A nurse saw him and had him on a gurney immediately. She called a doctor, who came right away.

"Young man, it looks like you got a problem. I'm Doctor Milton Hedley. Let's see what's going on here." He was avuncular in appearance, with bushy brown hair, heavy eyebrows, and small rimless glasses. Carefully, he took the red bandana off. "I'm going to have to cut that blood-soaked elastic sock off. What happened to you?"

"I hit a sharp corner with the leg."

"No, I mean in the first place. Why the elastic sock?"

"A horse fell on me when I was twelve. Is that gonna heal all right?"

"Give me time to get this sock off first . . . aah, there now. Say, that's one ugly looking leg. Still, that bleeding is where you hit it. If we can get that stopped, it ought to look as good as it did when you put that sock on this morning." He worked in silence for a while, got the bleeding stopped and bandaged the wound. "There now, that looks better. But I got to tell you, you can't walk on that leg for at least a week. When I say you can't walk on that leg for a week, do you understand that I mean every word? If you act brave and walk on it anyway, then there is a high likelihood you'll lose the leg. I'm surprised you haven't lost it already. Do you understand how serious this is?"

"Yes sir, I understand. I'll do whatever it takes to keep my leg. Do you have some crutches here?"

"I'm pleased to hear you say that. Yes, we have some crutches. We're going to move you to a bed, so you can spend the night here. By the way, what's your name?"

"Clyde Fuller."

"All right, Clyde. I'm going to give you a sedative to make you sleep. I'll look at the leg again in the morning. If everything looks all right, then we'll arrange for crutches. I want to see you every day for a week. Is that clear?"

"Yes, sir. I'll do what you say."

Clyde slept soundly under the sedative, but awakened before the hospital began to buzz. The events of the previous day hit him with force. He could see Elmer dying under the totally unexpected fusillade of bullets that snuffed out his innocent life. Then Clyde himself had put one bullet into the man who shot Elmer, but there was no way to know whether he had killed the oaf or not. No one had seen him shoot the man, so even the miners on the mountain, if they were forced to talk, could not say what he had done when he went squirrel hunting. Still, he wondered if the police were looking for him, and if he should confess to the shooting. What if the man was still alive? It would be foolish, he thought, to confess to merely wounding a man. Besides, the police would want to know where the rifle was that he used. If he told them the truth, he'd get a lot of innocent miners in trouble. He decided to keep quiet and see what developed.

A tray of food was brought to him. He wolfed it down, for he had not eaten anything since breakfast yesterday, except for the bread and jam given him by the miners. The doctor arrived at eight-thirty and tossed a newspaper at Clyde.

"I assume you can read. The news might take your mind off yourself. Seems like there isn't much news these days that doesn't deal with violence. Only last evening, there was some kind of shootout over in Matewan. Company detectives against the chief of police and a bunch of miners. If you don't want the paper, I'll give it to one of the nurses."

"No. I can read. Much obliged."

"Think nothing of it." The doctor removed the bandages and exclaimed, "Aah, that looks much better. I'll re-wrap this and get you some crutches, and you can do whatever you have to do in town. Did you say you were from Fayette County? I know a doctor who practices over that way, for the United Mining Company."

"Sure, I know him. He's the one who first treated my leg, after the horse fell on it. Named Doctor Stevenson."

"Yep, that's the one. Looks like he did a pretty good job in saving your leg. Now, I expect you'll be even more careful with it."

"I'll do whatever I can to keep that leg."

"Are you just passing through?"

"I got a ride in yesterday with a man comin' from near Oak Hill. I heerd there was work in this area and come to look. I was lookin' for a place to stay last night when I . . . uh, run into the corner of a big box in the road that I didn't see."

"That is consistent with the kind of wound you have. Is your friend still here?"

"What friend?"

"The one you got a ride with. I was thinking he might take you back home, and you could let that leg heal some more."

"Oh, him. No. I don't even know his name. I hitched a ride with him. I think he said he was going to

Huntington, or someplace." Clyde did not know where Huntington was, but as he was limping to the hospital the night before, he heard one man tell another he was going to that city. He was troubled by the thought that lying was getting easier for him.

"That's all right. You can get a room here and come see me every day, until I tell you when you can walk on that leg again. Understood?"

"Yes. I'll do it. Maybe I can get a room nearby?"

"There are a number of rooming houses within a block of here, to the right when you leave the building. Why don't you come back here tomorrow about ten o'clock?"

"All right. . . . Uh, Doctor Hedley, could I ask you something?"

"Of course. I bet you want me to write your parents?"

"No. My mama is dead and the Old Man Jack don't care much for me. You're an educated man, an' I was wonderin' if you could explain how all this fightin' around the mines got started."

"Well now, that's a big order and I've got patients to see. I understand they don't teach much about mining in the schools, which is a shame, since it is the most important entrepreneurial activity in the State, and has been since most of the timber has been cut. I'm pleased to see a young miner interested in history. I don't see that often. I can take a few minutes to enlighten you, I suppose. You probably know that West Virginia was mid-wifed by the Civil War because mountaineers, who had no plantations and therefore no slaves, saw no advantage in breaking up the country. You already know that the State is home to vast strata of precious coal. Absentee landowners managed to get control of it all about fifty years ago." He paused as if deciding whether he wanted to say more.

Clyde said, "I don't know about such things."

"I didn't think so. West Virginia," Doctor Hedley continued, "is the saddest State: small, nature's bounty, indescribable beauty, scandalous wealth for a few, and poverty for the many . . . isolated . . . backward. It is a green forested blanket with deep wrinkles lying between the south flowing Ohio and north flowing Shenandoah, home to the eternal New River and the historic Potomac. Valleys so deep that sunshine is limited." He looked at nothing in particular as if talking brought painful memories.

Clyde stared at him.

Hedley continued, "Hardy inhabitants fled the sea coast in the eighteenth and nineteenth centuries, to gain

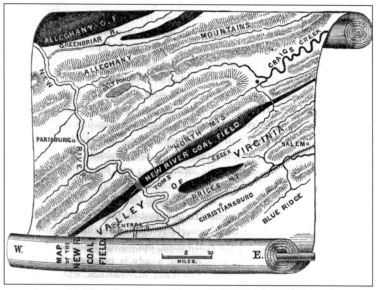

An early work on coal mining published in 1866 featured this map of the New River Coal Field.

seclusive security from being where few others wanted to be." He looked at Clyde and wondered if the lad was comprehending what he said. He started to rise from his chair and then, changing his mind, settled down again.

"The extreme tensions between miners and coal operators in the southern part of the State could be traced to opportunity, greed, and extreme capitalism. As early as 1890 or 1900, in the northern region, operators and mine unions met together and agreed on a wage scale, based on different environmental conditions. Haulage rates and distance from markets were calculated so as to be fair to all areas, which gave all operators a level field on which to market the precious mineral. The union accepted these conditions, since they promised more security. I know these things because my father was one of the union negotiators."

He rubbed his chin and added, "he was killed in a gas explosion two years ago . . . . He scrimped and saved enough money to send me to medical school . . . I sure miss him."

"I'm sorry. I didn't mean to make you sad," Clyde said.

"It's all right. It's just that some of these things are pretty fresh on my mind. About twenty years ago, huge deposits of coal were discovered here in the southern region, and the operators who opened those new mines were not bound by the earlier accomodation. The new operators announced that they would not permit unionization under any conditions, which allowed them to pay lower wages and thus threaten the survival of mines outside their region. The southern operators, however, forced the miners to sign 'Yellow-Dog Contracts,' saying that they would never join a labor organization. The southern operators refused to meet with miners as a group, and hired special guards, known as 'private detectives,' to drive away any miners suspected of being pro-union. By these developments, unionization in the north became threatened, emboldening the leaders there to take whatever action seemed necessary to defeat the southern operators. Both the northern operators and the unions felt that the southern companies were their enemies. That's the situation you've got yourself into. Do you really want to work here?"

"Not when you put it that way. Thanks for telling me about things. I never heerd of that stuff before. It's shore interestin'."

"No trouble. Good luck."

It was into this environment that Clyde Fuller, crippled and almost illiterate, was destined to find his position in life.

Violence and savagery, however, were not peculiar to the inhabitants of West Virginia during the first third of the twentieth century. Nevertheless, those people connected with coal mining, especially in the southern part of the State, faced both on a regular basis. Violence to human bodies was endemic to coal mines: from cave-ins, gas explosions, electrocution, carelessness, and poor management. Every miner knew every day of his life was precarious. Savagery, however, stemmed from the peculiar relationship of two groups of people: mine operators, who were intensely committed to running the mines without dealing with labor unions, and miners, who were just as intensely committed to forming unions. Unions, consequently, were the constant subject of conversation among miners.

Chapter Three

Doctor Hedley went on his rounds, and Clyde worked with a nurse who adjusted the crutches for him. He stuffed the newspaper in his belt, wrapped the end of the pillowcase around his wrist, and made his way carefully to the street. Four houses away, he saw a sign, "Rooms to Let," and made his way there laboriously. The landlady showed him a room on the first floor for seventy-five cents a night, four dollars a week, or eight dollars if he wanted board. Clyde took the room and board for a week, then closed the door and sat down. Quickly, he opened the newspaper dated May 20, 1920, the first one he had ever tried to read. With effort, he read the headline: "Mayor and Others Killed." Hands trembling, he started down the column, painstakingly uttering each syllable out loud:

"A small war occurred in Matewan yesterday, as the chief of police led a group of armed miners against a group of company detectives. When it ended, seven detectives, the mayor of Matewan, and two miners lay sprawled either on the road or railroad tracks, or in the doorway of the hardware store.

"The sequence of events is not clear. Apparently, the mayor, John Sitco, Sid Hatfield, and the miners, were con-

Miner's friend Sheriff Sid Hatfield and his twin pistols.

fronting the group of detectives at the entrance of the hardware store. Suddenly, a shot rang out and the chief of detectives, Avery Murphy, fell. At the same time, Hatfield was seen drawing both of his pistols and he and the miners with rifles began shooting. Return fire came from the detectives, who pulled their weapons from shoulder holsters. The mayor was mortally wounded, and three or four detectives died. As the other detectives scattered, the miners picked them off. A dying detective rolled over and fired one shot at a miner, who died on the tracks.

"The mystery involves the question of who fired the first shot. Some miners say the shot seemed to them to come from up on the mountain, but others said Avery Murphy pulled his pistol and shot the mayor. Hatfield said he shot Murphy after Murphy killed the mayor. Murphy's brother, Homer, was also killed, but his brother, Cedric, survived along with three other detectives. The three detectives say that Hatfield fired the first shot, the one that killed Avery. Cedric Murphy, however, said that during the confrontation he was sure he heard a shot from the mountain that killed his brother.

"The detectives had arrived in town only two days ago, and drove all the miners from their homes. Some miners went elsewhere looking for work, some took their families to other places and then returned to fight with the chief of police, and some families moved to a temporary tent camp on top of the mountain.

"A spokesman for The Aggregated Coal Company said he believed the miners were planning to form a union. 'The Company,' he added, 'had no choice but to fire the Reds and, of course, we couldn't let them live in our houses unless they worked for us. We'll need those houses for new hires.'

"Sid Hatfield said he investigated the alleged shot from the mountain. He informed this paper that there was no evidence that any of the miners in the tents had killed the detective. Instead, he said he had killed the detective after the latter had pulled his pistol and shot the mayor.

"Hatfield also reported that there were rumors that the store manager had seen Murphy shoot a man in cold blood and that he had helped a companion bury the victim. Hatfield said he examined the grave himself and determined that it was indeed a fresh burial, but the identity of the victim remains unknown. It was rumored that there had been a young man with the victim, but he had run away shortly after the killing and his whereabouts is unknown. The store manager,

John Kavalli, has himself also disappeared."

The paper went on to give details about each of the victims in the Massacre of Matewan, as the paper insisted on calling the catastrophe. An editorial, uncharacteristically placed on the front page, said, "As long as miners are hell bent on forming unions, the mine operators will be forced more and more to resort to violence to protect the American way of life."

Clyde had grown weary reading that far and acknowledged that he did not understand the meaning of some of the words. He put the paper down and concluded that only he and God knew who had killed Murphy. In an attempt to be humorous, he said aloud, "If God don't tell, then I won't. Besides, it's possible that a shot from Hatfield's group was actually the fatal one."

He looked about his room which contained a bed with a thundermug under it, a dresser with a mirror, and a small bookcase. Clyde had never been in a room with a case filled with books, and could not imagine who might read them. He examined the case carefully and recognized a black leather-bound Bible. Tediously, he read the titles on the spines of the other books: *The Last of the Mohicans, Ten Thousand Dream Interpretations, Proofs that the Pope is the Antichrist, Little Women, The Legend of Sleepy Hollow, Tom Sawyer, Up From Poverty, The Rover Boys, Can Jews be Loyal Americans?, The True Story of the Spanish American War, David Copperfield, Can Catholics be Christians?, Should Negroes be Permitted to Go to College?,* and *Bible Stories for Children.* It took every bit of learning he had to struggle through the titles, but added to his growing awareness that he ought to learn to read better. He committed himself to trying to see a newspaper every day, if possible.

He was called to dinner at six o'clock and joined three other roomers, all men. All three wore dress suits and had shiny shoes, while Clyde had on an open-neck grey shirt, denim pants and brogans. He told himself that someday he would be dressed as the men were.

"Well, young man, you seem to have a bit of trouble getting around," said the oldest of the men. He was distinguished looking and fat, with white hair. "I'm Leroy Gant, of Pittsburgh Steel Supplies, on the road trying to sell steel products to the mines. This here is Harvey Spelling who sells patent medicine, and this is Doctor Arnold Farthingham, a mining engineer. Who might you be?" Spelling was nearly bald, slight of build, with a red face. Farthingham was tall, with a long mustache, a square-jawed rugged face, and sharp blue eyes, all crowned by thick eyebrows and an explosion of dark brown hair.

"I'm Clyde Fuller from Fayette County and a coal miner."

"A coal miner? At your age? That just doesn't seem possible," Gant said.

"I have to make a living somehow."

"Of course you do. But shouldn't you be in school? You must not be more than seventeen."

"I'm eighteen," Clyde responded, determined not to lie about his age any further.

"What does an eighteen year old know about the mines? Are they starting you in as a trapper boy?"

"No. I did that when I was thirteen. I have also loaded coal and laid track, and have studied electricity a little bit."

"I know that is hard to believe," Doctor Farthingham said to the others, "but I've run into this sort of thing all over the southern part of this God-forsaken State. Taking kids out of school just so they can get a job in the mines. Is that how you hurt your leg, Clyde?"

"No, I hit it when I jumped . . . well, I tripped over a wooden crate I didn't see in the street." Why, he wondered, was lying getting easier?

"I hope you won't be on the crutches long."

"The doctor says I probably can walk again next week. I hope so, 'cause then I have to look for work."

"So many people have been fired in Matewan," Gant said, "that I'm sure you can find work there, but it's probably not a safe place to work, since that bunch of Reds killed so many guards. I certainly wouldn't work in a mine that was not well guarded."

"I was in Blair last week, and they're hiring now," said Farthingham.

"Much obliged," Clyde said. "I sure don't want to work in Mingo County. Where's Blair?"

"It's here in Logan County."

"I think I wanna get away from here, maybe a little farther north."

"They're hiring in Kanawha County, too," Doctor Farthingham said.

"Then maybe I'll try there." Clyde liked the feeling of being an adult talking casually with other adults.

"I'd rethink that, if I were you," Gant said. "Here in Logan County, you don't have to join a union to work. Free men shouldn't have to bow to the wishes of a gang of socialists."

"That seems pretty harsh to me," Farthingham

said. "I've known a lot of union men who weren't socialists, who simply wanted to be organized in defense of their interests as the operators are in defense of their's."

"I'm sorry to say it, Doctor Farthingham, but I find that view naive. There are not only socialists among the unionists, but also communists, syndicalists, and anarchists. These people would like to overthrow the government and try to run things themselves."

"Surely you exaggerate, Mr. Gant. The operators are well organized. They not only have their own hired guards, called detectives, but they control the local police, the prosecutors and the judges. Because of them, miners have been killed in cold blood, beaten senseless, fired without notice, evicted from their hovels along with their wives and children, and no branch of government will lift a hand to help them. How would you have them defend themselves?"

"Why, let them sign contracts as free individuals, promising a fair day's work for a fair wage," Gant said. "Remember, the operators want the coal mined, so they are not enemies of the miners. They control the mines and the miners are simply workers, obligated to do what the operators know should be done."

"Are you suggesting, Mr. Gant, that a single, uneducated individual is an equal partner in negotiating with the mining companies, with their sophisticated operators, lawyers, and managers? The lone individual and the corporate giant are equals?" Farthingham's heavy brows almost touched as he frowned.

Gant scowled at Doctor Farthingham. "Oh, the miner doesn't deal with the big evil company, only with the hiring agent. He can agree to work under the company rules or go elsewhere and work."

"Suppose the only work available is mining, not in a town but in a vast region the size of a state? Suppose the various mine operators have organized and conspired to set the same harsh standards throughout the region? Is the lone miner still an equal partner in the negotiation?"

"You sound like a socialist, sir!" Gant's face was red.

"I thought we were talking about equality in employment relationships. Surely, claiming something is equal when it's not cannot be dismissed by calling it socialism."

The two men, clearly accustomed to this kind of give and take, continued to eat their meal, but were so intense in their discourse that they seemed to be unaware that Clyde and Mr. Spelling were also at the table. Clyde, however, had stopped eating and was frozen with his fork in mid-air. He had never heard such language, and was especially enchanted by words that evoked emotional attachment by their users. They talked as if their ideas were of universal human importance, yet neither one had mentioned either God or the Bible, at least not yet. Clyde, his mouth open, drank in every word.

Gant looked angry. "You probably also support taxation of the better classes of people to provide free public schools."

"Of course I favor free public schools. Don't you think it promotes the general welfare to produce a literate population?"

"The general welfare! That's more socialism!," Gant said, his face turning red again.

"That's also the purpose of the American system, as spelled out in the Preamble of the Constitution," Doctor Farthingham said. "Do you think it serves the general welfare to permit corporations to unite and make the rules, while the masses are kept in ignorance and forced to negotiate their livelihood as individuals?"

"Don't you see that forcing the companies to deal with unions is an egregious restraint of trade? The courts have said so."

"It seems to me that the companies also were engaged in restraint of trade in bloody Mingo County, when they closed their mines rather than negotiate with the unions."

The two men pushed their chairs back from the table. Gant took out a cigar, clipped the end, struck a match, and carefully lit the stogie, blowing a large smoke ring above the table. Doctor Farthingham tamped a pipe full of tobacco from a tin, lit it, and puffed. Each watched the other and still seemed unaware of Clyde and Mr. Spelling.

"Will you concede me this point?" Doctor Farthingham said. "Society is better as all parts of it receive, not just negative rules of behavior, but benefits that make their life rewarding. Why should only the fortunate few reap all of the good things in life, while the large majority is composed of individuals who toil alone under rules they had no hand in shaping, for returns that barely provide sustenance? Democracy means that everybody has a voice in the rules of society. As a profound thinker said in the middle of the seventeenth century, 'the poorest he that is in England hath a life to live as the greatest he.'"

"Pure socialist bunkum, filled with emotional,

sympathetic appeals," Gant said, hitting his closed fist on the table. "With that kind of thinking, you are probably pleased that women--emotional, tender, caring women--have now been given the vote."

"Yes, of course."

"I predict," Gant said confidentially, leaning forward and placing his hands on the table, the cigar held between his forefinger and middle finger, "that in a few years, women will escape the steady hand of male guidance and begin to act like autonomous individuals. They will change the marriage bonds. They might even start wearing men's clothing and doing men's work. Can you imagine a woman in the mines?"

"I hardly think that will happen."

"Why not? If you change the natural order of human relations, who knows where it will end? I suspect that softhearted women will support the labor unions. In fact, they'll go even further, and interfere with international affairs and even possibly in warfare. Mark my word, the world is changing and not always for the better. That's why, to return to our subject, if we want to maintain America's growth, we must resist all efforts to treat miners, individually or collectively, as equal to the hard working explorers, inventors, investors, and operators who are the backbone of our economy."

"It's just as clear to me," Doctor Farthingham said, "that workers are as necessary for economic growth as managers and investors. Who would dig the coal if it were left up to the operators? Therefore, since workers are also an essential ingredient in mining, there's nothing undemocratic or socialist in granting them a voice in the economy." He paused and looked around the table at Mr. Spelling who seemed to be asleep and Clyde who appeared to be frozen in fascination at the conversation. "I'm sorry to say it, Mr. Gant, but we have monopolized the conversation. Perhaps we can get a reaction from our silent comrades."

"I guess we did get carried away," Gant said, puffing his cigar.

"Tell me, Clyde," Doctor Farthingham said, "how do you feel about our discourse?"

"It was very interestin'," Clyde said.

"Come, come, now. Very interesting is not much of a response. In the first place, you can substitute the word 'damn' for 'very' most of the time and not change the meaning of the sentence. Interesting is a word you use when you don't want to give a reasoned response. Damn interesting in this context is almost insulting. Our discussion might be informative, or nonsense, or reasonable, or dangerous, or inspiring, but interesting doesn't say anything useful about it. Speak up. How do you feel about unions?"

"Well, it makes it possible for miners to speak with one voice, and makes it better for all."

"Don't you see," Gant said, impatiently, "that that is socialism? You're trying to run the mines."

"I don't see that, sir," Clyde said. "We ain't trying to run the mines, just bargain over a few things that we need to make a living, like a living wage, payment in cash instead of script, and fair prices at the company stores. We risk our lives to go into the mines, so shouldn't we all get together and bargain over it? The operators sure don't risk their lives, and they're united against us."

"All I can say," Gant said, "is that you're trying to

destroy the American way. Our only hope lies with the Supreme Court." He puffed his cigar, and added, "We'll never agree, I suppose, so maybe we'd better change the subject."

"It's quite clear to me, Mr. Gant," Doctor Farthingham said, "that you've got a different perspective of the problems than I have. As I observe what has happened in Europe and in the northern states, I'm convinced that unionization will spread throughout the country, including West By-God Virginia. Capitalism has continued to function even where there are labor unions. They're part of the cost of doing business. In fact, what better role can government play than to try to make the contest more even? Sure, the miners are selfish and seek to promote their own ends, just as the owners and their operators do. That's a perfect situation for the creation of a means of arbitration. That's something for government to set up."

"As I said, we'll never agree on those things . . . . You staying in Logan long, Doctor Farthingham?"

"No, I'll be leaving tomorrow. Got to get back to Morgantown and to the School of Mining at the University."

As unusual as it was for Clyde to break into an adult conversation, he fairly blurted out, "Do you mean there's a school for minin'?"

"Of course there is," Doctor Farthingham said. "Who do you think locates the coal, plans the extraction, prepares the ventilation, measures for gas, designs the tipples, and trains the engineers and management? When it gets to the work you do, engineers and scientists have spent many years preparing for it. That's what a school of mining is for."

Clyde hung his head in embarrassment and said no more, even though the others tried to include him in their conversation. He knew things now that he had never thought of before and it would prey on his mind until he did something about it. No other conversation among the boarders proved as compelling to him.

Chapter Four

Clyde was born in 1902 in the southeastern part of the State, near the New River, where labor peace had been fairly well achieved. When he was twelve years old, neighbors predicted that the boy's future was not promising. No good, they said, can come from a boy who quits school at age ten and can barely read and write.

Clyde's mother died from blood poisoning from a gash in her leg that resulted from being pushed into a scythe blade in the barn by a nervous cow. Clyde had just turned ten at the time. Although he could not comprehend it at that early age, the tragedy became a turning point in his life.

When his father informed him of her death, Clyde attempted to run to his mother's bedroom, where she had lain for the few days before she died. His father restrained him.

"Not now, son. The neighbor women are preparin' the body. You go outside and wait awhile. I'll call you when you can see her."

Clyde was crying uncontrollably and blubbering, "but I want to see her now. I don't want her to be dead. Please, Daddy, tell her to come back."

"I cain't, son. You see, God works in mysterious ways. He's called Mama to heaven. Some day we'll see her again."

"Why would God do that? We need her."

"It's not up to us to question the ways of the Lord. We just got to trust him, come what may."

"I don't want to trust no God who takes my Mama away."

"You got to, son. There ain't no other way. Why don't you just set out there in the yard 'til I call you."

Reluctantly, Clyde stepped down from the front porch and walked to a tree in the yard, from which he could see the road. He had on what had once been a white shirt, knee britches with holes, knee-high socks draped around his ankles, and high-top shoes. He was crying disconsolately as he backed against the tree and slid down to the ground. He saw women enter the house with covered dishes, and men gather to talk in low voices on the porch. Shortly, a horse-drawn hearse arrived and six men came out to carry the casket into the house. After awhile, his father came to him.

"Now, son, we can go in and see Mama."

Jack Fuller, to the boy's surprise, took his son's hand as they entered the living room. The room was crowded, not only with people, but with the open casket. Clyde looked at his mother, seemingly submersed in ruffled white cloth. He cried again, until his father picked him up and carried him out onto the front porch. When Uncle Charlie, his mother's brother, and Aunt Nell arrived, he clung to them like they were his parents. By the time he saw the casket lowered into the ground, he was almost emotionless, drained, completely empty of any sense of being, of hope, of purpose.

After that, he felt there was no place to call home. He stayed in school, because it was something to do. Besides, where could a ten-year-old go? The mountains of southern West Virginia did not invite a child to settle down alone.

Clyde did fairly well in school, until near the end of the fourth grade. One day in early May, in the hallway, Billy Landrum pushed him over the kneeling Jason Pelt. As he fell, his left arm slapped the corner of the wall harshly and Clyde scrambled to his feet in pain and anger. Without thinking, he punched Billy in the nose, drawing blood, just as Mrs. Thompson screamed, "Don't do that, Clyde! What's wrong with you, anyway? As soon as I stop Billy's nosebleed, I want to see you."

Clyde went to his seat in the classroom for grades four through six and waited. Shortly, Mrs. Thompson came in. "Clyde, you know better than to fight in the hallway. Now, I want you to apologize to Billy and then we can get on with our lessons."

"But Billy shoved me down and hurt . . ."

"Enough of that. I don't want to hear any excuses. I saw you deliberately hit Billy in the nose and I demand that you apologize to him."

"Don't I get to say nothin'?"

"No. I saw what I saw. Either you apologize or I'll expel you for the rest of the school year. That means you won't get promoted to the fifth grade."

"I won't 'pologize. I didn't do nothing wrong."

"Then you're expelled until you agree to apologize."

"What does spel mean?"

"The word is expel and it means you can't come back to school, until you say you're sorry for hitting Billy."

"But I ain't sorry."

"Then when school is out today, I'm going to take you to your father and tell him what happened. Maybe he can talk some sense to you."

The other children were released at four thirty, but Mrs. Thompson seemed unwilling to send Clyde home to an empty house. Since his mother had died, she often wondered what Clyde did after school, until his father got home from work. This day, she would keep Clyde with her until after five when she thought Mr. Fuller would arrive. At five-fifteen, she said, "All right, Clyde, it's time to go. Let's talk with your father."

They walked out of the little schoolhouse nestled into the side of a hill, followed a path downward through the woods and came out to a narrow valley that seemed crowded with a road, a creek, a Virginian railroad and a row of houses. Each house was surrounded by a tiny patch of open ground, where a small truck garden could be cared for. The Fuller house also had a small shed nearby, where a cow had been kept until Clyde's mother died and the cow had been sold. Although Mrs. Thompson talked about the spring flowers and the new leaves on the trees and how beautiful the weather was, Clyde remained sullen all the way home.

They arrived just as Jack Fuller walked up.

"Wal, if it ain't Miz Thompson with my boy. Come on in and set a spell."

"I really don't have time, Mr. Fuller. I'm here because Clyde got in a fight at school and bloodied Billy Landrum's nose?"

"Is that a fact? Why did you do that, son?"

"Because Billy pushed . . ."

"I'm sorry, Mr. Fuller, but I'm not here to debate

the causes. I saw Clyde hit Billy in the face with his fist, something I don't tolerate in my school. I'm here to tell you that I will expel him until he apologizes to Billy. If I expel him, he won't get promoted to the fifth grade."

"That sounds serious, Clyde. Why don't you just tell Billy you're sorry and that'll be the end of it."

"I'm glad you see the right way, Mr. Fuller. So I'll just leave you now and get on to my place. You know what has to be done."

"Thank'ee, Miz Thompson. I'll sure talk to my boy here and I'm sure he'll do the right thing."

"Good-bye, then."

"Good-bye."

Clyde's father was not a mean man, but he had strong views on certain subjects. "Ignorance," he said to anyone who would listen to him, "that's what makes people poor. Book larnin' is the only way to survive in this world. Look at them what has money, and you'll see they was edicated. I ain't gonna support no kid of mine who won't go to school. I never had the chance when I was a young'un, but my boy is gonna go to school."

To Clyde, he said, "Now listen, son, I 'spect you to go back to school tomorra and do whatever Miz Thompson tells you to do. Your chance to be something rests only on schoolin'. So you be a good boy and do like I say."

"Look here, Daddy, look at my arm." Clyde pushed the left sleeve above the elbow and revealed a fresh bruise and evidence of a friction burn. "See what Billy done when he pushed me backward over Jason. I was mad and I hit him for it. Why don't he get punished, too?"

"Now I ain't gonna get involved in no kid's quarrel. If your teacher says you gotta 'pologize, than you gotta do it."

"I won't do it."

"Wal, then, maybe I got to persuade you a little." He grabbed Clyde with his left hand and pulled his belt out of his pants with his right.

He struck Clyde eight times on the buttocks, whose only response was "Ouw."

"Now you're going back there and do like I say or I'll give you more of the same."

"I don't care. Beat me all you want to, but I ain't gonna say I'm sorry when I ain't."

Jack Fuller stared at his son with a bewildered look on his weather-beaten face and walked into the house, thoroughly defeated. He wiped a tear from his eye and smoothed out his long, white mustache, and said softly, out of earshot of Clyde, "Oh, Martha, Martha, why did you have to go so early. I need you so much."

Clyde skipped school for the next two weeks, but his father never mentioned it to him. Once school was out for the summer, and Clyde had his eleventh birthday on June 16, there was nothing to talk about until the fall term began. He was delighted, however, when his father gave him the birthday gift he wanted--a .22 single-shot rifle with an octagon barrel. He did not know that his father had skimped for the last six months to save the five dollars with which to buy the gun. Clyde practiced shooting every day, so that by fall he would be ready to hunt for rabbits and squirrels. His arms were so steady that he became a marksman with the gun.

During the summer, Clyde's difference from other children began to show up clearly. He played some with friends his age but tired of it in due course and turned to things about which he was curious. He liked to note how things grew on the patch of ground that his father tended. He planted corn and string beans together, so the vines would climb the corn stalks. He also planted some lettuce, tomatoes, pumpkins, cucumbers, peppers, and potatoes. Something about watching the earth produce intrigued him.

He went to the Pilgrim Holiness Church each Sunday morning with his father, where he was told that God was good and merciful, even if he did allow his mother to die. He missed her a great deal and often cried at night.

On the first of September, Mrs. Thompson sent word that if Clyde would apologize she would let him enter the fifth grade. Jack Fuller was pleased. "Just think, all you gotta do is say you're sorry. Then you can go on with your schooling. Don't that sound good?"

"I won't say I'm sorry when I ain't. Besides, didn't Jesus say it was a sin to lie? I'd be lyin' if I said I was sorry and I wasn't."

"Then you gotta find somewhere else to live. I won't support no son who won't go to school when it's free. So make up your mind, either say you're sorry or find somewhere else to live."

Although he knew it was an extreme position, Jack was certain it would bring Clyde around to his way of thinking. The next morning as he prepared to go to work, he noticed that Clyde had put on some clean clothes, so he concluded that the boy was returning to school. When he got home that night, Clyde was nowhere to be seen. Jack walked the mile over to the boarding house, where Mrs. Thompson stayed, and was told that Clyde hadn't been in school that day. He went back to his house, saddled his horse, and searched much of the valley to no avail. He stayed away from work the next day and, joined by a few miners who were not working, searched the valley again.

That night Charlie Crabtree, the late Martha Crabtree Fuller's brother, rode up on his horse. "How are you doin'?" Charlie asked, as the men shook hands. "It must be pretty hard without Martha, I mean the loneliness and all."

"Yes. It's been awful. More'n that, Clyde has run off."

"Jack, Clyde walked all the way over to my house. Got there this morning. That's got to be thirty miles. He was plumb wore out. Said you had run him off, because he refused to tell some kid he was sorry he hit him. I left him asleep on the porch and come over here as quick as I could."

"What am I gonna do with that boy? He ain't really a bad kid. Works hard around here. I told him I won't support nobody who don't go to school, an' I mean it. Schoolin' is the only thing that can get a body out of these hills and into the real world."

"I never did rightly understand what you mean by the real world. What would be better'n living here in the mountains?"

"It's a fact. You don't understand. You see, Charlie, I lived for five years in Newport News, right down on the ocean. I seen land that was flat, where you could visit a neighbor by goin' north, or south, or east, or west. People lived in all directions. Here, it ain't so. We live in giant ditches with little streams running in the bottom, and trees, and cliffs, an' mountains filling up the big banks. Why, I bet if you could get up in one of them airyplanes and look down here, you'd swear that God had used giant claws to dig out these ditches we call valleys. And who's our neighbor? Why, someone living up the valley or down the valley. There are people living no more that three, four miles from us we don't even know is there. Why? Because there's a giant pile of rocks, an' dirt, an' trees between us and them that we call the mountain. I tell you, we live down here crouched in our ditch and other people of West Virginny live in their ditches. There just ain't no way you can form a community out of such arrangements. That's why everybody goes his own way and don't take no concern for his neighbors. I say it ain't natural. Goes against the grain of the way God intended humans to live."

"Why'd you come back here, then?"

"Timberin' is the only kind of work I know, so I had to come back where the timber is. An' I was good at it, till I couldn't swing no double-bladed axe no more. Then I switched to driving the tram engine and hauling timber to the mines. But I didn't go down in the mines. Worms, and snakes, and rats, and skunks make holes in the ground, but that ain't fer me."

"I know you've always said you wished you could move out of these mountains, and I guess it makes sense to you, but I just don't follow you. I also know how you feel about schoolin' and how you mean what you say. Clyde seems pretty upset. Why don't you let him stay with us for a while, at least through the win-

ter months? I got a lot of work he can help me with.
Maybe I can give him two bits every once in a while.
That keeps boys happy. Wha'da you say?"

"That's kind o' you Charlie. I hate to do it, but I
ain't gonna raise no kid o' mine to work like a rat in a
hole in the ground. If he cuts that course for hisself,
then so be it . . . . All right. You can let him stay with
you for a while. Maybe he'll come to his senses and
want to come home soon. I hope so."

Clyde was admitted to the fifth grade near his
uncle's house, but played hooky most of the time.
Schooling didn't interest him. He roamed the woods,
trying to identify the trees. Once, he found a hickory
limb slightly bent and used it to make a bow, and then
gathered straight reeds to make arrows. He went hunting a lot, but only took a catch to his uncle's house if it
were late afternoon, when his Uncle Charlie and Aunt
Nell would think he had searched for game after
school. He took the squirrel or rabbit to the back porch
and, using his hunting knife, eviscerated it, removed
the head and skin, and cut it up for Aunt Nell to cook.
He especially liked them pan-fried, but observed that,
"Aunt Nell makes a stew from fresh catch that even a
rich Yankee would like."

Frequently, Clyde saddled his uncle's horse and
explored the countryside. He was always fascinated by
the occasional sight of a Model T Ford and carefully
examined the underside when he had the chance. The
source of power for the machine intrigued him. How,
he wondered, did it manage to take the place of a
horse? Clyde stayed with his aunt and uncle on through
the next spring, although he never told them he hadn't
passed the fifth grade. He spent his twelfth birthday

with them, and his uncle seemed happy to have him spend another summer working the small patch he called a farm. Clyde realized he was growing closer to them than to his father. Aunt Nell baked apple pies like his mother's, and cakes too. She treated him like the son she never had. Yet after a year, he was certain he ought to be going home soon. His father came to see him twice, but only invited him back home on the condition he apologize to his teacher and to Billy.

Shortly after turning twelve, Clyde learned there was a horrible war going on. "Where is this place called Europe that people are talking about?" he asked Uncle Charlie.

"I think that's what people mean when they talk about the old country. I heerd my pappy talk about the old country bein' England, across the ocean."

"Is it far from here?"

"Yeah, I think so. Why do you ask?" As usual, Charlie was dressed in overalls and a red flannel shirt. He had a red face, sandy hair, and a kind voice.

"I heerd somebody say America might get into it. Do you think so?"

"Lord, child, I don't know. How come you're so interested?"

"Maybe the war will last long enough 'til I can get in it."

"Why would you want to do that? People can get killed in war."

"Yeah, but the soldiers get nice uniforms and shiny shoes."

"Well, I certainly hope you don't get your wish in that matter. Seems like strange thinkin' for a twelve year old."

"Old Mrs. Kropinsky's son came to visit her last week. He sure looked neat in his uniform and shiny black shoes. That's when I decided I would join the army when I get old enough. How old do you have to be to join the army?"

"I don't rightly know, at least eighteen, I 'speck."

"Let's see, that's six years, ain't it? I don't know if I can wait that long."

"They sure ain't gonna take no twelve year old, so I guess you'll hafta wait."

In the late fall, while he was still with his uncle and aunt, something happened that precluded his ever being in the army. He was riding a horse across a sleet-covered bridge, when the animal's feet slid out from under it. Before Clyde could jump off, the horse crushed his right leg under its belly. It then got up and strolled away, while Clyde lay on the bridge helpless. He was found in thirty minutes and taken to his uncle's house. A doctor arrived within the hour.

"I hate to say this," Doctor Stevenson said to Uncle Charlie, "but it looks like every vein in the boy's leg has been burst. If we take him to the hospital in Beckley, they'll probably amputate. What should we do?"

"He's my brother-in-law's boy, and I think we must get his father here as fast as possible. He lives thirty miles away. The way it's sleeting out there, I'd better hitch up the wagon quick like and get on my way."

"No. We'll go in my car. It'll be faster." He was wearing a full dress suit and tie, black shiny shoes, thin-rimmed glasses and a small white moustache. He was carrying a small black bag.

"That's mighty kind of you," Charlie said.

The two men, wearing heavy coats and hats, left the house and got into the doctor's Model T car. "Are you sure you gotta cut his leg off?" Charlie asked.

"Not absolutely certain. We might let him rest in bed for maybe two months, and then make him wear an elastic sock from his knee to the ankle. Sometimes that allows a person to keep the leg."

Jack Fuller returned in the car with Charlie and Doctor Stevenson and said he hated to see his son in that condition. He appeared to be worried. "You know, Charlie," he said, smoothing his long handle-bar moustache, "I have to work every day on the tram line, so there ain't no way I could stay at home and take care of Clyde. Do you s'pose you and Nell could look after him 'til we see how his leg is healin'? You've already done more for the boy than I have a right to expect, but he cain't take care of hisself in that condition. What else can I do?"

"Of course we'll take care of Clyde," Nell said. She had a pretty face, tied her hair in a knot, and always wore a white apron over her slim body. "We love him, and he has been a real help around here. Don't you agree, Charlie?"

"I shore do. We'll look after him. The doctor said he would have to lay in bed for maybe two months, so it ain't gonna be easy for him. It'll be January afore he's permitted to try to walk. The doctor said that maybe after a month he might let him try to get around on crutches, but he don't want no weight at all on that leg for a while. I'm sure Nell will do whatever hasta be done for him."

Clyde stayed with his uncle and aunt and let the

healing proceed. Shortly after New Year's, the doctor fitted Clyde with a heavy elastic stocking, from his ankle to just below his knee. "Now listen, boy, this might not work. I want you to put some weight on that leg, but only for a few minutes today. If you do all right, then tomorrow we'll try a little longer. In a week, I hope you can walk for twenty or thirty minutes. But there's something else. You can't wear this sock twenty-four hours a day. At night you got to take it off and let the leg breathe and then put the sock back on in the morning. To take it off, roll the top down toward your ankle, which is smaller than your calf and it should slip right off. In the morning, you have to stretch it on. If you can't learn to walk with this sock on, then you'll lose your leg. Do you understand what I'm saying?"

"Yes, sir. I do. I ain't gonna lose this leg. I'll learn to walk. You'll see."

"All right. Stand up and walk to me."

Clyde stood up, took a step and fell into the doctor.

"Doesn't surprise me at all. Those muscles are weak. Now try again."

Gritting his teeth, Clyde took a step and muffled a cry of pain. Then he took another step, and another.

"Stop now and rest," the doctor said. "I want you to do that again in about an hour, and maybe twice more today. I'll be back tomorrow, and we'll take a look at that leg again."

The doctor left the house, got in his Ford, and put-putted down the road. He calculated that before he had finished with Clyde, the total bill would probably come to five or six dollars. He had a regular income from the coal company, just to take care of mine injuries, which allowed him some free time to take care of cases like Clyde's.

Four months after getting out of bed, Clyde was able to walk two miles round trip from his uncle's house. Even Doctor Stevenson said he was now certain that Clyde could stand on his own two feet all day, if necessary. He could probably expect to take on regular work when he was old enough, as long as he didn't get an infection in that leg, and wore the elastic sock every day.

It seemed only natural now that he stay with his aunt and uncle at least through the summer. On June 16, he walked into the house for supper and was surprised by his aunt who was standing by the table with a huge chocolate cake topped with thirteen candles. "Surprise, surprise," she said. "You're finally into your teens and on your way to being a man. I must say, Clyde, that's it's a joy to have you here, don't you agree, Charlie?"

"Yes, indeed. Happy birthday, Clyde."

As he gave his aunt a big hug, she exclaimed, "My land. Look at that. You're already taller than me. I declare you're almost a man. I'm just so sorry your daddy don't seem to care about you."

"I think he cares," Clyde said, "but he wants to make me do something that's wrong. I won't lie just to go to school."

"Well, we'll see what happens when school starts again in the fall."

Clyde spent that summer working with his uncle on the garden and was pleased that his leg seemed to cooperate most of the time. Sometimes it ached and he often wished he could go without the elastic stocking.

"If it'll save my leg, I'd wear it on my head if I had to," he said when he felt especially conscious of his impairment. He got Aunt Nell to show him how to sew a stocking from elastic sheets, so he would always have extras. He accepted the fact he would have to wear such a garment the rest of his life.

In August, his father came to see him and to ask him to reconsider and return to school.

"I think your daddy's right," Charlie said. "Schooling is necessary to get by in these days. I heerd a man say just the other day that soon everybody would have to have some high school, just to get a job. Think about it."

"Don't you see," Clyde said, "that I'm too old to go back to school, for I'd be in classes with ten-year-olds and I just ain't gonna do it."

"Besides," Charlie said, "it might be better all around if you lived with your father. That's the way God intended for most boys to live."

"Don't you want me with you no more?"

"Yes, 'course I do. You've been a great help here and are welcome to stay as long as you want. I just meant that you might enjoy being home again."

"Well, I'm not gonna go back to school and that's final."

Chapter Five

The next morning after his father left, Clyde threw away his knee-britches and put on a pair of his uncle's overalls. He felt like an adult when he looked in the mirror on his aunt's dresser. So attired, he walked over to the office of the United Mining Company, about a mile from his uncle's house, and inquired about work.

"Sure, we got some work for boys that is fifteen years old," the hiring agent asked. "Are you that old, boy?"

"Yeah, I just turned fifteen. When can I start?"

"You're real anxious, ain't you, boy? That's good. Coal minin' ain't nice work, but it's one way to make some money, maybe enough to buy a girl something. I bet you'd like that. You go over there to where that slope is and ask for Dirk Schmidt. He'll make a trapper boy out of you."

Thus, by lying about his age, he got a job as a trapper boy. Trapper boys opened and closed doors in the passage-ways, to allow motors to get through, keeping the flow of air circulating throughout the mine. Sometimes air locks were created by using two doors, and sometimes canvas curtains were hung in the intersections of the tunnels to divert the flow of air. Clyde was to work under the supervision of a ventilation expert, known as a fire boss, one who checked a mine for evidence of gas. His pay was one dollar for a ten-hour day.

He got a room in a boarding house but missed the warmth of his uncle's home.

Clyde showed up at the slope on the appointed morning at six-thirty. Dirk Schmidt was waiting for him, holding a heavy cloth cap with a rack on the front, and a carbide lamp. "Here," he said, "adjust those straps so the cap will fit your head. You can buy your own after your first payday. It has to be tight enough so you can fasten this lamp on the front of the cap. See, the bottom of the lamp screws off and you drop carbide into it. Then in the top, you add a little water that drips into the bottom, creating a gas. When we light it, we get a flame. That's what you're gonna see with to work in the mines, probably for the rest of your life. Now, let that little hook fasten the lamp to the front of your cap, and put the cap on."

"It shore don't give much light," Clyde said, turning his head in different directions.

"Not out here in the open. When we get down where there is no light, you'll be surprised how much you can see. Are you ready to go?"

"Yeah," Clyde responded, but he was glad Dirk could not sense the apprehension he felt.

They walked into the opening and started a gentle descent.

"Now look careful, Clyde," Dirk said. "One thing you must never forget is that that heavy wire running along the top is death if you touch it. It's high voltage, and runs the motors. Don't ever get any closer to it than you have to. I seen a man once whose head touched that wire. It held the corpse right up there like it was alive, 'til they cut the juice off. Ya hear what I'm sayin'?"

"Yes, sir." They were now about two hundred feet into the mine and Clyde stopped and looked back. The entrance looked as small as a groundhog's hole. Except for dripping water, an eerie silence was becoming louder and louder to him.

"C'mon, Clyde. Let's keep going."

"I'm right with you."

The slight curve in the tracks informed them that they were making a gradual turn. Clyde stopped and looked back again, and saw only complete darkness. His dim light was reflected off the posts beside the tracks, and Dirk's silhouette was clear up ahead. Everywhere else, there was blackness. He held his hands up and seemed relieved to see them reflected in his lamplight, like long-lost friends. He looked to the side, between the posts, into side tunnels, and tried to sense what was beyond. He tried to remember the sun, but blackness seized him like an emanation. It seemed to be penetrating his pores. He wondered if he might become totally absorbed by blackness, if his lamp were to go out. Never had darkness seemed so alive to him, so sinister and ubiquitous. The temptation to turn and run back was overwhelming.

About every three hundred feet was a side tunnel at right angles to the main one, extending back twelve to fifteen hundred feet into darkness. The coal between the side tunnels was left standing as pillars, to hold up the top. Then the miners worked from the end of the side tunnels into areas called rooms, and gradually removed the pillars until they got back to the main tunnel. This allowed the top to fall in behind them, when the mine was worked out.

"C'mon, lad. You'll soon get used to it. The

silence and the loneliness get to you sometimes, but there are men who've worked in here for thirty or forty years, so loneliness and silence ain't fatal diseases. Are you gonna be all right?"

"Yeah, I'm okay. Thought I heerd something and stopped to listen."

"I felt the same way when I first started. You'll get used to it. Let's go. We'll soon come to a section where men are loading cars, so you'll see we're not the only ones here."

"Well, I ain't afraid. Let's go."

His supervisor told him where and how to hang the canvas and place the airlock doors, and the whole process interested Clyde. He studied carefully where the huge fans with eight-foot blades blew fresh air into the tunnels, and where, after feeding air to every working place, was then exhausted out by other huge fans, often on the opposite side of the mountain. The traps directed air into every working area. Within a year, he was able to anticipate almost every order of his supervisor, and understand what was necessary for good air flow.

"That's the smartest kid I ever seen," the fire boss told the section boss, Ellis Smith. "He's sure learning this job fast. Why, I bet you could put him with a coal loader and he'd soon learn how to set a blast and load his own car."

"Is that a fact?" the boss said. "I could use a couple more loaders, but I never trusted such a young kid before with blasting powder. You sure he can do it?"

"Sure, I'm sure. Why don't you put him in with that old Dago over in twelve section. He's the best there is with blasting. I bet he'll have Clyde trained in six months."

"That don't seem right likely, but on your recommendation I'll sure give it some thought."

"Well, you'll see. He's developed a big head over the success he's having, so don't be surprised if he sounds like a know-it-all. I'm sure he'll get over it in time. In fact, I'm gonna see if I can find another trapper boy, 'cause I think this one will be after your job soon."

"If he's that good, I'll have to use him."

The section boss watched Clyde for a couple of weeks, and decided that the fire boss was right, the boy was quick to learn.

"Clyde," the boss said at the end of a work day, "I've been watching you and like what I see. You've done a good job at trapping. How'd you like a chance to load coal?"

"The pay is on how many cars you load, ain't it?"

"That's right."

"Then I ort to try it."

"Good. First, I'm gonna put you in with Peter Costa so you can learn about blasting. That's not only dangerous work, but also a danger to the other workers, too. It's got to be done right. Okay with you?"

"I bet he's a Dago. Right? What can I learn from a Dago?"

"Hell, boy, you can learn a lot from him. He's the best blaster in the mines, and if you're too damn smart to learn from the best, then you don't belong in the mines. I'll see if I can get someone else to do the job." He whirled and walked away.

"Hey, wait. I'll give it a try."

"Let me tell you something," Ellis Smith said as

he turned again to Clyde, "in case you don't know it, coal mining is dangerous. The way we survive is for everybody to do his job right, and that means you gotta learn it right from the beginning. Now if you're too damn smart to learn, then I'll see that you don't work in this mine ever, because you'll be a danger to every miner who works here. If you wanna learn, then there's a lot of opportunity for you. Maybe in twenty years, you can even have my job."

"Look, maybe I spoke too fast. I'm willing to learn, and I'll do it with a Dago if I haft to. At least, I don't hafta learn it with no Nigger."

"Like hell, you won't. There's Niggers in here who know more about some parts of mining than you'll ever learn. There's times you'll be happy to ask their advice."

"I don't believe you, but I'm still willing to move in with that Dago. What did you say his name was?"

"Pete Costa. I'll take you to his section in the morning. Just get that chip off your shoulder."

"Okay. You got the control now, but I'm gonna have your job before twenty years."

"I hope you're right, cause we need good bosses. But you'll have to lose some of that cockiness before then."

"You just tell me what to do and leave my cock to me."

"You're a smart ass. I'll meet you here in the morning."

***

Clyde learned fast from Pete Costa and in six months was blasting his own coal face and loading the results in a coal car, and earning up to two dollars a day. He learned the importance of setting posts in his room as the coal was removed. He soon realized that he liked Pete Costa, but would never admit such a thing on the outside. People might think he was a Hunky-lover, and if he loved Hunkies, he might even be a Nigger-lover. He had to watch things like that.

He was now fifteen but claiming to be seventeen. America was in the war, but he failed his army physical due to his injured leg. He continued to work for over a year as a loader, and then talked his boss into letting him become a track man. In a few months, he could lay track like a more experienced man. All the while he was watching the electricians hang the high-powered cables that were necessary to drive the motors that hauled the coal cars in and out of the mine. At age nineteen (in reality, seventeen), he was apprenticed to an electrician, but never completed the training.

Chapter Six

Clyde Fuller lost much of his arrogance by the time he was eighteen. To Ellis Smith, the section boss, he said, "I guess I orta tell you that I like Pete Costa. He's really a nice man, and I like working with him. Also I been workin' with Bonehead Scott, that colored guy, and he's really good at layin' track. I got a lot of good tips from him. Besides, I understand what you said about every body bein' concerned with the safety of all. Makes you sorta know you gotta depend on a lot of other folks, and they gotta depend on you."

"Then you've learned a good lesson, son," Ellis Smith said. "You're a hard worker and have developed a good attitude. I think you can go as far in the mines as you want."

Clyde's teen years were restless ones. After he went to work at age thirteen, he found the hard labor drove him to bed early. However, on weekends when he was not in the mines, he fished or target-practiced, and hunted when the season was right. Although he kept his .22 rifle, by the time he was sixteen he was able to buy a .30 caliber rifle, with which to hunt deer. He became an expert marksman with it. Working, hunting, target shooting, and fishing occupied his time. He never once went to visit his father.

On Saturday nights while still only fifteen, he

began to frequent Elmer's Restaurant where he could buy a beer and no one questioned the age of a miner. He was certain that God frowned on what he was doing, but he felt he needed to learn something about life, and a lot of the miners seemed to find it in a bar. The bar patrons, sensing his youth when he first went there, teased him a lot about girls. "Hey, Clyde," one man said, "I seen you by the company store last week with a girl. So you've started courtin', have you?"

Others at the bar spoke up, saying "Clyde's got a girl. Clyde's got a girl."

Since he had not yet entered puberty, his response was usually, "Ah, you're just kiddin' me. I don't have no girl. Honest. You just leave me alone."

The men laughed at his impetuosity and marked it off as bravado; at the same time they admired the fact that one so young would be working in the mines. The ribbing, consequently, never got out of hand, and it made him more sociable.

Shortly before his sixteenth birthday, he began to face some peculiar wet dreams and acquired an interest in girls. He was unable to explore the ramifications of that fact, because there were no girls his age in the mining community, except for a few who were in school and whose parents would not allow them to consort with a near-illiterate miner. For a year, Clyde simply pondered his plight, but as he paid more and more attention to the miner's talk, he sensed a relationship between his feelings and girls. It was Elmer Yocum who served as a go-between for his libido and the consummation of nature's purpose.

"What'll you have?" Elmer always asked, but he knew Clyde would order a beer.

"The same. You know what I like," Clyde always answered.

"Yeah, I know," he said as he placed a bottle in front of the young man. Then he leaned across the bar and whispered, "But I got something else you might like. I hired a new girl today, and she sure looks like she needs to get laid. I'll introduce you, just because I watched you grow up right here. Let's see, you must be seventeen by now."

"Nineteen," Clyde lied. It always bothered him when he lied, but the one about his age seemed to be justified whereas the one about apologizing for hitting a boy seemed somehow to be different. He wondered if God would note the difference.

"You can say what you want, but I know how old you are. You're seventeen. You told me your real age two years ago. Don't worry. I ain't gonna tell no one. You must be getting' horny for some pussy, and the girl I mentioned is fresh and ready. You ought to get her before some of these creeps do."

"Why don't you get her yourself?"

"I'm too old for that now, but I remember what it was like when I was your age."

"Yeah, I'd like to meet her."

"Good. I got a back room that's empty if you want to use it."

"Thanks Elmer."

About 8:30, after Clyde had had two beers, Elmer said, "That girl's here now. C'mon back and I'll introduce you to her."

Clyde went with him to the back room. "Mary Ann, this here is Clyde Fuller, the feller I told you about. He sure has been hankerin' to meet you. You two have fun, now, y'hear!"

He left the small room which was basically used for storage, but contained two straight-back chairs and a daybed in the corner. Elmer always seemed to have a woman around and often sent customers back to see her. This was the first time Clyde had been invited to the back room, and he was nervous.

Mary Ann had short curly hair, a pretty face with bright lipstick, and wore a very low-cut bright green dress that barely extended to her knees and had no sleeves at all. Clyde remembered what a preacher had said about such attire, when he last attended church four years ago: "The way women are today is an abomination to God. Some paint their faces up worse than a red barn. Them that wears a dress that exposes armpits is as evil as one that exposes her knees. And the worst hussy of all is a woman who cuts her hair, 'cause the Bible says a woman's hair is her glory, and that means God don't want her to cut it."

Despite the preacher's warning about such women, Clyde gazed at Mary Ann with desire. The thought going through his mind was that at last he was going to see what a woman looked like. He was sure it was sinful, because it felt so good just to look at her. He stared at her, seemingly tongue-tied, until he remembered his manners.

"Do you want to set down?" Clyde asked.

"Yes. Yes, I would." They sat, followed by a long silence.

"What do you do, Clyde?"

"Work in the mines."

"Oh. That is so frightenin'. I can't imagine doing that. Ain't it scary down there?"

"Naw," Clyde lied, "only girls would show fear of a mine."

"But it's so dark. And there's cave-ins, and sometimes they explode."

"I know, but it's man's work and I'm a man."

"'Course you are. I can see it in the muscles of your arms."

"Are we just gonna talk?"

"Well now, what would you like to do?"

"I don't rightly know. You shore are pretty."

"Thank you. Do you like my new dress? I had it cut way low here in front."

"Sure I like it. And I like what I can see there in front."

"Oh, you are sweet. Most men would have it off me by now. Would you like to feel me there in front?"

"You mean your, ah, your titty?"

"Sure. Give me your hand. See, we'll place it right there next to my heart. Don't that feel good?"

"Yeah, that feels great. Can I see them?"

"Of course, honey. See how easy my shoulder straps slip off. There now, how do you like my titties?"

"They're, they're beautiful. Can I kiss them?"

"Well I hope so. I'm beginning to think you never been with a woman before. Is that so? C'mon now, tell me the truth."

Clyde's only answer was to turn beet red.

"I knowed it! You ain't never been with a woman before. C'mon, honey, and I'll show you what to do. First, let me get rid of this dress." She dropped the dress over a chair and Clyde saw a naked woman for the first time. He had not been aware that women had pubic hair and he stood there, entranced and curious, wondering if his mother had looked like that. Nevertheless, there was a growing physical eagerness. Mary Ann reached for his crotch and said, "You're getting the message, 'cause I can feel it in your pants. Take them off and join me on the daybed."

He did as she commanded and saw the target for his tool as she lay on her back. She pulled him down on her and as he slid into her he realized a sensation he had never felt before. It was over all too soon, but he was pleased at the release the experience gave him.

She said, "You were very good, and I'm so glad to have been a party to your christenin'. You may be the first virgin I ever had. It was fun. In fact, I almost feel like giving Elmer back his money. I hope you'll come and see me again soon."

"I shore do thank you, Mary Ann. You know how to make a man feel good."

"You're sweet, Clyde, but it's all in a day's work. Come see me again."

"I'll do it."

He returned to the bar and thanked Elmer.

"That will be the last time you get to do that here," Elmer said. "I have managed to keep the local police off my back by slipping them some money every week. They pretend I ain't here. Prohibition ain't enforced much in this state. Now I gotta close my entire business next month."

"No! I didn't know that. Why?"

"You don't pay much attention to the news, do you? Ain't you heard of the Constitution? Well, a new 'mendment was passed that says I can't sell no likker, not even beer."

"If you can't sell beer, where will we get it?"

"You won't be able to. Nobody can sell it. Nobody's gonna get to have any likker, not even in your home."

"You mean I won't ever be able to have another beer, because there won't be any place to buy it?"

"That's what I mean. All drinkin' is prohibited."

"How can they do that? Just take away a man's livin' like that, and then tell us all that we cain't ever drink again? It don't seem fair!"

"Fair! They got all the holy men in Congress and all the bootleggers together, and the women's temperance somethin' or other, and simply made a new law. Nobody is allowed to make a livin' selling booze no more."

"That's awful. When does the law take over?"

"I just got a notice here about somethin' called the Volster Act or somethin' like that. Here, let me get the letter." He reached under the counter and produced a sheaf of papers. "See, there it is. V-o-l-s-t-e-a-d Act. It says they're gonna destroy all my inventory, that's what I got on hand, on January 16, 1920. See, there it is right there. That's just a few weeks away. If I sell booze after that time, they'll throw me in jail."

"Can't you pay them off, like the locals?"

"No, 'cause they're Feds, an' can't be bought."

"What are you gonna do?"

"I don't rightly know. I usta work in the mines, but I got so I could hardly breathe, so I had to think of somethin' else to do. That's when I opened the restaurant and bar to sell hotdogs and likker. Now that the war is over, there just ain't no work around here 'cept in the mines. I guess I'll go to Oak Hill or Mount Hope and try to find work. If I cain't, then I'll hafta go back in the mines."

In April, after failing to find work, Elmer returned to the little village where he had run his restaurant nad bar and applied for a coal-loading job in the United Coal Company mine where Clyde worked. Because he was experienced, he was hired and began work immediately.

He went to Clyde's rooming house shortly after returning. "I just had to come by and see how you're doin'."

"It's good to see you, Elmer. I'm doing okay. Where are you working?"

"I'm over in number two mine. What do you do on weekends, now that the bar is closed?"

"I like to feesh and sometimes I stay out till dark. I'm goin' feeshin' this evening over in New River. Why don't you join me?"

"By god, that's a great idea. I've got an old pole some wheres. I'll get it and go with you. What time should I be here?"

"Come around four. I know where we can dig up some worms real quick."

Despite the difference in their age, they became close friends. When they were fishing on Saturday or Sunday, age did not divide them.

Clyde noticed that Elmer coughed a lot, and sometimes expectorated black sputum when he was not chewing tobacco, just as others of the older miners he worked with. "I seen a lot of miners cough like that. Is it something to do with the mines?"

"I don't know. I asked a doctor about it once, and he said a lot of miners had the same problem, but he didn't know what it was. All I know is it gets worse when I go back in the mines and improves when I don't go in the mines."

Chapter Seven

When Clyde arrived in Logan, after the shooting at Matewan, he was in the heart of medieval existence. Although he did not understand the terminology, Dr. Farthingham told him that southern West Virginia had by 1915 become a great feudal estate. The mine operators were lords; the hired police, administrators, judges, and politicians were yeomen; and the miners were serfs. Clyde left Logan deeply troubled by Dr. Farthingham's observation, not understanding where he fit in the strange nomenclature.

The leg he injured jumping onto the coal car healed as expected, and in a week he was able to walk on it again, using one of the spare elastic socks he carried with him. He went to Kanawha County, as he said he would, and was awed by the size of the capital city, the width and volume of the Kanawha River, and the small tugs pushing huge barges on the waterway. How, he wondered, can a city that big support so many people? What did they do to make a living?

He got work immediately nearby as a loader, and found great unrest among the miners. Although they had a union of sorts, they were still talking of demanding better working conditions, not only in pay, but in housing, in fairer prices at the company store, in the use of real money instead of script, and in better tools supplied by the company.

At Christmas 1920, Clyde went to visit Uncle Charlie and Aunt Nell. He took his aunt a meat grinder that fastened on the edge of the table, which she loved. To his uncle, he gave a box of twelve-gauge shotgun shells, greatly appreciated by a man who hunted a lot. After the turkey dinner on Christmas day, Clyde and Uncle Charlie retired to the living room to talk, while Aunt Nell did the dishes.

"I hear there's a lot of unrest over in Mingo and Logan counties," Charlie said.

"Yeah. Some people say it's just like war. Miners have been shot down right out in the open and nobody seems to care. Some miners have started to shoot company goons, just to try to balance things. They shoot from up in the hills and then disappear. I think that's what happened over in Matewan."

"What's it like where you work?"

"We got a union there, so the work ain't bad. The miners are unhappy there about what's happenin' farther south. If the operators win there, then the miners in Kanawha County might lose what benefits they already have. There's a lot of talk about gettin' their guns and marching on Logan, just to shoot the sheriff who hates miners and bows down to the operators like a slave."

"I've heerd of him. Heerd he deputizes the detectives the operators bring in to guard the mines and drive out all who have been fired."

"That's what I hear, too. What does deputize mean?"

"It means he makes them police officers just like hisself, so when they kill somebody, it's just like the law done it."

"That don't seem quite right to me. . . . Don't tell

Aunt Nell, but when I leave tomorra', I'm gonna take my high-powered rifle with me. I 'spect somethin' is about to happen and I may need it to protect myself."

"You be careful, now. Ya' hear?"

"I promise. I'll be careful."

Clyde returned to his job and listened very carefully to what was happening. Word was that the chief of police in Matewan, Sid Hatfield, had been indicted for the murder of two "detectives," Avery Murphy and his brother, Homer, in the battle of Matewan. In January 1921, however, the chief was acquitted. Shortly after that, Hatfield was indicted again, this time for the deaths of the other detectives who died in that battle. The trial was expected to begin in August in the city of Welch, in McDowell County, adjacent to Mingo County. Consequently, the spring and summer of 1921 were filled with rumors that instilled great unrest in the coal fields.

In July, Frank Keeney, President of the United Mine Workers in Kanawha County, called for a meeting of miners to discuss his plan of action. Clyde was among the first to arrive at a large park near Charleston.

"What I want us to do," Keeney said, "is to invade Logan County with thousands of miners whom the sheriff can arrest and overcrowd his jails. That will bring national notoriety to the plight of the miners.

"Listen to me, miners, the governor has refused to order the state police to protect our lives and our rights as free men. Now we must accept the reality that we are at the mercy of the organized company thugs, local police, state police, prosecutors, judges, legislature, and governor. Union organizers are being killed on sight in the three southern counties of Logan, Mingo, and McDowell, and anyone overheard speaking in favor of unionization is being run out of town. Sometimes, union men are tarred and feathered, and frequently beaten unmercifully. Fellow miners, we must now realize that our Constitutional rights of free speech and assembly, even our lives, are not being protected by any branch of the State Government. The Federal Government seems determined not to get involved."

Keeney's plan was aborted, however, on August 1, when it was learned that Sid Hatfield and his deputy, Ed Chambers, were killed by company detectives, as they walked up the stairs to the Welch courthouse with their wives. They had been promised safe conduct by the governor, provided they came to the courthouse unarmed, which they were. Hatfield's two pistols, in fact, were packed in a suitcase back in his hotel room. The two lawmen walked through a gauntlet of armed men in front of the courthouse, but on the stairs a number of shots rang out and each lawman was riddled with an unknown number of slugs. One of the detectives told the deputy's widow, while the bodies still lay where they had fallen, "We didn't go to Matewan to be killed last year, so it is only fair that Hatfield and Chambers be treated the same way. They're dead now. Go on home and find another man to support you."

As miners learned of the death of their hero, anger spread like measles throughout the region. A perfunctory investigation was held in McDowell County, and the detectives were freed on bond immediately. No one was ever tried for the murders. Harassment of the miners continued unabated. A large number of miners were held in jail in Mingo County without any charges at all.

Striking miners and their families endured life in a Mingo County tent colony for 16 months.

Although Keeney had called off his planned march after Hatfield was killed, armed miners nevertheless met on their own on August 20, in Marmet, near Charleston, and started a march toward Blair Mountain in Logan County. Recruitment was by word-of-mouth, and Clyde was a willing volunteer. He bought a cheap valise with many pockets to carry his few clothes and extra elastic hose. Most of the miners carried rifles and backpacks, and a few had pistols and/or shotguns. As they marched, they were joined by miners from other counties, particularly Fayette, Raleigh, and Wyoming counties to the east, as well as from the southern counties of Logan, Mingo, and McDowell, swelling the number eventually from eight to ten thousand.

Early on, someone tied a red bandanna around his neck, and soon everyone was wearing something red. They called themselves red necks, but were called Reds by the mine operators. The roads were filled with men dressed in every imaginable garb, from worn dress suits, to blue jeans, to overalls. Long lines of men could be seen snaking out of the valleys and crowding the main roads. Thousands of other people brought food to the marchers along the way. There were even a few doctors and nurses, identified by wearing headbands marked UMWA. The only looting occurred when the miners came to a company store and robbed it of provisions and guns. A few army veterans, some of them officers of the World War, tried to instruct the ragtag group in military tactics, and brought order to a few thousand. Many miners, however, being stubborn individualists, simply refused to conform to military drill. In fact, no one was in charge of the entire group. The miners constituted a mob with a single purpose.

As the crow flies, the distance to Blair Mountain was only thirty-five miles. The roads meandered down valleys and climbed mountains on S-curved turns with long switchbacks, repeating the same patterns on roads falling into a valley before rising again so steep that cars maneuvered them only in low gear and trucks monitored their load weights carefully before trying to cross them. The distance by road was about sixty-five miles. The miners reached Blair Mountain on August 26. Most were walking, a few came in cars, and some were on freight trains.

Clyde, being only nineteen and in reasonably good health joined other young men by helping some of the older men carry their rifles and knapsacks, some loaded with ammunition. "Thank ye, son," one man said to him after he took the man's load. He had white hair and a back bent from many years using a shovel in passages no higher than four feet. Black creases lined his face, and he was breathing hard. He was forty-five, but could easily have passed for eighty. "I sure hate to see a young feller like you get involved in somethin' like this. Why don't you leave it to us older ones? You could get killed or crippled, ya know. Me, I don't expect to see the day when we get our rights. I'm gonna fight for them till I die. You got a lot to live for. You ought to be out there tryin' to persuade the Feds to help us. That's the only way out that I see."

"Thank you, but I feel this is part of my battle, too. I've worked in the mines for six years, and I know how bad it is in this part of the state. I intend to do what I can. By the way, my name's Clyde."

"Six years, eh? Well I've been in the mines for thirty years, and I got to admit I'm about wore out. I think the mines is worse now than when I started. Pleased to meetcha, Clyde. My name's Abner. I was born and raised in these hills, about twenty miles from here. Never been no farther away from home than Charleston, but I didn't stay long. Too big a city for me . . . . Whee, the road sure is steep here. It's all I can do to breathe. Just go on ahead and I'll ketch up when I can."

"Pleased ta meetchu, Abner. Don't worry. I'll carry your rifle and sack and walk with you. I'll give them back to you at the top of the mountain."

"I 'preciate that, Clyde." He sucked in some deep breaths. "Let's set a while on this log, 'til I ketch my breath. You look to me like you're limpin'. What's wrong?"

"I got a bum leg from a horse falling on me. It's hurt worse than this before. I'll be all right."

"I'm just glad we got young fellers like you on our side."

"Thanks a lot . . . . Have you seen this kind of march before?"

"My, my, yes. I was in the battle of Cabin Creek, back in 1912. We was fightin' the company goons, like we might hafta do here."

"Nineteen twelve. I was only ten then. Never heerd of Cabin Creek."

"It's just a valley and next to it is Paint Creek, not far from here. They was coal companies on them two creeks that refused to recognize the union, even though all the other companies in Kanawha County had. We had an awful fight up both them hollers. Mother Jones come and talked with us. She'd just been freed from prison for encouragin' the miners to strike. She used some big words I didn't understand, but I'll never forget what her meanin' was. She said the operators hired so-called detectives who were their bloodhounds, but even they wouldn't treat their dogs the way they treat the miners. She was eighty years old then and shamed us by saying we should behave like men and stand up to these people who would deny us of our rights." He paused and stared off into space.

"I heerd of Mother Jones once," Clyde said. "I thought she wasn't real, like maybe some story somebody thought up."

"Oh, she was real enough. Had more gumption than most men."

Labor crusader Mother Jones is seen here with miners' children.

"She sounds like a good woman."

"The mine operators sure didn't think so. She stood up to every kind of abuse; made the men cringe a little to be talked to like she did. I heerd she's still living. Must be ninety by now."

"What was it like in the fightin' you mentioned?"

"I was in Cabin Creek when I got shot in the leg. Funny thing happened. A doctor treated my wound, named Henry Hatfield, related to that Hatfield clan in Mingo County. I didn't know till later that he was the governor of the state. Can you believe that! He was the first governor who tried to understand our fight. In fact, the only one."

"Did your leg heal all right?"

"Yeah, I guess better'n yours."

"What's it like to be shot at?"

"It ain't no fun, but when it's the only way to get fair treatment, sometimes you just gotta face up to the possibility of being killed."

"Did you ever kill a man?"

"I'm afraid so, just before I was shot in the leg. I was in the woods and saw one of them detectives up ahead of me. He heerd me coming and whirled to shoot me, so I put a bullet through his heart. I never seen such a look on a man's face. His eyes bulged out and he looked like he was gonna say something then fell flat on the ground, and twitched a little."

"How did you feel after that?"

"I'll tell you, son, shootin' people ain't my idea of fun. I hope you never have to live with something like that."

"I guess we better get on up towards Blair," Clyde said, cutting the conversation off.

The next day, as the march continued, Abner said, "Look at that fire tower up there. That's the top of Blair Mountain."

"So that's where the sheriff and his goons are campin'?" Clyde said. "It looks steep. Think you can make it?"

"Sure I can. I'm kinda heated up now for whatever comes."

Before reaching Blair, on the advice of mountaineers, the men left the highways and went into the woods to work their way toward their target. Part way up the mountain, Clyde stopped to look back down into the valleys and saw many thousands of men, all moving toward the mountain.

The newfound friends started up the steep part of the mountain, resting frequently so Abner could catch his breath.

"See that man over there with the beard and brown hat?" Abner said, as he sat on a log with Clyde. "He was a mine foreman till last year. When the operators found out he favored unions, they fired him. Because he'd been to high school, the school board hired him to teach in the grade school. When the sheriff found out, he fired him."

"That don't make no sense to me. What does the sheriff have to do with schools?"

"You sure gotta lot to learn. Don't you know the companies own everything in this region? Not only the sheriff, but they pay part of the salaries of principals and teachers. That way, they can control every aspect of schooling. The sheriff even boasted out loud that he was gonna run the man out of town because he liked unions."

Half-way up, they heard a volley of shots, including the staccato rattle of machine gun fire, and the cacophony of hundreds of crows that were routed by the noise. As the group that Clyde and Abner were in neared the top of Blair Mountain, under a fire observation tower, early in the morning of August 31, they were met by an organized band of sheriff's deputies, state police, and deputized detectives, under the command of the Logan County sheriff, Don Chafin, numbering perhaps two-thousand five-hundred.

The officers started shooting at the miners as soon as they came in sight, with machine guns as well as rifles. Six men were wounded on the first fusillade that

Militiamen and state troopers fire on attacking miners from atop Blair Mountain.

Clyde and Abner had heard when they were lower on the mountain. As they neared the top, Clyde darted from tree to tree, and sometimes threw himself flat behind a log and crawled on his belly to another spot. Gunsmoke filled the woods but fog was even more prevalent, and one had to be careful to shoot at the right target.

Clyde saw Abner behind a tree about sixty feet away. The old man apparently saw something move and stepped out from behind the tree to shoot. At the same time, Clyde saw the hat of a sheriff's deputy as he rose up from behind a log and fired at Abner. Clyde shot the deputy and saw him fall just as he was aware that Abner had also fallen.

Crawling as quickly as he could, Clyde found that the old man had been shot through the head and died instantly. To no one in particular, he said, "I'll be damned. Just like Elmer last year. It jest don't seem right for good men to die like this." He looked where the deputy had been, but could see nothing because of the fog, which kept opening and closing as it spread through the woods.

A man who had been accepted more or less as the leader of Clyde's group saw what happened and congratulated Clyde. "I seen it, boy, I seen it. You got that goddamn goon. That's one more so-called officer of the law we won't hafta worry about. How's the old man?"

"He's dead."

"That's five I know of. I jest hope we get as many of them."

The miners watched as some airplanes flew over and dropped bombs, but did no damage. Later, they learned that the planes were under the command of

General Billy Mitchell. Before the battle ended, Clyde thought he had killed another enemy. Although the officers were under military discipline, and carried government-issued weapons, they were being pushed back

One of 13 bombs, this one a dud, dropped from an airplane on striking miners at Blair Mountain.

by the motley crew of mountaineers, who greatly out-numbered them.

On the fifth day, word spread among the miners that regular army troops were heading their way. Bill Blizzard, another union official, sent word that, "We can fight the thugs of West Virginia but not the army of the United States." He also advised the miners to hide their weapons (there were numerous worked-out mines on the hillsides) and walk peacefully, unarmed, out of the hills as ordinary mountaineers who hadn't shaved for a week or more. Clyde had just passed the opening of an abandoned mine slope when word was passed to him. He rushed in and found a place to hide his rifle. He then walked down into the valley, looking like he had been out for a stroll. He didn't see a single miner carrying a gun.

The general in charge of the army made railroad flat-bed cars available for any miners who would come down peacefully. Soon dozens of cars were filled with hundreds of men, ready to return home. The general even promised the miners that they would not be bothered in the future by the local constabulary, a promise he could not keep.

That night the sheriff and the head of the state police took a group of seventy-five men toward Charleston, planning to capture someone, anyone, who could then be indicted as a ringleader. Clyde was in a group that camped out in a ballfield for the night, before returning home the next morning. "You know, it's funny," he said to a nearby comrade, "but I get the feelin' that somebody's out there in the woods."

"You must be dreamin'," a voice said. "Only miners have been coming up this way for hours. You must be hearin' some who ain't found a good place to sleep."

Hardly had the man finished speaking when about fifty lanterns suddenly brightened the area, and the miners, lying on the ground, saw themselves surrounded by a group of law-men with rifles and drawn pistols.

U. S. troops mounted a powerful searchlight atop Blair Mountain in their efforts to disperse miners.

"You're all under arrest as ringleaders in the murders of police officers on Blair Mountain," the sheriff said. "If anybody moves, you'll be killed here on the spot." Turning to his fellow officers, he said, "Put those chains and handcuffs on every one of these god-damn killers, and I don't care if you make 'em tight. These sons-o-bitches are likely to be facing the electric chair before too long."

Twenty-three miners were captured, and Bill Blizzard was arrested in Charleston. Clyde was one of the unfortunate ones, and he and the others were shackled, put on a railroad car, and sent to Logan. There, they were locked, six men at a time, in cells with three double bunks, with buckets for personal needs.

The next day, rather than murder, which would be hard to prove, the prosecutor decided to grandstand by charging all twenty-four men with treason against the sovereign State of West Virginia. He said that when these twenty-three plus Blizzard were found guilty, he planned to indict at least five hundred more miners.

The UMW president, Frank Keeney, visited the men in jail and presented them to Aaron Goldfine, who would be their defense attorney. "You boys are in the best hands the union can supply. Aaron is the best lawyer in this State and one of the finest men I know. So don't let it bother you none that he's a Jew. He's on your side."

Clyde had never met a Jew face to face, and stared intensely at Aaron Goldfine. To his surprise, the lawyer looked like other men. He wasn't sure what he had expected to see.

None of the prisoners in the Logan jail was recognized as the leader of the miners. Although Clyde was the youngest of the group, he stepped up to the bars and spoke to their defense lawyer. "We're awful confused here. First off, there musta been thousands of us on the mountain, so why pick on us? Second, the police never saw none of us with guns. Third, even if we wanted to fight, we never would fight against America. Then these goons grab us and claim we're the leaders of some gang. What's going on?"

"You are charged as being the leaders because you were the only ones they captured. Don't worry about the charges against you because they're silly. The State has a rigid definition of treason, so we're not totally defenseless. Also, West Virginia already has laws forbidding the private hiring of sheriff's deputies, so many of the people shooting at you were no more deputies than you are. What we have to worry about now is the fact that one of the local judges has now resigned his judicial office, in order to serve as the prosecutor in this case. He has simply moved from one hired-gun position to another. That may provide us a means to get a change of venue . . . ." The men stared at him. "You know, a change to another location."

Unwittingly, the mine operators decided that it might be difficult to convene a jury in Logan County that would convict miners, so they arranged to get the change of venue themselves. They hoped that a jury drawn from an agricultural county would convict. The trial was moved to Charles Town, in the eastern panhandle, the place where John Brown had been hanged sixty-two years before for his fight for freedom.

Clyde's leg bothered him quite a bit. The long march to Blair Mountain, followed by a week in jail while wearing the same elastic sock, had produced swelling. Although he removed the sock at night, to allow it to breathe, he could not get a clean one to change. The guards refused even to look in the bag he had been carrying where he had two clean socks. After two weeks, however, Aaron Goldfine persuaded the guards to let Clyde have his elastic socks, which reduced his pain considerably.

Being locked up in a crowded jail with little hope of getting out, possibly for years, depressed all the prisoners. Tensions ran high as men quarreled among themselves and were punished by the guards by reduced rations, which were not much more than broth and bread.

"By god," Clyde said, "I ain't gonna take no more of this. I cain't go but so far and no farther. The next guy that starts arguin' is gonna get a face full of my fist. We can't go on quarrelin' like this or we'll never get any real food. Besides, we may be here a long time, so we ort to be talkin' of escape instead of fussing. Why don't we put our information together and see how much we can find out about this place?" Talk of escape calmed the men down.

In January 1922, Clyde and his fellows, who had lost an average of fifteen pounds, were manacled and placed on a special train bound for Charles Town. "Well, whadda ya think, Clyde, are we gonna get out of this?" The speaker was manacled next to Clyde and the two had become acquainted while in jail.

"I jest don't know, Bud. It don't seem real, no how. Being chained here like this, traveling though country I never seen before. Going to what? To our death? Would they kill us for what happened at Blair, when there was thousands of others also? Besides, I ain't never understood what they're chargin' us with. Treason! Do you know what that means?"

"No. I always thought it was somebody who secretly fights his own government."

"That don't make no sense. When did we fight the government? When Keeney told us to put down our guns because the United States army was coming, everybody done just that. I ain't heerd nobody say he was against America. Have you?"

"No. As far as I know, every man I met was a loyal American."

"Things shore is strange."

When the train arrived in Charles Town, the prisoners were marched through the streets, still manacled to each other, to another jail. A crowd of angry citizens gathered in the street to protest the treatment. A local civil-rights lawyer was the leader of the protest. "This is no way to treat men who were fighting for their rights," he said. "What makes this whole case a sham is now clear when we have learned that the prosecutors are being paid by the coal operators. More than that, the State's attorney general has not even bothered to send an observer to the trial. Just because we don't have coal mines in this part of the State doesn't mean we aren't interested in fairness and justice. Coal miners are human, too. We may have a different concept of fairness from Logan County, but ours is based on the Bill of Rights of the Constitution."

The trial began in May, 1922. Bill Blizzard was to be tried first. Aaron Goldfine was up to the challenge he faced. "Your honor," he said to the black robed judge who looked properly somber, "My client has been charged with treason, so it seems appropriate to set certain standards for treason. According to the Constitution of West Virginia, as well as that of the United States, treason is clearly defined. Each person can be convicted only if there are two independent witnesses to the same overt treasonous act of giving aid and comfort to the enemy in time of war. Therefore, I beg the court to rule that my defendant must be charged according to the Constitution; which means the prosecution must be ordered to produce two witnesses to the same overt act, and must demonstrate that there was a time of war when the alleged treason occurred, all before any possible finding of guilt can occur."

"Your honor," the chief prosecutor said, "this court must consider the seriousness of the case. This man is charged with leading a horde of viciously armed men, who attacked officers of the law, killing a number of them and wounding dozens. They took the law into their own hands. Your honor must not be taken in by the emotional appeal of defense counsel regarding the United States Constitution. I beg you to resist this appeal which is designed to free these murderers, before there is even a trial."

The judge looked at the two lawyers, and pondered a while. Finally, he said to the prosecutor, "It is you who have charged Mr. Blizzard and others with treason. Would you apply a looser standard for conviction in this case than is spelled out in the West Virginia Constitution? Would you try for treason any person who killed a police officer? The standard proposed by the defense is reasonable and I grant it. Can you produce two witnesses to the same overt treasonous act in a time of war?"

"We feel that the standards are too high, but we

can still convict these men," the prosecutor said. "We are willing to try these man one at a time, and that's why we have chosen to try Bill Blizzard first."

Aaron Goldfine pointed out that the prosecutors were not connected with the Office of the Attorney General nor with any county law enforcement agency, but were attorneys for the coal operators. "No one here," he said, "represents the people of West Virginia, although it is their supposed representatives who have already aligned with one side against the other. It is the State that is on trial, not men who seek rights of free speech and assembly. If Blizzard is found guilty, then who else is safe from being charged with treason? If he is found guilty, then the State will stand out as in a condition of anarchy."

After a five-week trial, Blizzard was acquitted and the charges against the rest were dropped. Some newspapers noted that law and order had already broken down, coal operators were in control of the state, and there was therefore no government against which treason was possible.

The men were all released from jail.

Chapter Eight

None of the co-defendants understood fully what had happened, except that suddenly they were free. The judge, furthermore, ordered Logan County to pay the fare for any miner who wished to return to the south.

Clyde decided to remain in the north and see what mining was like there. He retrieved his bag and put a clean elastic sock on his swollen leg, and confirmed that forty-five dollars he had hidden in a side pocket was still there. He bought a bus ticket for Morgantown for a dollar, and was impressed by the Monongahela River, as it flowed northward toward Pittsburgh to join the Allegheny in forming the Ohio. Three dollars went for a week's lodging, and still another for food. He spent half a dollar to take a bus to Mannington, where he approached the mine foreman at a shaft mine for work. "How old did you say you are?" the foreman asked.

"I turned twenty last week, on June 16. I've worked in the mines for almost seven years, first near Oak Hill and then near Charleston. I was a trapper boy, then a coal loader, a track man, and a motor man, and I've had a little training in electricity."

"That's impressive for a boy your age. We do need a track man, so report here at six tomorrow morning."

Clyde reported as asked, and was laying track at

five p.m. when the foreman came to him. "Look, kid,"
he said. "I was wrong about needing a track man. In
fact, we don't need any workers right now. I brought
your pay for the day, so why don't you take it and
leave."

"That don't seem quite right," Clyde said. "I can
see by just looking around that you got a lot of track to
lay. Is there something wrong?"

"The super made some calls and found out you're
a socialist who was in that gang that fought at Blair
Mountain. We don't want no troublemakers here, so
go!"

"Well, I'm a union man and I bet the union'll help
me."

"Don't count on it. The union here does pretty
much what they're told. We pay them a little bit more
than other places and that keeps them quiet."

Clyde left the mine and went directly to the union
office, a little shack near the company store. He
knocked and a fat man appeared, smoking a cigar.
"What can I do for you?"

"I'm Clyde Fuller from down south and I was
hired to lay track yesterday and fired awhile ago."

"What for?"

"The foreman said he didn't need any workers,
and besides he thought I was some kind of trouble
maker."

"What kind of trouble did he accuse you of."

"Said I was in that group of miners that fought at
Blair Mountain, but nobody ever proved I fought
there."

"Were you there?"

"What difference does it make? I'm a coal miner

and a member of the UMW. Ain't you gonna fight for me to keep the job?"

"Look, we done worked things out here and don't need no one to interfere. The company pays us more and we promise not to cause trouble. I can't do a thing for you."

"You're no better'n a scab!" Clyde yelled as he left the office. He then went to Pursglove and visited the union office first.

"I happen to know this mine needs workers. With your background, you can be used in two or three places. If I was you, I wouldn't say I was from the southern mines. It makes a lot of people nervous. Me, I like what some fellows did on Blair Mountain, but if you was there, I'd keep it quiet. Get me?"

"Sure, I get you."

"Good. The mine foreman, named Chip Kelly, is a pretty decent guy. Go see him early tomorrow, at number three shaft."

"Much obliged."

Clyde got a job at Pursglove in number three shaft, and stayed two years. He proved especially valuable, because he worked at different tasks while there.

In late 1922, he learned that the United Mine Workers of America had abandoned its efforts to unionize Mingo and Logan counties. Two million dollars had been poured into the struggle, but the financial power of the mine owners could not be overcome, even though it had been in other parts of the state. Miners in those two counties continued to work at subsistence wages, long hours, inflated food prices, and poor housing. Elsewhere, conditions were only slightly better.

After two years at Pursglove, Clyde moved to

Scott's Run and got more experience. Always, he was moving. He kept thinking about Logan County. He was certain he had killed Avery Murphy, the detective who had killed his friend, Elmer, back there at Matewan; and he felt strongly he had killed a deputy and one other person at Blair Mountain. He heard that the newspapers kept back issues, so he went to the newspaper office in Morgantown and asked if it was true and could he see one.

"Sure. What're you looking for?" a young woman asked.

"Well, I'd like to see the papers for August and September, 1921. Would that be possible?"

"That's easy. They are piled up in a back room by month. I'll bring the ones you want to you. You can read them at one of the tables. There are paper slips nearby, if you want to take notes. You're not allowed to take the papers outside this room."

"Thank you."

He found the papers that described the Battle of Blair Mountain and laboriously read them. Two sheriff's deputies and one detective had been reported killed on the second day of battle. That was something of a relief, because Clyde thought he had shot at the deputy on the first day. He also couldn't be sure he had killed another man in that battle. He was somewhat bothered by it, but after all, they were shooting at him. He recalled that he probably had killed the man who shot Elmer, but wondered why he thought of it so often. He acknowledged to himself that he might be a murderer, but wondered why he didn't feel like one.

In 1925, at age twenty-three, after more or less continuous work and living frugally, Clyde bought a used Model T Ford for one hundred twenty dollars, and learned to drive it. He began to roam the countryside on Sundays, when it was not raining or snowing. One experience of trying to drive in rain soaked tire tracks that sank the car to its axles was enough to keep him at home unless the weather cooperated. The Ford meant that his restlessness could now be met by getting acquainted with the area surrounding Morgantown.

When he was not working, and not exploring, he spent his time trying to understand things. He now read a newspaper every day, but references to New York, Washington, or Chicago seemed like dream places; not that they were pleasant dreams, but rather a chimera which he wanted to visit and hoped to avoid. Always the papers were filled with bad things: wars, murders, theft, conflict, strikes, crooked politicians, and women wearing short dresses.

Clyde Fuller was by now clearly a bright, but uneducated man. He was of average height, had a handsome face with a chin dimple, and straight black hair. He had all the qualities of an intelligent person, a curiosity about the world, a hope to understand it, and the devotion of many hours speculating about meaning and purpose. However, he lived in a world dominated by the educated, the professionals, the doers, the leaders, the molders of opinions. Because he was uneducated, he had to stand by while events he did not fully understand swirled around him. He lacked the basic tools for grasping life and always felt left out.

In 1925, a fellow miner invited him to a party held at a Church in Blacksville, only ten miles away.

"It's just a party," his friend said, "at the Methodist Church. It won't hurt you and you might meet someone you like. You don't seem to have many friends here. Why don't you come?"

"Methodists? Are they real Christians? I've heerd of them but never went to no church."

"Well, don't worry. We're not going to no church service. There'll be some lemonade, and coffee and tea, and some cookies and pies. Everybody will just get acquainted, and maybe play some games, like musical chairs."

"I don't know how to play games. Maybe you better go without me."

"So you're afraid of a little fun, are you? Want to hide in your room?"

"No. I ain't afraid of nothin'. I'll show you. I'll go with you."

"Great. We'll leave here about seven o'clock on Saturday. We'll go in my car."

At the party, a young man asked Clyde what he did.

"I'm a coal miner," Clyde said.

"I'm sure glad I don't work in the mines," the man said. "I've been following all the tension in the southern mines, and it seems to get worse and worse."

"Of course it gets worse and worse. Miners is shot-at all the time and killed right out in the open if they support a union," Clyde said, as other people gathered around him as he spoke.

"When the miners tried to form a union in Matewan, the company fired all of them. That even led to a gunfight between the chief of police and some company thugs. Ten men were killed right in front of the hardware store. The companies were too powerful and bought off the judges and police, and hired their own private police force. To this day, there ain't no union in Mingo or Logan Counties. The miners are treated just like they're shovels or picks, not human beings. When they do get work, their pay is reduced by being forced to buy food at the company stores at prices higher than at other stores. They can be fired if they don't buy at the company store." He smiled at the young men and women who had gathered around him.

"You've all heerd of the trial of a bunch of miners in Charles Town. Well, I hafta admit that I was one of the men, 'cause I was in the Battle of Blair Mountain. The judge freed us." He never mentioned that he had been in Matewan.

"Mining is real dangerous, as you know, but not all mines is the same. Here in this region, we ride straight down in the mines in a cage, but in the south, we walk right into a hole in the side of the mountain, called slope mining. I think I like slopes better than shaft. Something else I've noticed here is that there ain't as many coal mines in the northern part of the state as in the south.

"Another thing, the valleys are deeper in the southern part of the state than in the north. We got a lot of high mountains there. My Old Man Jack called the valleys ditches. Once, I hopped a freight train to go to Logan, and the valleys was so close that you could only see the sun about four or five hours in the middle of the day. Logan is beside Mingo County, where the Hatfield and McCoy fight took place. That's a real wilderness, and there's people living back in the hills who ain't never been to a city. They're good folks, even if they do drink and fight a lot."

"How can they drink a lot? Isn't there prohibition

there?" a woman asked.

"Shore, but those hillbillies got stills hidden up in the mountains where they make white lightening, sometimes called mountain dew. The feds discover the stills every once in a while, but they cain't get them all, and the corn likker still flows. If you know how, it's easy to get a drink, but many people think it's too powerful. It'll knock the socks right off you."

"Did you ever drink the stuff?"

"I tasted some of it once, but it didn't do much for me. I like to keep a clear head all the time. I'll be honest and say that the one thing I miss is beer."

He talked a great deal and was pleasantly surprised that people actually stopped to listen to him, and even to raise questions. He felt good about himself.

One portly young woman, about his age, especially caught his eye, so he maneuvered around to meet her. She had listened intently to him talk, but never said a word. She was about five feet tall, had a beautiful round face, was somewhat heavy for her height, and was wearing a black dress to mid calf, her hair bunched into a top knot that fit the times.

"Well, my pretty woman, did you like my stories?" he asked.

"They were interesting. Did you tell everything?"

"What do you mean?"

"You talked a lot about yourself, but I suspect you didn't really reveal who you are."

"I'm just a poor hillbilly who works in the mines."

"Oh, it's clear that you've had a lot of experience in the mines, but you must have started when you were very young. Could you go to school and work the mines, too?"

"You know how to bring a man down, don't you?"

"Please forgive me. I had no thought of belittling you. I'm so sorry. Can you forgive me?"

"Shore I can. Will you join me in having a cup of coffee?"

"Yes. Of course. What did I say that troubled you, or don't you want to talk about it? Maybe we ought to change the subject. By the way, I'm Kate Morris."

"Pleased ta meetchu, Miss Morris. My name is Clyde Fuller. You sure are pretty, ma'am."

"Thank you, Mr. Fuller. You have a kind way about you. Where do you live now?"

"Near Scotts Run. You raised a fair question and I ain't gonna ignore it. It's just that I can't hide my poor schoolin'. I only finished the fourth grade and a little bit of the fifth, then I went to work in the mines when I was thirteen."

"Thirteen! That's amazing. I didn't know any child that young could work in the mines. It must have been a frightening experience."

"I wouldn't admit it at the time, but it was pretty scary. It was the darkness. I jest couldn't git used to the darkness. I had the feeling that it was draped 'round me like tight fittin' clothes. 'Course, after a few years, I couldn't tell whether darkness was the real world or whether light was. Does that sound strange to you, ma'am?"

"Not really. I think I understand. I've never been closely involved with mines, myself, and so what you say is interesting. My father works for the oil company, patrolling the gas lines that run across the fields. So even though mines are nearby, mining is strange to me. . . . What does Old Man Jack mean?"

"He's my daddy."

"You must have a bad feeling about him."

"Well, we didn't see eye to eye. He whupped me with a belt for not going to school, and I was so stubborn that I refused ever to go to school again. My mama had died, so I 'spect my daddy didn't know no better. You know, sugar tastes better'n vinegar."

"How did you live?"

"I stayed with my uncle and aunt till I got a job in the mines. I've seen my daddy only about four times in the last six or seven years."

"How awful!"

"Enough about me. I'd like to meet your daddy some time. He has to be nice to raise a woman like you. Would you mind if I come to visit you a week from next Sunday, and meet your folks?"

"I think that would be nice. I live in the fifth house on the left, after you leave Blacksville on the west. Think you can find it?"

"Sure. I can count that high. About three o'clock?"

"That would be fine."

Chapter Nine

Armed with a dozen roses, Clyde went to see Kate Morris at three o'clock on Sunday. He parked his Model T Ford beside a picket fence, walked up on the porch with a colonnade set against a white house, nestled on a hill side. Kate answered his knock on the door.

"Hello, Mister Fuller. It's nice to see you again."

"It's nice to see you too, Miss Morris. I hope you like these roses, and I have a box of chocolates for your mother."

"They're beautiful, and I'm sure mama will like the candy. Come on in and meet my parents." She led him into a funereal parlor, with a carpet of dark floral design, dismal stuffed chairs and davenport, some heavy carved small tables, and poorly lit lamps with black fringes hanging from the shades. Clyde blinked his eyes, trying to get used to the darkness. A couple in their sixties sat in the chairs.

"Mama, daddy, this is Mr. Fuller, whom I met at the party at the church a week ago last Saturday. My mother and father, Jeremy and Mildred Morris."

"Pleased ta meetchu, Mr. Morris and you too, Mrs. Morris." Clyde shook hands with each and said to Mrs. Morris as he handed her a box of candy, "I hope you like candy."

"Thank you, Mr. Fuller," she said without any enthusiasm. "It's my understanding you're from the southern part of this State. Do you plan to stay in the north long?"

"I never really thought of it, but I guess I'll stay as long as I can find work."

"What kind of work do you do?" Mr. Morris asked.

"I'm a coal miner. Worked in the mines for ten years."

"Ten years! You must have started as a kid," Mr. Morris said.

"Yes. I was only thirteen. I've learned a lot of different jobs in those years. I can hold my own with about any job they is in a mine. 'Course, I ain't got used to these shaft mines yet. I like the slope mines best."

"I guess there isn't much future in the mines for a person without much education," Mrs. Morris said. "At age thirteen, you probably hadn't even finished the sixth grade."

"That's right. I only got part of the fifth grade. But I'm a hard worker, so maybe I can learn some more some day."

"Well," the mother continued, "it's awfully sweet of Kate to invite you over for a short visit. It's likely Mr. Boone will drop by later this afternoon. He has been to college."

"Mother!" Kate said. "I don't think that's fair. After all, we've just met Mr. Fuller, and he's merely visiting us to get better acquainted. Come on, Mr. Fuller, let's take a walk. I'll show you the orchard."

"Yes, I'd like that," Clyde said, looking at Kate's parents with a puzzled look.

They walked out of the house down a path that led

to the peach orchard, two acres of heavy-laden trees.

"I don't think your mother likes me," Clyde said.

"I don't think it's that. She has always said she hoped I would meet and marry a banker, or a doctor. She never looks on coal mining as a suitable occupation for anybody. I'm so sorry for what she said and your embarrassment."

"Don't be. She may be right. After all, miners is nothing but rats working in holes in the ground."

"That's an awful way to think of yourself."

"Actually, I think a little higher than that. Someday, I'm gonna be a fire boss. Then I'll have something to say about a mine. Men will listen to me."

"How do you become a fire boss?"

"First, you gotta know mining. Then you hafta study and pass some tests. I'm still learnin' mining, but later I'll think about preparin' for the tests."

"That makes sense. I like to see a man with ambition."

"You do? Then maybe I can see you again?"

"There's another party at the Methodist Church in two weeks. Would you like to come?"

"Sure I would. Just give me the date and time and I'll be there. Will they have more of that lemonade?"

"I'll see that we have plenty."

"Thank you, Miss Morris. I find you very kind."

"That's nice of you Mr. Fuller. If you will permit me to call you Clyde, you may call me Kate."

They saw each other every two or three weeks, usually at Kate's house or at some public gathering. When he took her for a ride in his Ford, they were chaperoned by one of her parents.

For Clyde, the meeting with Kate was the beginning of a valuable friendship, at least at first. She had completed the ninth grade in school, but went no further because there was no public high school in the surrounding area. She was able nevertheless to help him with his reading and he soon found the daily paper easier to cope with. He even improved his grammar, but not to perfection.

After a courtship of a year, he asked her to marry him. When she agreed, he said he must also ask her parents. Her father assented to the marriage, but her mother opposed it.

"He's nice enough," Mrs. Morris said, "but has no future. I'm sure you'll regret it, Kate."

Despite her mother's warning, Kate seemed determined to marry Clyde, her first suitor. They were married in the summer of 1926, when both were twenty-four years old. There were only ten people at the ceremony, because her parents, as her mother said, could not afford a large wedding. Clyde's contribution to the wedding was to buy a grey suit with vest ($20.00), a white shirt and blue tie ($2.00), and a pair of shiny black shoes ($8.00). "I won't look as good as you," he said, "but we'll look nice standing before the preacher together. Don't you think so?"

"Don't belittle yourself," Kate said. "You look very nice in your new suit. And your shoes just sparkle. To me, you look like a successful man."

Their honeymoon consisted of a hotel room in Morgantown and a chance to eat at a good restaurant. After a meal of meatloaf, potatoes, and gravy, they went to their room where Clyde hefted her into his arms, crossed the threshold, and laid her on the bed.

Sitting on the edge of the bed, he leaned over and

kissed her. "Hello, my sweetie. Want me to help you get undressed?"

"No! I mean not tonight. We don't have to rush things, do we? Why don't we just rest tonight and then go further tomorrow night?"

"I don't understand. We're married. Don't that mean we get to make love? I've been countin' the days. I expect it tonight."

"I'm a little nervous," she said, watching him closely. "I've never done this before, you know. Do I have to take my clothes off?"

"Of course you do," he said. "Let me help you and it can be fun."

"No. You stand outside the door and I'll get ready for bed. Don't look so disappointed. I'll let you do it tonight, although I'd rather wait till later. I understand men have strong needs, so I'll do my wifely duties."

"Why can't I watch you undress? That thought excites me."

"That's evil. No lady would think of such a thing. You must go out, while I get ready for bed."

Reluctantly, Clyde went outside the room and killed time by using the bathroom at the end of the hall. After ten minutes, he knocked on the door and heard her say come in. She was lying in bed with covers tight under her chin.

"I hope you won't mind if I undress," he said.

"Do you have to take all your clothes off?" she asked.

"Shore. I sleep naked most of the time, anyway. Why would you object? Don't you want to see your husband naked? I always thought most women do."

"I'm not most women, and I find this kind of talk

offensive. Get in bed and do what you have to do."

He crawled into bed and moved to her. "My god, what are you wearing," he said, "a flannel gown in July?"

"It's the only thing I'm comfortable with."

He threw the sheet off, and grabbed the loose gown, and pulled it up far enough to see her full breasts. Below her rotund belly, were the brown pubic hair and the object of his longing. He spread her legs and knelt between them, his organ ready. He paused and looked at her, apprehension on her face, then rolled over to the edge of the bed and sat up, his face in his hands.

"I can't believe what I almost done," he said as if she were not there. "God must be punishin' me for something I done years ago. Here I thought I finally got a woman that can satisfy a man's needs, and who can help me to better myself. Then I find out she's a cold fish, uninterested in what can please a man, even if it's her husband."

Kate rolled over to him and grabbed his shoulders. "I'm so sorry. I was trying to be ready, but I guess it takes women longer than men. I'm sure in a few days it will be better, as I get used to what is expected of me. I hope you won't get angry with me again. I know I shouldn't be like this. I know that I'm supposed to help a man get relief, but I was scared. Now I see that you're a gentle man, I'm willing to try it again. Here, I'll even take my gown off . . . There . . . Do I look all right to you? Will you try once more to enter me?"

"You look fine, just as you're supposed to. I'd like to kiss your breasts."

She thrust her chest out and he proceeded to function as the situation called for.

After that, their frequency was less than he desired and more than she wished, but a son was born to them nine months after the wedding.

It was not a marriage described in romance novels. Clyde, as he matured, became loquacious, stood out in a crowd, was highly opinionated, especially about politics which he was trying to understand. He tried to develop an interest in other people, but almost always found himself the most interesting topic of any conversation. He became a first-rate storyteller, especially with tales about the mines.

Kate was taciturn, almost invisible in a group. She had little interest in people outside the family, but to her family she devoted every ounce of her commitment. Anyone who became a friend came to her; she sought out no one. She had no interest in the news or what was happening in the world. She had an inexhaustible tolerance for listening to Clyde speak and never, at least in front of her child, disagreed with him.

Early on, Kate said, "I've been observing you, and I've never seen anyone so restless. From everything I hear you saying, you're not pleased with whom you are. You want something more."

"I do want something more. I'm just a coal miner without an education. I keep looking for a better way. Maybe some day I'll find it."

"It won't come to you. You've got to make it happen. There's a School of Mine Extension right in Morgantown at the University. They have night classes and some on Saturday. You ought to consider it."

"I already heerd there was a school for mining there. They wouldn't take in a fourth grader, would they?"

"You won't know till you try them."

It was too frightening a thought and he procrastinated about it.

"Look," Kate said. "You already have twelve years experience in the mines, and from what you tell me, you've worked in every type of position. At least, go talk with them."

Finally, to keep her from continually nagging him about it, he decided one day to do it. He dressed in his one suit, put on a necktie, shined his black shoes, and wore a cap instead of the straw hat he liked to wear. He drove his Ford across the river and up the hill to the campus, which looked vast and imposing to him. He found a place to park and, alighting from the car, saw that young people were everywhere, possibly making fun of him. Red brick buildings had strange names on them. There were no meaningful signs, and he did not know which way to turn. He stood by his car in total bewilderment. Since he was well dressed, he hoped that he fitted right in. The only problem was what to do next. Which way should he turn?

"Hello there. You look lost. May I be of help? I'm a professor here, in English. Are you looking for the administration building? Most people are at this time of year."

"No. I, uh, don't know what building I'm looking for, but I would like to go to the place where they learn mining to people who ain't in college."

"The word is aren't, not ain't, and it's teach, not learn. I suspect you want the Department of Mining Engineering, which has some extension programs. Go right over the hill there and you'll see a sign that says

Department of Mining Engineering."

"Much obliged," Clyde said, wondering what the man meant by saying the words weren't ain't or learn.

He walked over the hill and saw a building with the appropriate sign, a large red brick edifice, with wide cement steps leading up to wide doors. Young men, well dressed in suits and tie, were scurrying in and out. Clyde entered the building and looked down a long hall, with numerous doors opening off the hallway. Beside the closest door, he saw the name of Professor Rufus L. Ledbetter. On the next door was Professor James Starling Jones. He walked down the hall until he came to a door marked Dean, from which much activity was visible through a large window. Inside was a counter, with a young woman behind it, her hair in a bob. "May I help you?" she asked, as Clyde approached cautiously.

"Yes. I'd like to see the boss, if I could."

"The boss?" she said, suspiciously.

"Yes. If he's in."

"If who's in?"

"The boss. The man who's in charge here."

"Oh, you must mean the Dean. Is that the person you want?"

"I'm not certain. What does a Dean do?"

"He's in charge of the College of Engineering."

"Does he have anything to do with mining?"

"Mining engineering is one of the areas of his concern. Maybe if you told me exactly what you want, I could help better."

Clyde was twisting the cap he held in his hands and trying not to yield to the temptation to turn and flee. "Well, you see, I heerd there was people here who could learn a man how to become a fire boss, and I was just inquirin' about it."

"Let me have your name and I'll see if the Dean can talk to you now. I'm sure we can help you some way."

"Thank you. My name is Clyde Fuller."

"Thank you, Mister Fuller. Won't you please sit down while I tell the Dean you're here."

Clyde thought she seemed real accommodating, and he hoped the Dean would be also.

The young woman returned quickly. "The Dean will see you now, Mr. Fuller. Please follow me." She led him to a door off her work area and told him to go right in.

He saw a man, fully suited, with white hair, sitting behind the largest desk he had ever seen. In front of him was a sign that read, Professor Cyril Humphrey, Dean. "Come in, Mister Fuller. I'm not certain from what the secretary said about you, but I surmise you may be interested in entering the Engineering College. Is that correct?"

"I don't rightly know. I heerd they was a school here where you can learn a man how to get papers for fire bossing, and I wanted to hear about it."

The dean smiled slightly, and then, with complete kindness, said, "I suspect you haven't finished high school yet. How far have you gotten in school?"

"I finished the fourth grade and took a little of the fifth."

"Yes, I see. I suspect you're really interested in the mine extension program. For that, you'll want to see Professor Darrell Kelly. Let me call Doctor Kelly and see if he's in."

He dialed a number and then said, "Hello, Darrell. This is Cy. I have a gentleman here who is interested in the mine extension program. Can you see him now? . . . Oh, that's great. I'll send him right down."

Turning to Clyde, he said, "Doctor Kelly can see you now, and his office is on the next floor down. Go right on down, because he's waiting for you."

"Much obliged. I'll do it."

Clyde left the Dean's office bewildered at the complexity of it all. There seemed to be professors everywhere, and he wondered how they were all kept busy. He had started this inquiry, and he was determined to see it through. He found a door marked Professor Darrell Kelly and knocked. "Come in," came a rough voice from inside.

Sitting behind a desk, just as large as the Dean's, was a man who looked to be about forty. He had piercing eyes, was dressed in a brown pin-stripe suit, and smoked a pipe. Clyde could not imagine what they could keep in so large a desk.

"Doctor Humphrey said I ort to see you."

"Yes, he called me. What can I do for you, Mister . . . let's see, that's Fuller, isn't it?"

"Yes. Clyde Fuller. I heerd you have a program that can learn a man how to become a fire boss. I have worked in about every position in the mines now for twelve years, trapper boy, coal loader, motor man, track man, some electricity. I've studied how they're ventilated and that interests me a lot. I've worked in about six different mines now."

"Well, it looks like you may have the kind of experience we want in the miners who enter our extension programs, but I wonder if you have the reading ability to pass the courses. How far did you get in school?"

"I finished the fourth grade and took a little fifth, and I read the papers regularly."

"I doubt that you could read at the level we require."

"Look, my wife has a good education, and she has been helping me to read. I take a newspaper every day and read all the front page and most of the other pages, except for sports. I been trying to get myself prepared for this place. Can't you give me a chance? I been wanting a place like this so bad my mind won't let me think of nothing else. Maybe you got a test you can give me to see what I know."

"That's rather unusual. Still, perhaps we can see where you are. You certainly seem motivated and that's a big part of being successful. Tell you what I"m willing to do, if you have the nerve. I have here a blank map of a mine that I use for the first test I give to my ventilation students. I give them thirty minutes to ventilate the mine. Most of them make mistakes, which is only natural, since it's the first test. They have to read the descriptions of conditions here in the margins, and then use a red pencil to show the flow of air that is needed. If a student makes eight errors, he fails and cannot continue the program. Four or five errors are a C. Two or three errors are a B, and no error is an A. Are you willing to try your hand at it?"

"Yes. I think I can do it."

"If you can do it with no more than twelve errors, it would be a good sign that you might be able to pass our program. Come over here to this work table, and I'll time you when to start."

Clyde was led to a large table from which papers

were removed, and he was given a chair and a red marker pencil. "You may start now," Kelly said.

Clyde spent twenty minutes laboriously reading the descriptions, the locations of the fans, the height of the coal seams, the different passageways, and pockets where gas had formed. Kelly smiled indulgently at how much time was taken in reading the conditions.

Suddenly, Clyde swung his pencil over the paper, leaving long red marks in places and short ones in others, drawing in barriers where needed. After seven minutes, he announced that he was finished.

"Don't you want to take the time that's left to double-check you work? You've got three minutes, you know."

"No. If this ain't right, then I ain't learned nothing in twelve years."

"Well! You certainly aren't weak on conceit, are you! Here, let me have it and mark out the errors." He sat down at his desk with the map and, taking his heavy black pen, began to trace the proper air flow for the mine. He went through it quickly without making a mark, then frowning, retraced the examination with greater care, again making no mark on the paper. He looked up, scowling.

"I don't understand this. Are you making fun of me? How did you know how to ventilate that mine?"

"I told you that I've worked at a number of mines, and I've always studied how they are ventilated. I find that interestin'. Besides, it's important for miners' survival. Soon, the proper way seemed clear. Why are you angry?"

"I'm not angry, just startled. This would have gotten an A on my first test, after eight hours of lecture and some practice sessions. Yet you got it right the first time, without any lectures or practice. Why do you want to go to school?"

"So I can get the certificates that will make me a fire boss."

"You may be slow in reading, but I am now convinced you can do the work. I'm happy to accept you into our short course in coal mining. The next session starts in January. We'll give you special lectures on ventilation, gasses, geology, safety lamps, mine fires and explosions, timbering, and mine law. There'll be a lot of homework. I presume you plan to continue working?"

"Yes. I have to work to feed my family. I have a wife and small son."

"I understand, but I suspect you can do it. Here's a packet of papers you need to fill out and a schedule of classes, all at night or on Saturdays. Welcome to our mine extension program."

"Thank you very much. I can do the work."

"Somehow, I believe you. Good luck."

As Clyde walked into the hallway, he saw Doctor Farthingham coming toward him. "Hello, Doctor Farthingham," he said, "remember me? I'm Clyde Fuller. We met at Logan in a rooming house in 1920."

"Clyde Fuller? Yes, yes. Of course I remember you. The young coal miner. What brings you to West Virginia University?"

"I've been admitted to the School of Mine Extension. They're going to learn me to be a fire boss."

"I'll bet they teach you more than fire bossing. Still, I'm delighted to hear of your ambition . . . Logan? Yes, it's coming back to me now. You arrived there about the time of that shootout in Matewan. Isn't that right?"

"Yeah. I guess it was about that time." Clyde shifted his weight and looked at the floor.

"You know, I often thought that maybe you were that young man the papers mentioned, who ran away after his friend was killed. Would you be the one?"

Clyde swallowed hard. "How could that be, sir? Remember, I was on crutches when we met."

"Yes, of course. I should have remembered that. I guess you tend to forget details after seven years. You seem to be getting around all right now."

"Yes, my leg healed like the doctor said it would."

"It's nice to see you again, and I wish you the best of luck."

"Thank you, sir." As Farthingham walked away, Clyde thought to himself: I ain't gonna let what he said stop me. I been accepted here, and I'm gonna succeed. I know I can do it.

He spent the fall of 1927 practicing reading with Kate, and even bought some books on mining, to practice on. The books were filled with technical geological terms that he never did learn, but he still benefited from them because they provided a general feeling with which he could identify. He started the formal program in January and soon found every evening, after eight to ten hours in the mines, devoted to either lectures or homework. Kate sat at the kitchen table with him, helping him to read every page. Often he blurted out, "Yes, now I see it. I know exactly what they mean. Makes me feel good to know I understand this stuff. I appreciate your helping me read it."

"I'm glad to do it. Don't you realize that you're

reading much better than just a month ago. Your vocabulary has grown quite a bit, especially with words that apply to mining. It's such a pleasure to see a man so motivated."

"You got to admit, I always told you I'm gonna better myself, and I think I am right now. What I'm doin' will pay off, you'll see."

"Oh, I believe you, Clyde. I think you're going to prove my mother wrong."

"Well, you know that ain't my main goal, but it will be nice if I can better myself, so she has to admit it."

He led his class with a 4.0 grade record and graduated on July 21, 1928. He took a certificate in Mine Rescue Training at the same time, and passed the state examination for First Class Mine Foreman the following October. The news reached him in the mail.

"Look here Kate. I done it. I got my certificates. I'll go see if that old Ford will start while you get Jimmy ready. We'll go down and look at a new car I've had my eye on."

"Are you sure we can afford a car? Will you make enough money?"

"Sure, I'll get a lot more. We've got the money saved now for a car. It'll only cost about three hundred dollars for a new Willis Whippet. I'm gonna get that much now out of the bag." He went into the small bedroom, opened the bottom drawer of a chest, took out a small bag, and dumped the contents on the top. "Kate," he called out, "we've got a little over three hundred fifty dollars here, so we'll be okay."

"All right, Clyde, if you say so. I've always worried about having that much money in the house, so if it goes into a car, it probably won't be stolen from us. I still wish you'd put our savings in a bank."

"You know I'm afraid of banks. If it makes you feel better, I'll put what's left over from buying the car in a bank."

He got the little Whippet for two hundred seventy-five dollars and felt that at last he was beginning to look successful. "It's a good feeling to have something like this, ain't it?"

"Yes. It does feel good," she said, settling into the front seat of the new vehicle. "You deserve it. You've worked hard for what you have. There are not many men who could have done what you've done, considering your background."

"Do you think maybe it's stubbornness?"

"Partly. You also have a curiosity about things and you catch on quick."

"Maybe you're right. A man can't just live in a rut. He's got to try to see over the top if he can."

Chapter Ten

Clyde got his first job as fire boss at Pursglove, where he had previously worked. At the end of his first run, he walked up to the notice board at the entrance of the mine labeled Fire Boss Report, and wrote the following: "Mine Clear. Mine Temp. 58, Oct. 20, '28. Clyde Fuller, Fire Boss." He smiled like a child at Christmas, every time he filled out the Report.

The stock market crashed a year later. Other fire bosses had seniority over him, so Clyde found himself without work. "Fire bosses are needed in the southern part of the state," the general mine foreman told him. "You should try there. I hate to see you go, but I don't know of any openings here in the north."

Clyde loaded Kate and his son in their small car and headed for Logan, leaving some furniture with Kate's parents. Although the mines were working only one day a week, sometimes two, it was necessary for a fire boss to make a run through to be sure no gas had accumulated. Clyde was able, as a result, to get work right away at Whitman in Logan County and was given a fire boss run, always twice and sometimes even four times a week.

"Since there's another baby on the way, we must be thankful that you get as much work as you do," Kate said, only weeks before she delivered a stillborn son.

Clyde noted that she was gaining weight.

"You know, Kate," Clyde said one evening after supper in October 1931, "I got a bad feeling about the mine. There's lots of methane gas down there and also a lot of very fine coal dust. You put those two together with a spark and it will explode. I'm afraid of it. I've tried to get the mine foreman to blow in a lot of rock dust, which suppresses the coal dust, but he claims the owners don't have the money. He says the depression is as hard on them like it is on us. Can you believe that? He'll risk an explosion, rather than spread a little rock dust."

"What are you going to do about it?"

"If it gets any worse, I'll have to quit or you won't have a husband."

"Oh, Clyde! It's really that bad, is it? We're doing well here, so that'll be a big step to lose this job. Where would you go?"

"I think with my papers, I can get a job some place."

"Well, do what you have to do."

The very next week he went over the head of the mine foreman to talk with the superintendent, George Holman, who was new on the job and was as hesitant to spend money as his predecessor. Clyde told the super that rock dust needed to be sprayed over the bug dust to help reduce flammability.

"No way, Clyde. You know we can't afford that. See if you can't get more air in there. That'll take care of things."

"But George, I've done all I can do without rock dust. That section is gonna blow on us if we don't do something about it."

"You fire bosses are always seeing scary things. You worry too much. I simply won't approve spending any more money on safety, and that's that."

"Then I quit. I got a family to support and my son won't have a father if I stay. Get yourself another fire boss."

"It's not very bright of a man to quit in the middle of a depression, when he has a good job. You must be crazy. Screw you. I'll find another fire boss."

When Kate learned of his act, she asked, "What can we do now?"

"Kate, I'm sure that mine will blow, and I don't want to be in it when it does. If I've learned nothing, it's when gas has become dangerous. I'm gonna drive over to Rossmore. I heerd they need a fire boss there."

Sure enough, he was hired the very next day in Rossmore, and moved his family there to a company house. The coal camp lay in a valley wide enough to handle rows of houses five abreast, as well as a creek, a railroad and a road. He was given a little four-room house with running water and a privy near by.

Despite the setback, Clyde seemed always to keep his sense of humor, though Kate often disliked it. On the drive to Rossmore, the round knob of the gearshift came off and Clyde dropped it between his legs. "I'll put it here with the other balls," he said with a grin.

"How dare you!" Kate said. "How can you even think of such a thing with Jimmy in the back seat?"

"He's not even four yet. You're being too critical."

"You know I don't care for sex jokes. It's simply something people don't talk about."

Clyde frowned and said nothing, gripping the steering wheel tightly.

Later that same trip, Clyde brought a smile to Kate's lips as he passed a 'Stop Ahead' road sign. "If I see a head rolling down the road, I'll shore stop it."

One week later, since he had not received his final paycheck from Whitman, he went back to that mine office to collect it. As usual, when he was not going to work, he wore his one dress suit and tie and shiny black shoes. The general office, the payroll office, the company store, and a barbershop were all located in a large brick building on the side of the hill opposite the opening to mine number four. Clyde collected his back pay, stuck it in his coat pocket, walked out onto the porch of the building, and looked across the small valley at the slope he had worked in only a few days before.

Suddenly, the ground shook, and as if in slow motion, he saw a red ball of fire far back in the tunnel heading for the entrance, gathering speed as it neared the exit, and belching out into the open air in a massive fireball, racing toward the valley. The roar of the explosion was deafening, as heat spread all the way to the office building, scorching the paint off cars parked nearby. Clyde threw his arms up to shield his eyes, and was thrown back against the building. As the holocaust subsided, he saw fire everywhere near the opening. Burning furiously were parts of the tipple, some posts still standing, the remains of tram cars loaded with coal, and the shack of the man who collected checks from loaded cars. Sirens were now screaming, and dozens of people were running toward the mine, most of them wives and children of the miners.

"Oh, my god," Clyde said to no one in particular, "it blowed just like I said. That close to the surface, I know just where that pocket of gas was." Clyde was

A rare print published in 1869 illustrates the effects of a mine explosion.

muttering to himself as he ran toward the open slope, unmindful of the scorched arm that had protected his face, and the dress suit and tie he was wearing. The superintendent ran out of his nearby office and saw him.

"Clyde, for God's sake, help us. You know that section better'n any man. Will you go in there with me and see what it's like?"

"Shore. Let's get some hats and lamps first."

The superintendent ordered a man standing nearby to get them hard hats with headlamps and batteries and also a safety lamp for detecting gas. Clyde and the super put on the steel hats and hung the electric lamps on the fronts, letting the cord hang out the back of the hats and down to the battery which they fastened on their belts.

"I'm shore glad we don't use carbide lamps like we used to," Clyde said. "It would've blowed before now with that live flame."

"I'm sure you're right. I just hope there's no methane left in there now," the super replied.

As people recognized the two men, they stepped aside to let the pair pass. Everyone looked apprehensive and many women were crying. At the opening, they could see some posts still burning. "We cain't go in there until the posts stop burning," Clyde said. "As long as there's open fire, we know the methane has been exhausted. It's being fed by oxygen now."

"Here come some firemen with hoses," the super noted. "We can go in with them."

A water wagon drove up and five firemen grabbed hoses and dragged them into the opening. They sprayed the nearest burning posts, producing sizzling and smoke. "Look," Clyde said, "that smoke is being blowed right out of the pit. That tells us that there's ventilation from the other side of the mountain. We gotta find out which tunnel is getting' air, how many men are in there, and how much top has filled the passages. C'mon. We've killed enough time."

The two men walked forward cautiously into the dark, and Clyde commented that he could feel air passing by. "Look. The air is coming out of that passage. In fact, I'm certain I saw a light back in there. Yes. There are four or five lights coming this way. So that passage is okay. The explosion was down this left passage, just where I knowed it would be. You can stay and meet those men if you want to, but I'm gonna go down this tunnel as far as I can."

"No. They're getting out all right. We'll see if anyone was damaged where they were soon enough. Let's see what's ahead of us here."

They walked forward five hundred feet and then stopped cold. Boulders the size of tables blocked their way. Above them, the top looked like a huge overturned saucer, two hundred feet in diameter.

"Looks like the top of the mountain collapsed here," Clyde said. "I can still feel some air. It's coming over the top of that rock, so that means that there may be some live men on the other side. 'Course, the air could be whistling through cracks between rocks, too small for a man to get through."

"You're right, Clyde. We have no choice but to see if we can get men in here quick and start clearing a path through this pile of rocks. I'll go out and round up a crew. You coming with me?"

"No. I'm gonna go meet those men we saw com-

This 1869 print captures the horror of a mine collapse.

ing out. They'll soon be at the intersection."

Clyde met a group of five men coming out of the right tunnel, each smiling to be so close to the entrance.

"How bad is it?" he asked. "Are there any dead? Where was you when it blowed?"

"We were in that section over there," one man said, pointing to his right to the tunnel where Clyde and the super had found the cave-in. "Suddenly, the ground started shaking, then there was an awful roar, and the air was sucked out of our place. Right away, though, we were able to breathe again. When we started out, we ran into another group of nine men. We traveled together until we got about two thousand feet down that tunnel where you just come from, when we were stopped by a mountain of rock. The five of us decided we would backtrack about half a mile and use a cut-through, but the others said they were afraid it was closed too, so they decided to wait and try and see if they could move enough of that rock to get through."

"That means there are probably a half-dozen or more men under that rock pile," Clyde said. "The super has gone to get a crew in here as fast as he can, and if you want, you men can start trying to move some of the rock, although I know we won't move much until we get equipment here. I think I'll retrace your steps and see what it looks like from the other side, and tell those men that you got out okay."

"I'm sure a good friend of mine is under that rock, so I'm gonna stay and do what I can," a man said.

"So'm I," the other four said, almost in unison.

"Thank you, men. I know how you feel," Clyde said as he turned and walked into the forbidding viscera of disturbed nature. There were sounds ahead of him; rocks moving. He stopped and looked around carefully. Another step and a rock the size of a five-gallon bucket fell to the floor in front of him. He waited and listened, and the rumbling noise abated. If this passage was blocked before the other nine men got out, they might never get out. He had to go on. Another thousand feet and he heard an enormous crash behind him. He knew that there had been another cave-in, possibly where he had just been. He looked at his safety lamp for detecting gas, and saw that it was still burning oxygen. He found the cut-through and shortly thereafter the nine men, who were running to meet him.

"Oh God, Mr. Fuller, am I sure glad to see you," a young man said. "How did you get behind us?"

"Glad to see you Spike, and you too, Jeremy, Curley, Baldy, and Art. I don't know you other men." He peered into each man's face. They introduced themselves as Joe, Steve, John, and Pete.

"I come by the cut-through," Clyde said. "That's how the other five got out. I come here to find you and see what it looks like from this side. Hurry and follow me. Something fell behind me back there, so we may be in trouble." He walked away from the men even as he talked, and they moved quickly to catch up with him.

"Whadda you know, yet? Anything?" a man said.

"Not much. The top of the mountain fell in right in front of where you was and filled up probably five hundred feet of tunnel, maybe more. Those five men that left you found what I'm shore is the only way out. Let's just hope it ain't blocked now."

The men walked through the cut-through and up to the point where Clyde had encountered falling rock.

There, in front of them, was the passage blocked by a pile of rocks from the top.

"Oh God," Spike murmured.

"Don't panic, men. This whole area has been cleared of coal, probably four hundred feet in each direction. So, George, you and Baldy go to the right, and Art and Curley go to the left and see if there's some way around this pile. The rest of us will see if we can get over the top."

The men walked into the black, their reflected light soon disappearing with them.

Clyde and the other five scrambled as high as possible on the rock pile but were stopped by the top. They dropped back onto the mine floor as the others returned.

"We walked about four hundred feet through there and found this pile of rock ended against an uncut coal surface," Baldy said. "There ain't no way of getting around it that way."

"We found the same thing," Art said. "About three hundred feet. No way to get by."

"Oh God," Spike said.

"Look, son, it looks bad," Clyde said, "but there are worse situations. We got air in here, so we won't suffocate. I see all you men got your lunch pails, so I bet some of you still have coffee, or tea, or water in yours. That's what we'll need if we have to wait a couple of days." They were each carrying a cylindrical lunch pail with a top tray for sandwiches and the bottom for liquids.

"Two days?" Spike asked.

"I said maybe," Clyde said. "Look. We can't move that rock by hand, so we'll have to wait till they get to us from the other side. They know we're here, so they'll start digging soon. I expect we can hear them digging once they start. Here's what we must do. We don't need all this light, so everybody should turn off their light and save it till we need it. The flame on my gas lamp will give us what light we need for now. Let's just set down here and rest and see how much liquid we have."

Each man opened his lunch pail in the dim light. Four of them each reported that he had at least a quart of coffee left, two had an equal amount of tea, two had a quart each of water, and one had only a cup of water.

"Not bad," Clyde said. "We'll drink the coffee and tea first, and save the water till last. Hold off as long as you can before having a drink . . . I hope you're willing to share with me," Clyde chuckled nervously, as if he were ashamed to beg. With all seriousness, however, the men agreed to share their liquid with Clyde.

Three Catholics began to utter a prayer, two fundamentalists were on their knees praying silently, and Jeremy, the only black, started to sing "Swing Low, Sweet Chariot" in a beautiful, bass voice. The sound reverberated in their dark space and seemed to trail off down the tunnel from which they had come. The praying stopped as everyone listened to Jeremy. The mellifluous tones penetrated each man's feelings, as if directed to him alone. The song being finished, the men sat alone with their thoughts for what seemed like a long time, but was only a few minutes.

"Jeremy," Clyde said, "you got a nice voice. Bet you sing in a choir some place."

"Thank you, Mr. Fuller. I do sing in a choir, but I also sing solos about every Sunday. I like to sing.

Makes me relax."

"How long you been in the mines?"

"Oh, Lord, I been in the mines, let's see, thirty years now. I'm forty-eight and I started when I was eighteen. Loaded most of the time, but sometimes I laid track. I make more loadin' than track, and my missus likes it better when I load. I don't know how much longer my back is gonna cooperate with me. How about you?"

"I started when I was thirteen and that was sixteen years ago. Done about every job till I got papers for fire bossing."

Each man felt the need to describe his years in mining, which ranged from forty-two years down to seven months. The youngest was Spike, and the men listened to hear what he would say.

"I'm only eighteen," he said, "and I've worked in the mines only seven months. I'm scared shitless! How do you men act like this is just ordinary? We're gonna die here. You know it."

"No, no, Spike," Clyde said. "We ain't gonna die here. You just wait. We'll hear some digging before long. Besides, you heard that Joe and Baldy have both been in cave-ins and they got out all right. We're gonna make it . . . Wonder how many kids we got between us?"

This started the men to talking all at once. Among them, they were fathers to thirty-three children. Joe, in fact, had a son who had just started work in the mines. The men talked until they grew weary and sat and listened.

Time passed. A quarter-cup of coffee was passed around. One by one the men got up, walked into the dark to urinate, keeping the dim light from Clyde's safety lamp in sight. Silence again.

"This blackness sure makes you think of sunshine, don't it?" Jeremy said.

"And my wife and kids, too," said Steve. "Seems to me I think of them more when I'm inside than when I'm outside. Wonder why that is?"

"I think when you're in here, you think 'bout what's most important in life," Joe said. "I thought a lot 'bout my boy and hoped he wouldn't go in the mines. You know how boys is. When they get to be twenty, they think they know everything."

"That's not fair," Spike said. "I sure don't feel like I know everything. If we get out of here, I'm gonna think again about working in the mines. There's gotta be a better way to make a living."

"Not if, son," Clyde said, "only when. I'm sure we'll hear some evidence before long that they're coming to get us. We simply have to wait till they can get some heavy equipment in to start moving the rocks. . . . Well, I'll be doggone, I believe I hear some noise now. Yes, yes, don't you hear that clinking noise?"

The men perked up and each agreed that picks and augurs and some simple motorized shovels made the sounds. Small explosions indicated that large rocks were being split on the other side of the cave-in. Clyde looked at his watch. "Midnight," he said. "It'll probably take them eighteen to twenty-four hours to break through to us, but I'm sure we'll make it. Sing us another song Jeremy."

The men were rescued twenty-eight hours later. They had drunk all the coffee and tea, and had precious little water left. They were sore from sleeping on the

packed earth, and each man arose with obvious stiff-
ness in his joints. The superintendent was the first to
break though and shake hands with each of the men.
All ten of the men turned their lamps on and hugged
each other in turn, except for Jeremy. No one hugged
him, until Clyde noted he had been overlooked and
grabbed him with a bear hug.

"Jeremy," he said, "you helped us a lot. Your
singing and your positive attitude kept us all perked up.
You're a hard worker and a good man. Much obliged
for all you done."

The others hugged Jeremy in turn, and everybody
smiled in relief. Then Jeremy emitted a deeply resonant
laugh. "Mister Fuller, you sure do look strange with
that suit on and a necktie. You dress like that for work
every day?"

"Well, whadda you know?" Clyde laughed, and
the others joined in. "I forgot about that. Come over
here to Whitman to pick up a paycheck. Guess I'll hafta buy me another suit now, and a necktie too. This one
sure ain't gonna clean up, not even with soap and
water, but it's worth it."

"It was sure a comfort to have you come back in
and find us and wait it out with us. We're all grateful,"
Jeremy said. The other men, all at once, also told Clyde
how much they appreciated what he had done for them.

Each man was greeted at the entrance by crying
spouses and other loved ones. Kate said, as she hugged
Clyde to her expanding bosom, "You were so right.
How did you get involved here?"

"It blowed while I was here. I had to help, since I
know that section so well. We just got caught in loose
rock that fell from the top without an explosion. I got-

ta ask the super a question." He turned and walked over to the top official.

"How bad is it, George? How many men are likely to be under that big slate fall?"

"We've examined the roster of men working when it blew, and calculate that five were in the part where the explosion occurred. They're under that pile in the left fork. When we knew you men were in the right fork, we stopped digging in the left and started on your side. Knew we couldn't do a thing for any man under that big pile."

"Do you need my help in moving that rock fall?"

"No. You were in there almost two full days. That's enough for any man. Go on home and get some rest."

When they arrived home, Kate said, "I shudder at the thought that you might have been in the mine when it exploded. I lost a baby there in Whitman and I sure don't want to lose a husband, not when I'm pregnant again. What an awful way we have to live to survive in this world."

On February 25, 1932 another baby was stillborn, and buried in the snow-covered cemetery on the hillside. A month later, Kate rejected Clyde's request for intercourse. "No, not tonight. I'm just too frightened that I might get pregnant again. I can't stand the thought. If you were willing to use rubbers, I might consider it again, but not without any protection at all. Can't you understand how I feel?"

"Can't you understand how I feel?" Clyde said. "I'm a man and a man needs a woman almost every day. And you know that rubbers feel like washing your feet with your socks on. I've told you that many times.

Are you gonna be a woman for me or not?"

"It takes two to do it, and that means my desires must be heard too. Don't you care how I feel?"

"Shore I do, but what's marriage for if it don't include sex? Part of the price you hafta pay is that you might get pregnant. That's always been the risk women run, if they get married. Why did you get married then?"

"You just don't understand what it's like for a woman to lose two babies. I can't stand the thought of its happening again."

"Does that mean we ain't ever gonna have sex again?"

"Not until you buy some rubbers."

"That's like castratin' a man." He got out of bed and spent the night on the couch, suspecting that this was the beginning of constant tension between them. Kate put on weight.

Clyde was working two to four days each week, so the family lived better than most of the miners. After a year in Rossmore, Clyde said to Kate, "I've got some bad news. There's a lot of gas in this mine that worries me. It's in the same seam of coal that Whitman is in, and I'm afraid the gas is just as strong. If I can't get the super to help us to control it, I'll quit. I ain't no use to you and Jimmy dead. It just don't look like I'll ever get ahead, but I gotta keep trying. I'll just hafta find a safer place to work."

"I know it's a big decision, but I'd rather have you alive than dead, no matter how long it takes to find work. Do what you have to do. I just wish there was some other kind of work you could do. You ought to try to get ahead by looking for other work."

"Mining is all I know. I always dreamed of having a little farm someday. I'm sure I could make a go of it. I don't have no money; besides, I done spent eighteen years in the mines. I cain't change now. This depression makes it almost impossible to get ahead."

"I know, but I live in fear every day you're at work. With the depression on, I don't think any other kind of work will be possible for you. It's an awful way to live. I certainly don't want to make it any harder for you than it already is. I'll support you in whatever decision you have to make. We'll get by somehow."

"Sometimes it seems like they ain't no God. Poor people have a hard time. I agree, we'll make it somehow."

Without warning, in 1933 Kate received notice that her father had died of a heart attack. There was not enough money for her to attend his funeral. "Don't worry about it," Kate said. "I can't help him now, and it's just part of suffering people who are poor have to put up with." It was clear that she was terribly disappointed and engaged in silent grieving. She became more and more non-communicative, and she and Clyde seemed to recognize that they really had very little in common.

"It makes me damn mad to be so poor," Clyde said. "Some day, I'm gonna be able to deal with a situation like this, you just wait and see. I won't be poor all my life."

Even so, he told the superintendent at Rossmore four days later that he quit. He went to a number of mines, before landing a job at Blair, under the hill where he had fought back in 1921. He only got, on average, two days of work each week at the new mine, but it kept the family alive. The regular miners, if they were lucky, got one day every three weeks.

While the depression looked as bad as ever, Clyde continued to maintain that there still was hope, but Kate seemed to have very little to say about anything. Part of the basis of his hope was due to the fact that the National Industrial Recovery Act had been passed by Congress as part of Roosevelt's New Deal. That Act required employers to bargain collectively with labor unions. That was the slow beginning of improved conditions for miners, but it did not provide new jobs: the Depression continued unabated through the 1930s. Operators stopped using detectives to guard the mines, and miners openly talked about their commitment to a union.

Six months after taking the job at Blair, Clyde got the news that the mine at Rossmore had exploded, killing eight men, including the fire boss who had replaced him. "The only comfort I get," he said, "is that I got a pretty good idea when a mine is safe and when it ain't. Makes me wonder if God is looking out for me. How else can you explain how I have survived?"

One Sunday, he stuck a flashlight in his hip pocket and went up on Blair Mountain to see if he could find the old abandoned mine where he had hidden his rifle in 1921. He was certain he had been under the highest point of the hill when he was fighting, near the fire tower, so he attempted to find that first.

After two hours, he found the right hill. He searched for four hours in heavy underbrush, before he found the mine slope he thought might be the right one. He had laid his rifle on a beam between two posts about two hundred feet inside, close enough to the opening to allow some dull light in. However, the flashlight was necessary for details. Some posts were still standing, but most had rotted, letting the top collapse in places. Gingerly, he made his way to the point he was looking for. A rotted post and beam lay on the floor of the mine, but behind the beam, where it had fallen, was his rifle, the stock rotted where it had lain in wet dirt, and the barrel rusty. He took it home and showed it to Kate and Jimmy.

"I bought this rifle myself when I was about fifteen. Had to hide it when the union told us to do it, and then come off the mountain. That's when I was captured and sent to Charles Town, where the judge throwed our case out. Sure brings back a lot of memo-

The author lived in this typical miner's dwelling at Stotesbury, West Virginia, in 1935-37.

ries. Think I'll keep it and see if it'll clean up."

Clyde left Blair, not because of gas, but because he could not stand to remain in one place very long. He moved to Helen where he stayed two years and then moved to Stotesbury, both in Raleigh County. Where he lived didn't seem to matter. The southern coal towns during the depression were always in valleys; always drab; always with black creeks; always with electric motors hauling lines of cars out of the earth like segmented worms after a rain; always spewing, hissing locomotives pulling long serpentine trains loaded with the black cornucopia; always with poor housing; always with salaries eroded by script and gouging store prices; and for Clyde, always the hope that the next town in the next valley in the next seam of coal would somehow be better.

Conjugal relations between Clyde and Kate had been absent for over three years, because Kate was adamant about any more sex, unless condoms were used. She was quietly pleased when Clyde refused to use them. As the tension between them grew, she put on more weight, and by the time they moved to Stotesbury, her five foot two frame carried two hundred forty-five pounds.

"Why do you let yourself go like that?" Clyde asked. "You know I can't stand fat women, at least not as fat as you are. Your thighs have got to be a foot thick in diameter, and your stomach must be at least fifty inches around. Your breasts look like truck headlights, and your buttocks bounce up and down when you walk. What's wrong with you?"

"You don't understand, and I don't care what you think," she said, crying.

"I'll tell you one thing. To me you're no longer a woman, just a ball of fat that washes clothes, fixes meals, and takes care of Jimmy."

Stotesbury was nestled in a narrow valley with high mountains on each side. The Virginian Railroad ran along one foot of a mountain and the Chesapeake and Ohio ran along the other. A black, soot-infested creek ran between them, and houses were built in short rows where the landscape and space permitted. In the only level spot between the creek and the Virginian was the brick home of the superintendent of mines, which Clyde looked at longingly every day as he walked by. A narrow road ran above the C&O, and then cut between houses to meander along the tracks and go by the bath-house, company store, a small wooden-frame hotel, a tipple and six sets of rails for storing railroad cars till they were loaded, another row of houses, and finally Mark Twain School, before heading up the side of the mountain overlooking McAlpin. A community church nestled on the hillside overlooking the C&O. On the hillside above the Virginian was the Boy Scout cabin.

The house Clyde and Kate moved into in Stotes-bury was larger than most of the mining houses, but not as large or nice as that of the general mine foreman. The Fuller house had a second floor with an outside stairway to a small apartment upstairs that Clyde rented out. The privy was about sixty feet back of the house. Unlike the poorer structures, the Fuller house had running water in the kitchen. The house of the superintendent was in sight of the row that Clyde moved to.

***

Clyde paid little attention to his son, until 1937 when the lad was ten years old. Then he began using every opportunity to steer the boy from mine work.

Cars filled with coal, graded by size at the tipple, line these West Virginia tracks. (Courtesy Norfolk & Western Railway)

"It's like a rat in a hole in the ground, that's what it is," Clyde said. His face was craggy now, lined with count-less little streaks no larger than a hair, each bearing evidence of twenty-two years in the mines. He still had black hair and stood straight, despite the hours every day that he walked bent over as he moved from work place to work place. Often, the first thing he wore out in his work clothes was the back of his denim jacket, from rubbing against the roof of the low passageways. Despite their lack of communication, Kate sewed his elastic bandages for him, and he was able to have a fresh one each day for his leg. That, he had learned to guard very closely.

On a Saturday afternoon in July 1937, Clyde invited Jimmy to join him in climbing the mountain back of their house. It was steep enough in places that they had to hang on to small trees to navigate their upward trek. As they came to a beech nut tree, Clyde picked the small burr, still forming in early summer, and showed his son the tiny triangles of nuts. "In the fall, these nuts will be good to eat," he said, "even though they're kinda hard to get to. We'll enjoy pickin' them."

"Why can't we eat them now?"

"They're too green. We hafta let them grow more."

As they climbed further, Clyde showed Jimmy a hickory nut tree. "Now this tree also produces good nuts, and they're easier to open. You can crack the shell with a hammer, but it has another purpose. When I was a boy, I'd look for a good straight limb from a hickory tree, an inch in diameter, about four or five feet long, and cut it off. Then I'd clean the bark off, and maybe trim the ends a little and put it in water for a few days. After it soaked, I'd bend it into a bow by tying a small rope from end to end. Then I'd look for some straight reeds and I'd have me a bow and arrie."

"My teacher calls it an arrow. Can we make one?"

"That's a great idea," Clyde said, as he took a knife from his pocket and cut a limb the size he had describe. "Well soak this when we get home. Let's climb on to the top now, where we'll see a beautiful sight."

Twenty minutes later, they crested the hill and found a log to sit on. Clyde sat and looked at his son for awhile, then said, "When I think about it, I don't believe God ever goes down in the mines. He jest leaves that part up to the devil. Yes sir, the devil runs the mines down there close to hell. We ain't no different than the rats that run around down there all the time. It ain't no place for a man, son, and I hope you'll remember that when you're growed."

"Why don't you like working the mines, Daddy?" Jimmy asked.

"Like it? Jimmy, when you ain't got no education, what is left for a man to do? Shore, I'd like to have a little farm, maybe down in Virginny, where the mountains ain't so close, but farms cost money, and I ain't got no money. So all I can do is fire boss or section boss in the mines, and maybe become a superintendent some day, and thank God for letting me get certificates for them jobs."

"Is that what you were doing when we lived in Morgantown? I remember Mama talking about it. She said you studied a lot."

"That's right. I started to work in the mines when I was thirteen, just a little older'n you are right now. I dropped out of school when I was ten and just bummed round. Your granddaddy wouldn't support me, lessen I stayed in school, but I was full of the devil and wouldn't do what he said. So he kicked me out of the house. I stayed over two years with my Uncle Charlie and Aunt Nell, but you ain't met them yet. They was good to me. After that, I could either hire out as a farm hand and earn my vittles and board or go to work in the mines as a trapper boy, where I could have a dollar or maybe a dollar and a half left over after paying room and board. So I went to the mines. That was in 1915. By 1927, when you was born, I worked in a lot of positions in the mines, so I went over there to the Mine Extension School at the university and asked them to learn me mine bossing. They said no, 'cause I dropped out of school after the fourth grade. I finally talked them into letting me take a test to see what I knowed, and they let me in. Your mama helped me to read the lessons. I graduated with A's because I already worked in most every position in the mine. That's what is helping us to live when many people are hungry. I always get to work two days a week, and sometimes I work as many as six days a week, because I'm a fire boss and I hafta report on any gas. Most of the other miners are lucky if they get one day a month."

"What would you do if you couldn't work in the mines? Mister McKinney drives a laundry truck, and Mister Bennett works in a grocery store. Would you do something like that?"

"No, I'm afraid that coal mining is the only skill I have. I don't know nothin' about laundry, and I shore ain't made to be no grocery store clerk, but you don't hafta be like I was. I can't say it enough, but education is the only real salvation out of these mines and these hills. There simply ain't no salvation in this world without education. I promise you that as long as you stay in school, I'll help you any way I can, but if you drop out of school, I expect you to move out of my house the next day. Do you hear what I'm saying?"

"Yes, sir. I like school and can't hardly wait for the

A typical West Virginia coal miner of the 1930s.
(Courtesy Farm Security Administration)

next term to start. Don't you like the mountains? They're so pretty."

"I shore have to agree with you there. Look over there and you'll see the proof of what you just said. There ain't nothing so pretty as that green mountain. In the winter, when the big oaks an' beeches, an' sycamores all have snow piled on their limbs, with the pine trees scattered all around covered with snow, it's jest like a picture. I'm sure God loves mountains, 'cause he made them so pretty. What I meant by getting out of the mountains is that there are better jobs outside West Virginny than here. We can see how humans are destroying what God made by lookin' down there to the right at that dirty scar that we have put on God's green earth. That black tipple with the covered convey-or running up the side of the mountain is surely a insult to God. There ain't nothing can be done about that now, so we better go on back home. Your grandma is com-ing to visit us, so we got to be there when she comes. She probably won't be with us long. The house will be kinda crowded with her there."

Jimmy smiled lovingly because this was one of the rare times that his father took notice of him; he always seemed to be preoccupied. He took his father's hand, as the two began their descent back into the valley, sliding down steep slopes and laughing uproariously. When they got home, Clyde took the oval wash tub, poured about four inches of water into it, and bent the limb into a curve. "In a couple of days, we'll be able to tie a small rope tight to each end and then we can shoot arries with it."

"That sounds funny, calling them arries."

"I always called 'em arries, so I guess I always

will. Look! I think your grandma is here."

Kate's mother, Mildred, had just arrived, brought by car by one of her cousins. She was eighty, but seemed spry enough. She greeted Jimmy and Kate with enthusiasm, but was very formal with Clyde.

"Hello, Clyde. How have you been?"

"I been okay, I guess. Here, Jimmy, take you grandma's bag into the house."

They spoke as little as possible, because Mildred had never really forgiven Kate for marrying Clyde.

Mildred was startled at Kate's weight and spoke to her as soon as they were alone. "No one in our family ever looked like that, Kate. It must be a hard life to cause a woman to let herself go like that. Are you and Clyde getting along?"

"Yes, Mama. We are," Kate lied. "As well as can be expected. You know that men have different interests than women. I guess I just haven't been paying attention to how I look. I'll try to lose some weight."

"Well, you know that most men can't stand women who are grossly fat, and that's what you've become. Maybe you've become fat just to turn him off. That will only drive him to find someone else. Is that what you want?"

"Oh, no. I just want him to leave me alone and help me to raise Jimmy, but I don't want him to see other women. Doesn't marriage mean he has an obligation to stay with me?"

"It does, but that doesn't mean he'll stay if you won't satisfy his basic needs. Do you understand what I'm saying?"

"I suppose so. Maybe I'll try to lose some weight," she said without conviction.

Chapter Eleven

In Stotesbury, Clyde made three momentous decisions: to devote more time to Jimmy, to run for the
West Virginia House of Delegates, and to join the
Wolves. When Jimmy was eleven, Clyde went with
him to help him join the cub scouts. Jimmy took the
bow and arrow Clyde had made and proudly showed it
to his comrades. Clyde spent one night each week helping Jimmy earn his badges, and father and son grew
closer.

While he revealed very few of his plans to Kate
(men just don't do that sort of thing), he had to tell her
he planned to run for the State House of Delegates.
They were seated at the kitchen table and he simply
blurted it out: "I'm gonna run for the House of Delegates." She did not offer any encouragement.

"Why," Kate asked him, as she sat in a chair
mending socks, "why would you want to run for
office? Don't you have enough to do? You generally
work ten hours a day in the mines when you get work,
you tend a garden that gives us vegetables, and spend
some of your evenings at meetings. You only get to see
Jimmy two or three nights each week and only if there
hasn't been an accident or trouble in the mine. Now,
you want to run for a political office. Why are you so
restless? What drives you? I simply can't understand
you."

Clyde arose from his chair and paced the floor. He had a look of rage on his face, more pronounced than Kate had ever seen. He was struggling to control himself. "You don't know a god-damn thing about me. Cain't you get it through your head that for years I've resented living most of my waking life in a hole in the ground like a rat? Cain't you imagine what it's like to walk in darkness all day long wondering what people up on the earth are doing, in God's bright sunshine? It ain't real down there, I tell you. It ain't real!" Scowling, he rubbed his hair back again and again with both hands. Kate cried, and begged him to speak quietly, since her mother, who was outside somewhere in the yard, might hear him.

He seemed not to hear her. "Every morning when I go in to boss a section there's a bunch of men with faces you can recognize, and they all look like humans. When we come out, every man has a black face that blends in to his black shirt and black hands and black jacket and black pants and black shoes, and there ain't nothing that you can see but the whites of their eyes. We ain't human no more. We're just black blobs with two eyes. We gotta come out of that blackness and try to understand what's going on on the earth. No fat slob of a wife is gonna make me like it. I want to run for the House of Delegates because that's one place in a democratic country where poor people can be elected. Maybe I can learn something there that will help me to escape the black prison I hafta visit every working day. An' I tell you now, I'll be damned before I give up on bettering my life. Do you hear me? Dammit, I said, do you hear me?"

"You're frightening me," Kate said, tears flowing

down her cheeks. "I never saw you like this before. Please don't yell at me any more. Mother might hear you. Sit down and calm yourself."

"I'm calm," he yelled. "Don't you see! I'm calm. Maybe if I had a wife, I'd be calmer."

Kate held her apron up to her face, crying profusely. "It seems like it was better when you only got two or three days a week," she blubbered. "Now, you're gone all the time. You seem to have a life outside this house, but I don't. I need something, too. Can't you see that I need something, too?"

"I'm up to the point where I'm making four or five dollars a day when I get work, so I figger I have a right to spend some of it in trying to better myself." He paused, then yelled again, "I've tried to get you to go with me to some of the meetings I go to, but you always say no. It looks like you ain't gonna help me to better myself. Besides, it's clear to me that you don't want to be a wife, just a mother and someone who cooks my meals and stuffs her mouth all day."

"Please don't run for office," she said, her head bowed.

"I got to. An' if you won't support me, I know others will. I don't want to talk about it no more." He looked at the folds of fat, spat on the floor and walked out muttering, "Goddamn sow."

He started to go to the grungy saloon by the side of the railroad tracks and buy a beer, something he rarely did. To do so he had to pass a small open field where boys were playing baseball in the long summer twilight. Jimmy yelled, "Watch me, Dad, I'm up to bat next."

Clyde forgot the beer and watched, and was

rewarded when Jimmy made a hit. He sat down on the rail and watched his son for an hour, proud of his hits, and understanding of his errors. "That was a good game you played," he said as he and Jimmy walked home at dusk. As they entered the house, he was relieved to find that Kate had gone to bed.

Clyde spent twenty-five dollars of his own money to have posters printed up for his political campaign announcing himself as the candidate who supports the working man. He never formed a campaign committee, nor even knew that he should. He drove up and down throughout the county, and he and Jimmy tacked his posters on utility poles. Occasionally, someone would ask him why he was putting up the signs and he would make his campaign speech. "I've lived in this State all my life, and I think it's time the people got the chance to vote for a coal miner. That's what I am. I'm a coal miner and a Democrat. I want to go up there to Charleston and speak for the coal miner."

"What specifically are you going to propose?"

"Why, things that is good for miners. I told you, like better wages and better working conditions."

It was only after he ran into the posters of other candidates that he discovered they were all running as the representative of the working man. Furthermore, he learned, the other candidates would speak to any group they found anywhere. "I jest can't do that," he said to his son, "walk up to a group and start spouting off. That'd be intrudin'." He learned that the other candidates had campaign chests, some with as much as three hundred dollars to spend on radio and newspaper advertisements.

Out of a field of seven primary candidates, he

came in fifth, and that may have been because the two lowest vote getters were Catholic. He was crushed. It was a sad defeat, and he thought about it often. He wondered if God was punishing him some way, maybe for killing Avery Murphy in what many would call cold blood, even though the detective had killed his friend, Elmer. Would God be interested in something like an election?

"Dad, I'm glad you lost," Jimmy said. "It means you can be home more. I miss you when you're not home."

"Thank you, son. That does help me to see it all in better light. Let's walk up to the company store and see if they've still got that big Hershey bar for sale."

"Great! I love Hershey bars."

The next day, Clyde walked out of the mines with Tom Mitchell, another section boss, who had become as close a friend as Clyde ever had, which were few.

"I was sorry to see that you lost the primary vote, Clyde," Mitchell said as the two entered the bath house.

"Thanks, Tom. I guess money is more important than I thought. I couldn't afford any radio time, an' only had a few handbills to pass out. Runnin' for political office ain't as easy as it sounds."

Both men had black-streaked faces and hands, and bug-dust-covered clothes. Each went to a thin chain that was locked to a steel ring protruding from the wall, unlocked the chain and lowered a steel basket from the high ceiling that contained clean clothes. After showering, they put on the clean clothes and pulled their work clothes up to the ceiling in the wire basket. Few mining companies were as considerate in providing a bath

This modern bath house of the 1930s featured clothes hoists for security purposes.
(Courtesy Pocahontas Operators Association)

house with a means of protecting their things from thieves.

"I know I have no desire to be a politician," Tom Mitchell said. "But I have a lot of respect for someone who's willing to make that sacrifice."

"I'm glad I tried it, but I ain't gonna do it again. I heerd you gotta have a lot of money to run for the state senate, and you hafta be rich to run for other seats. Frankly, it don't seem right to me that only rich people should be in government."

"I agree with you," Tom said, "and we ain't gonna solve that problem ourselves. I've been watching you since you arrived here, and I like what I see; a family man, sends your kid off to Sunday school every week, speaks your mind openly, and still get along with most people. Still, I heard you knocked a man down recently. Is that true?"

"It shore is," Clyde said, buttoning his shirt. "He called me a nigger lover, just because I approved the right of colored people to vote. If they're gonna live here, then they got to have a voice, too. I've seen too many good colored workers here in the mines to treat 'em bad. Makes me think of Jeremy Holmes over at Whitman, as good a man as I ever knowed. Spent two days with him trapped under a cave-in. Made me want to know him better."

"I thought for a while you were going to join the Klan."

"I thought about it, 'cause I thought it might help me get elected. Then I heerd that they believe the colored people are going to overthrow the government. I tried to find some proof, but they wasn't any. Then I read in the paper that President Roosevelt calls the

Klan a bunch of cowards. Well, I cain't stand being thought of as a coward, by nobody, much less by Franklin Roosevelt. So I never joined."

"You certainly are bold to talk that way. The Klan don't like to hear any criticism, so watch your step."

"I ain't afraid of 'em."

"Just watch your step. I know it's nice to belong to some kind of club, and I hope you'll consider joining the Wolves. That's an organization of public spirited men who help little crippled children and meet every Saturday night in Beckley to have good food and fun. They're lawyers, and judges, and teachers, and other important people in the Wolves. Just the sort of people you ought to know. I'm a recruiting officer, so that's why I'm telling you this. Why don't you join me for a visit on Saturday night, as my guest? We'll take my car and leave about six-thirty. Wha'd'ya say?"

"That's kind of you. Shore, I'd like to look at it."

"That's good news, Clyde," as the two parted outside the bathhouse.

"Kate," Clyde said as he arrived home, "something interestin' happened today that I hope you'll be pleased with. Tom Mitchell invited me to go with him to Beckley Saturday night and have dinner at the Wolves' club. He wants me to join. That's a respectable organization with a lot of successful men. Not jest anybody can get in the Wolves."

"How can you do that? Why don't you think of my needs once in a while? Do you want to join a men's club just so you can get away from me? It's certainly not something I could enjoy."

"You don't know nothin' about the Wolves, so keep your mouth shut. There's lots of men in the

Wolves who never worked in a mine, and some of 'em don't have no more education than I do. I've got to join the Wolves to see if I can discover the secret."

"From what I hear," she blubbered, "all they do is have a meal, drink beer, and watch strippers. That's not what I need."

"That ain't so. You jest keep spoutin' off about things you don't know nothin' about. They help the needy. Look in the papers, an' you'll see where the Wolves are always helpin' people. An' when they have dinners, it helps us get acquainted. I get to meet important people. An' what's wrong with a little entertainment now an' then? Tom says that some of the wives even stay and watch the dancers, when they have them. You're tryin' to hold me back."

It was at this time that the greatest challenge to Clyde's marriage occurred. Kate's mother, Mildred, who had been visiting for six months, had a stroke. She was paralyzed on her left side and could not speak. The stroke occurred in the night, and Kate had found her in a filthy bed the next morning. Clyde went for a chiropractor, who had an office in Beckley. The doctor looked at Mildred and pronounced that she had had a cerebral hemorrhage and would not live long. He did not recommend any therapy.

Kate became her mother's twenty-four hour nurse. Every day she changed soiled sheets and washed them on a washing board. She fed her mother mainly soup because the stroke victim had trouble eating solid foods. A routine set in that involved Kate's getting up at five o'clock, fixing breakfast for Clyde and packing his lunch, changing the linen on Mildred's bed, fixing Jimmy's breakfast, feeding her mother, washing and ironing clothes, feeding lunch to her mother, fixing lunch for Jimmy, changing Mildred's soiled bed, washing more clothes, fixing supper, washing dishes, checking on Mildred, helping Jimmy with home work, and going to bed with the observation that she was tired. The routine stretched out for months, then for years-and she added another thirty pounds to her weight.

***

"Daddy," Jimmy said one cold January night in 1938 after a fresh snowfall, "Mama says it's all right with her if it's all right with you for me to stay with Bud Hogan tonight. We want to ride our sleds first thing in the morning. It's Saturday tomorrow, you know."

"Shore, that's all right with me. Bud's a fine boy and responsible, too. An' he does a good job as assistant scoutmaster. Where will you ride?"

"Down the hill from Mark Twain School."

"That's kinda steep, ain't it? Also, there's a turn in the road. What if there's a car coming?"

"We keep someone down at the bottom to signal if a car is coming. It's the best place to ride around here."

"All right, but you be careful."

"Thanks, Dad."

At ten o'clock the next morning, the sheriff knocked on the door of their house. Clyde answered, and paled when he saw the uniform.

"Mister Fuller?"

"Yes, I'm Fuller," he answered with a sinking feeling that he had finally been found out about the Matewan killing.

"I've got some bad news. Your son was sledding

down the hill at Mark Twain School and met a car coming up. He swerved to miss the car and ran under the rear end of a parked car. The differential ripped his back open and . . . I hate to say it . . . but he's dead."

Clyde's face turned ashen and Kate, who was standing in the background, screamed and fell into a chair, which collapsed under her. "How could it happen?" Clyde asked with anguish and disbelief. "Jimmy said they always had a guard to watch out for cars?"

"Apparently the guard, an eight-year old boy, got to rolling a snowman and forgot to look."

Clyde and the officer helped lift Kate up from the floor and placed her on the couch. After the parents had cried awhile,the sheriff asked Clyde if he would come with him to make the funeral arrangements.

When he returned to the house, Kate said, "How can we take any more? Life is so hard. Now the only thing I have to live for is gone."

"I'm still here."

"No. You've been gone a long time already. Now there's nothing to hold you here. All is lost. What's left in life?"

At the funeral, people were standing in snow listening to the minister read the Twenty-third Psalm. Kate was not there because there was no one to look after her mother, and besides the path was too steep for her bulk to maneuver. As the minister started to speak, Clyde said, "I want to say something."

"You?" the minister said. "That's most unusual."

"I still intend to say something." He stood at the end of the casket and spoke to the small crowd of mourners standing among the tombstones, all in heavy clothing and gloves. "My son is gone. Did I make life pleasant for him? Not in his first ten years, I'm shore. As he got older, I told him about the mines. I told him not to work in the mines, like a rat in a hole in the ground. I helped him to get into scoutin'. Can I say I done all for him I could? I don't think so. My son is gone. I know it will be hard to think about for the rest of my life. Good bye, Jimmy." Tears rolled down his cheeks as he turned and walked down the hill and to his lonely house.

The minister completed his sermon and the weary people left to return to weary homes.

Two weeks later, on Saturday, Clyde joined Tom Mitchell for the visit to the Wolves. It would help him adjust to the death of his son. He was so impressed by the friendliness of the members he met that he told Tom he was willing to be nominated for membership. He scraped together the fifty dollars for the initiation fee, and was given a date when he would be sworn in.

After he was nominated, the president of the order sent Clyde some material and told him to memorize it. He struggled for a number of days, before he finally memorized the full paragraph of the oath of admission: "To the Benevolent and Reverent Order of Wolves (BROW), I hereby pledge to our God and our country my faithful obedience to their laws and that I will, in brotherhood and fellowship, congregate and share in BROW comradeship, in fun and seriousness, and support its efforts to make offerings of our wealth, paltry though it may be, to relieve the suffering of the poor and needy."

Clyde and Tom Mitchell drove together the fifteen miles from Stotesbury to Beckley for the swearing in ceremony, in a building called the Wolves' Den, which was attended by seventy-three men. On this serious occasion, visitors were not permitted in. The president of BROW, Hayden Lange, a high school teacher, addressed the attendees.

"Fellow Wolves, it gives me great pleasure to announce that one Clyde Fuller has applied for membership in our sacred organization. Our brother, Tom Mitchell, has nominated Clyde and assured us he is an upstanding citizen, a fire boss and section boss in Stotesbury, born and raised in West Virginia. I need not remind you that the Benevolent and Reverent Order of Wolves is an ancient organization, having been founded at the end of the World War. Its members constitute the backbone of our society: bankers, businessmen, entrepreneurs, ministers, teachers, politicians, policemen, foremen, and bosses. When we speak with our loud voice, the community listens. It's an honor for me to welcome one other distinguished citizen to our august group.

"Clyde Fuller, please come forward." Clyde walked to the front of the room. "Please get down on your knees, Clyde Fuller." Clyde obeyed. "Have you learned the oath required of all Wolves?"

"Yes, I have."

"Please recite it."

Clyde dutifully, and somewhat haltingly, recited the oath. The president stepped forward and placed his right hand on Clyde's head. "By the authority given me by the Benevolent and Reverent Order of Wolves, I now pronounce you a member with all the rights and privileges appertaining thereto. You may arise now and shake hands with all the members who are here tonight."

The members came forward, introduced themselves and shook hands with Clyde. Afterwards, drinks were served followed by a dinner of fried chicken. At that time, some of the members' wives were admitted. The president told Clyde that for most meetings, wives, sweethearts, and other dates were welcomed, and dancing usually followed the meal, accompanied by a small band consisting of a pianist and guitarist; and sometimes they were entertained by dancing girls who liked to remove their clothes.

On the way home, Clyde was enthusiastic. "What a swell bunch of men. And friendly too. Why, one man said he was a banker, another said he owned that big hardware on Kanawha Street, and another said he was a professor at the junior college. Yet they all treated me like an equal."

"You are their equal. Why would you doubt it?" Tom asked.

"I dunno. It's just not the kind of crowd I been in most of my life. I just decided it. I'm gonna see if I can get a job at Sprague. It's right on the edge of Beckley. I could walk to the Wolves' meetings if I hafta."

"You must have really been impressed. I told you it was the right group to join. I'd hate to see you leave Stotesbury, but I heard they're looking for a section boss at Sprague. So if you're serious about moving, good luck."

"Of course, I'm serious. I'll go to Sprague first thing on Monday."

"Boy! When an idea sets you on fire, you don't stand still on hot coals, do you? What will Kate think of a move? Don't you have to talk it over with her first?"

"No. I make the decisions in my family. She'll haf-ta go along."

Clyde found the job at Sprague, and was willing to show his thoughtfulness by giving Kate a month to get things ready for the move. He found a house near both the mine tipple and the boundary of the City of Beckley. It was on a rough slate road from mine residue. The rent was twenty dollars a month, but Clyde felt it was worth it to be so close to both the mine and the city. His seven year old Pontiac was not running well, so he was pleased to be near enough to the mine and the city of Beckley that he could walk to each easily.

He had to carry the frail body of Mildred out to a car for the ride into the new place, which resulted in constant screaming on her part. For Kate, the move was a mere interlude on her numbing life. The house had two bedrooms, so Mildred had a room of her own. There was a large opening, but no door, between the bedrooms, which once and for all effectively killed any opportunity for connubial activity, in the unlikely chance that they might engage in it.

On every possible occasion, Clyde talked about the Wolves and dropped the names of prominent members. Life was hard, but maybe the Wolves would help him to cope. He resented his mother-in-law but was totally hobbled to do anything about her helplessness. When he was depressed, he thought of Avery Murphy, that thug over in Matewan that he shot. *Why*, he wondered, *does that man's name haunt me, especially when I've got a lot on my mind?*

Although many men brought their wives or girl-friends with them to Wolves' meetings, Clyde could not find any way for Kate to join him, in the unlikely event that she might be willing.

"Even if I could find someone to sit with my mother, I have too much work to do," she said. "Besides, I don't see any reason to be traipsing around with self-important men. I'll bet that if you just stayed in one place long enough, you'd get promoted, probably to mine foreman, or even general foreman. I just can't understand why things always seem better some place else. I suppose if you got to go, you got to go."

"I told you, you jest don't understand. Here I am gettin' close to forty and still my life is just like a rat in a hole in the ground. I've got to see what's out there in the world above ground. I just got to, and since you ain't my wife no more, I'll do it by myself."

"I just hope what you find will include your family."

"Don't be silly. I always took care of the family, didn't I? Have you ever gone hungry? Of course not! Just look at you."

"I guess there's no use arguing," she said, her lips and three chins trembling.

"That's right. A man has jest gotta do some things on his own. If his fat slob of a wife won't help him, then he has to go alone." Referring to her obesity always started her to crying, usually for an hour or more.

Even as a fire boss, Clyde hardly made enough money to allow him savings of any appreciable amount. As late as 1939, coal operators defended the prices in their stores. Clyde decided to try to get around the expectation, not the stated requirement, that all managers were to trade at the store. Any miner could draw script out of the payroll office for any day he had worked. These were slugs with holes in them indicating their various values. Each dollar of script was worth around ninety cents at any bank, sometimes only eighty-five cents. This provided ready cash when necessary, at less than face value. At the company stores, however, any item marked a dollar might be bought at private stores for sixty to eighty cents. So miners were doubly penalized. Only those who did not take an early draw on their wages would be paid in cash, but almost all miners found it necessary to take some script each pay period.

By careful planning, Clyde managed over five months to save enough money to buy a month's supply of food at a private store. He had formed the habit, after Kate became so fat, of buying groceries every Saturday. Even if she could walk and carry groceries, she simply could not get away and leave a man to care for her mother.

Clyde selected the A&P for his store and was delighted at the amount of food he could buy for fifteen to eighteen dollars, for what before would have cost him twenty to twenty-five dollars at the company store. At the end of a month, Amos Wilson, the superintendent, sent word for Clyde to come see him.

"Well, Clyde," he said, "I hope you and your wife are feeling better."

"I don't know what you mean," Clyde said. "We haven't been sick."

"Glad to hear it. Then I suppose you've been fasting. I didn't know you were a religious man."

"Fasting? Why would you think that?"

"I happened to notice from the store records that you haven't bought any food the last month. What else could account for it?"

Clyde, visibly angry, clenching his fists, said,

'Yeah, I guess we did fast some last month."

"Glad to hear your explanation. I hope you like working here. I'd hate to see you leave. I'm sure that things will work all right once you get to eating again."

"I guess you're right. I'll watch that from now on."

"Good man! Keep up your fine work."

Clyde was caught in a bind. He could probably get work some place else, but it would be away from the Beckley area. The thought of moving Kate's mother again was depressing. Even more uncomfortable, would be moving from the nearness of the Wolves' Den.

"I know one thing," he told Kate, "if I ever become superintendent, I'm gonna make the company store compete with the A&P, and I'm gonna pay the men a full dollar for every dollar they earn. It looks like the only way I can better myself is to try to move up in mining, or to get acquainted with other men who are successful. It shore is humiliatin' to be treated as nothing but a tool for the mine operators. I just gotta get where I can have some influence."

In late fall of 1939, Clyde and Tom Mitchell and Tom's wife, Sally, were having dinner at the Wolves' Den. Clyde, as usual, wore his one grey suit, white shirt, blue tie, and shiny black shoes, and noted that the other men were similarly dressed. Food was served buffet-style and the odor of chicken, beef and pork filled the air. There were bowls of green beans, corn, mashed potatoes, sweet potatoes, gravy and corn bread, as well as lettuce and carrots on the side. Apple pie and chocolate cake were available for dessert. Each person took his own plate and found a place to sit.

Clyde and the Mitchells were seated at a round

table with chairs for six. A strange man and woman came toward their table carrying food trays. "Hello. My name is Daniel Monroe and this is my wife's sister, Angelica Patterson. Everybody calls her Angel. The other tables are full. May we join you?" He was rotund with a round face and a pleasant smile, and premature white hair in abundance.

"Of course. My name is Clyde Fuller and this is Tom and Sally Mitchell. Tom is section boss at Stotesbury and that's what I do at Sprague."

"I'm into mining hardware, myself. Represent Pittsburgh Steel," Dan said. "I'm just visiting the local Wolves, but I belong to the order in Charleston."

The five seated themselves, with a vacant chair between Clyde and Angelica. Clyde stared at her, petite, pretty, black hair, rouged cheeks and lips, full bosom in a low cut dress, and before he could regain his whereabouts, thrilled to the lilting sound of her bubbling voice.

"Oh, it's so nice to meet men like you. I just can't imagine what it must be like to work down in a hole in the ground, in all that dark. I mean darkness is all right when you're cuddled up with someone warm, but frightening when you're alone with only your thoughts. Don't you agree with me, Mr. Fuller? I'll bet you like to cuddle up, even if it's not dark. I do declare, Dan, I forgot to get a drink before we sat down."

"I'll get you one," Clyde said, before he realized it. "What would you like? There's elderberry wine if you like it."

"Oh, I do think that's nice of you, Mr. Fuller. I'll have a glass of white wine. Don't you agree, Dan, that it's nice of Mr. Fuller?"

"Yes, I'm sure Mr. Fuller can get a drink for you."

Clyde returned with the drink and re-seated himself.

"Thank you, Mr. Fuller," she said.

"You should have tried the elderberry wine. It's very good," Mrs. Mitchell said.

"Normally I would, but since Mr. Fuller was kind enough to get me some white wine, I'd better drink that for now. I couldn't expect a man to get a drink for me and then not drink it. That wouldn't be fair. I'm a person who believes in fairness. Thank you."

"Let's enjoy our meal," Dan said, "and hope Maisie gets here soon."

"Of course," Angelica said. "I keep forgetting that some men are tied to their wives' apron strings. I think that even a married man ought to have a lot of freedom. I bet Mr. Fuller isn't tied to someone's apron strings, are you?"

"Well, now, uh, I guess I never thought of myself that way," Clyde said, blushing. He had stopped eating while she talked.

"Well, I knew that just from looking at you. The way you carry yourself, like a man who knows who he is. Don't you think he looks strong, Dan? I know I do."

"Hush, Angel. You're just flirting. What's got into you? That's not like you."

"I always say that there's nothing wrong with flirting with a handsome man, that's what I always say." She sipped her wine. "It just seems to me that there are a lot of strong, handsome men who work in the mines. There were always manly looking miners every place I used to go with my second husband." Clyde was aware that she had smiled and winked at him, and wondered if the others saw it from where they were sitting.

Just then a woman carrying a tray came to the table and Dan got up. "Let me introduce my wife, Maisie. These are Tom and Sally Mitchell and Clyde Fuller. They're section bosses. Move over Angel, so Maisie can sit down next to me."

Maisie was Angel's sister, in appearance as well as vivaciousness. "It's such a pleasure to meet you all. Has my sister been bending your ears? She's a talker, you know. I'm late because I wanted to get my hair done. I hope it looks all right. Do you like it, Dan? I always believe your hair looks all right if a man likes it. What do you think, Dan?"

"Your hair looks great, any way you wear it," he said.

"Isn't it wonderful to have a man like that? I just get goose pimples when he talks to me like that."

"I doubt these people are really interested in your hair, Maisie, so let's change the subject and see how the Mitchells are doing."

Angel moved into the chair next to Clyde and continued their conversation. "How long have you been working in the mines, Mr. Fuller?"

"Twenty-four years," Clyde said as the others at the table turned away from Angelica and talked among themselves.

"Twenty-four years! I can't believe it. Why you can't be more than thirty now. Did you start as an infant?"

"Thank you, Mrs. Patterson, but I'm getting close to forty."

"I'm not a Mrs. My husband ran away three years ago, and I had to divorce him. Got a nice settlement out

of it. More than from my first husband, the beast . . . ."
She paused as if remembering. "I'm so sorry about my
language. That just slipped out. But let's not be
gloomy. Just call me Angel. Everybody does. I sure do
miss my husband. Do you know what it's like to sleep
alone, Mr. Fuller?"

"Well, you know it's possible for a man to be alone
even if there's somebody else in bed. You can call me
Clyde."

"Why thank you, Clyde. I don't know why, but I
always thought Clyde was a masculine name, virile,
and powerful and able to do anything that men do, if
you get my meaning. I sure understand what you mean
by being alone, even when someone else is in bed with
you. Silence and a cold back can be very lonely. You're
a man and know how to get what you want."

"Yes, I guess I am a man, sure enough. I ain't
always got what I wanted."

"I bet you get most things you go after. Now admit
it, don't you get most things you want?"

"Maybe I do," he said, looking thoughtful, "maybe
I do."

They continued talking in this light vein and soon
finished their meal of roast beef and potatoes. Clyde
got them each a piece of apple pie, which they ate in
silence.

"Oh, the music has started. Let's dance," she said
to Clyde. "I just love to dance."

"I don't know how to dance."

"Of course you do. Everybody can dance. You just
get close to somebody and follow the rhythm. Surely
you've done that!"

"No, I never have. I never even tried. I jest cain't

dance."

"You mean you're a fraidy-cat? You're actually afraid to try?"

"I ain't afraid of nothing."

"I won't believe you unless you at least let me show you how easy it is." Her soft hand clasped Clyde's callused one and he found himself yielding to the pull. As they moved away from the table, she turned and faced him. "Now first, stand close to me. There! Doesn't that feel good? Put your right arm around my waist and hold my right hand in your left, and I'll place this hand on your broad shoulder. Now as I step back you step forward, then we'll both step sideways, then you step back and I'll step forward. See! It's simply a big square. That's not hard at all."

Clumsy at first, he soon felt the rhythm of what she was doing. He was aware of her perfume and of her breasts pushing his chest. Her black hair fell in waves to her shoulders. He looked down into her smiling face and perfect teeth, pulled back, and said, "It's getting late and I just got to go home. I hafta get up early you know."

"I'm sorry. Maybe you'll be back next Saturday. I'll be in Beckley for a few months, maybe longer, and I'll need someone to escort me here. Would you like that?"

"Well, yes. I suppose I could be your escort. Maybe I can bring . . . " He started to say Kate. "Uh, I might not get back next Saturday."

"If you do, here's my address and phone number. Give me a call." She had written the information on the back of a grocery order she found in her purse, which he put in his jacket pocket.

Chapter Twelve

Clyde walked hastily out of the Wolves' Den and north on Kanawha Street, before cutting off to his house. I've got to get ahold of myself, he thought. That Angel is the most temptin' thing I ever seen. She don't mean nothin' by it, but she sure knows how to make a man feel good. Still, maybe I better not go back to the Wolves' meeting next Saturday.

Kate and Mildred were asleep when he arrived. As he slipped in besides his bulky wife, she awakened and spoke quietly. "I smell perfume. Have you been with a woman tonight?"

"Of course not. Or maybe I should say, I been with a lot of women. Many of the men bring their wives to Wolfe meetings, you know. I ate at a table with three different ones. Maybe they had on perfume. Do you hafta complain all the time."

"Well, I don't want you to even touch me smelling like that. Good night." She turned her wide back to him.

"I don't like that, Kate. Cain't you think about being a wife just once for a change? I'm especially in the mood tonight. I don't care if you are fat or if your mother hears us. I need a woman."

"Well, I care. Besides, you keep forgetting to buy rubbers, and I don't intend to get pregnant again. I've told you that many times. I've got a life to live, too. Maybe I need to get away some time."

"How can that be with your mother bound to a bed?"

"If you really wanted to, I bet you could find some way, and I don't mean to some place where you can rub shoulders with the rich. I mean, I need some time to call my own. I've been nursing my mother every day for over two years. I don't intend to get pregnant again. How could I survive it? What I would really like would be to have some time in the afternoon when I could read. Who knows, I might even want to learn to drive a car and do some visiting? If you want me again, you've got to change, and I've got to have some relief somehow."

"Damn it. You've become a nagging woman, also. I can't stand nagging women, especially fat ones. You've got to change, too. Are you gonna be my wife or not? I ain't gonna put up with this much longer."

"Then you'd better change."

"The only change I want to make is to better myself, an' I'm gonna do it. If you ever want me again as a husband, you'd better get rid of that fat."

Kate was crying, and Clyde got out of bed quietly so as not to awaken Mildred and went to the couch in the living room, where he slept fitfully for five hours when it was time to get ready for work. Kate got up and fixed his breakfast, but neither spoke a word.

Clyde decided that he would miss the next meeting of the Wolves but wondered why he should. As late as Saturday morning, he was still determined to miss the meeting. As he arrived home from work that evening, Kate said, "I hope you'll stay home this

evening and help me celebrate my mother's birthday. I
think she recognized me today and tried to say something."

"That don't mean nothing. She's eighty-two years
old now, and ain't gonna get any better."

"At least, you can stay home tonight and be with
me for a change. I'm so lonely since Jimmy died. I
don't want you to go to the Wolves. I . . . I demand that
you stay."

"Demand? You still don't know me, do you? Well,
no woman is gonna tell me where I can go. Now I hafta go. My staying here ain't gonna bring Jimmy back."

He dressed in his one suit and tie and stalked out
of the house at seven-thirty. He walked over to
Kanawha Street and started into town, mulling over the
question of whether to go to a movie or to the Wolves'
meeting. Although it was a hard decision, he chose to
go to the movies where, for ten cents, he saw Clark
Gable in a romance. He missed much of the movie's
plot, however, because his mind kept drifting to what
he regarded as a crisis in life. *I need a woman like any
man does. But when you cain't get one, what are you
supposed to do? Go to a whore? I jest cain't do that. I
might get a disease. Then there's Angel, who has sure
stirred me up. I know I don't mean nothing to her, but
she knows how to make a man feel good. Maybe I can
go on back to the Wolves' meeting hopin' she won't be
there. She asked me to escort her there. Would that be
wrong? What am I gonna do? I suppose I'll wait till
next Saturday and see how I feel.*

He didn't like to miss a meeting of the Wolves, but
Angel had complicated things. He missed the next two
meetings of the order, and then decided he had to do

something. He would go to the next meeting but not call Angel. As he walked toward the Wolves' Den, he found Angel's phone number in his coat pocket, and could not resist going into the drugstore and calling her. "I just now decided to go to the Wolves' meeting, and you said you needed an escort. Are you still in the mood?"

"Oh, Clyde, I'm always in the mood. I'll be ready by the time you get to the apartment."

He walked the half-mile with a troubled mind. He was, after all, a hard worker. He had always taken care of his family. A man also needs companionship, and right now he wasn't getting any, and hadn't for the last six, maybe seven, years. What could be wrong in escorting Angel to a supper? Just listening to her talk would make him feel good, and beside, she was pretty to look at. She might even want to dance again, and he would get to feel her body against his. She came to the door dressed for the evening, looking as ravishing as before, and just as bubbly.

"How nice it is to see you again, Clyde. I've thought about you a hundred times since we met a month ago. I was afraid you didn't want to see me again. Did you know you have that kind of impact on a woman? I'll bet you didn't even know. Why, I think you're blushing. I like that in a man. Makes me want to mother him."

"I've thought about you, too. You're such a nice woman. I find it hard to believe you want me to escort you."

"I told you. You're a strong handsome man. Maybe it's that cute dimple in your chin that I find so attractive. Well, shall we go?" She put her arm in his and they walked two blocks to the Wolves' Den.

They picked their food from the buffet and she led them to a table for two, although Clyde had first headed for a table for six. "Don't you just love these cozy little tables for two? They're so romantic. Don't you agree?"

"Yes, I agree, Angel. Do you mind my saying so, that is, well . . . uh . . . you sure are pretty."

"Of course I don't mind. How could a woman object to something that sweet from a man? I just love it when men say sweet things to me. You can say those things any time you want to."

It got easier for Clyde to escort her to the Wolves' Den and after two months of doing so every Saturday night, they became friends, in the sense of being comfortable in each other's presence. They avoided any talk of intimacy.

After they had known each other for six months of regular dining together, usually followed by dancing, Clyde realized that their closeness was too much for him. One night, as they were eating, he prepared to either break it off or get more involved. She helped him by suddenly observing, "Why Clyde, I think you're looking down my dress. Do you like what you see? Makes me feel good to see a man look at me like that."

"I'm glad you like to be looked at, 'cause the way you're dressed, in that pretty outfit, it's hard not to look."

"Don't you see, all women dress to be looked at. Some women just make it hard to see what's there. Now you just eat your meal and forget about my, uh, front."

"I never seen a woman like you before, so full of

life. I'm glad I finally joined the Wolves."

"Did you come here to meet someone like me?"

"Oh, no. I come here to see if I can find a way of living that is better than the mines. You know that working in the mines is no better than being a rat in a hole in the ground."

"Oh, how awful. A man ought to enjoy his work. We're not on this earth very long, and ought not spend it suffering, especially if we can escape it some way. I do believe you're trying to better yourself, and you see life passing you by. You don't smile very much, do you? Is life really that sad?"

"Right now, I don't think there's much to smile about, but when I look at you I feel like smilin'." They were eating chicken with their fingers and enjoying it. He was drinking a beer, and she had a glass of white wine. "In fact, the thought of you all last week made me smile."

"That's much better. You have such a warm smile. I like that in a man. A smiling man just melts my heart."

"Are you always like this? Surely you must have had some unhappy moments in your life."

"Yes. Yes, I have. I told you my second husband left me. That was because I can't have any children, and he said he wouldn't live with a woman who can't bear him a son. He just walked out. Never left a note or anything. He owned a coal mine in Mingo County. I got a lawyer and we sued him for divorce and a pile of his money. So now I'm just a free woman."

Clyde looked startled. "Mingo County, eh? Did you ever live there?" He had to be careful and not even hint that he had been in Mingo County, when Sid Hatfield killed those goons. It was possible that she might be setting him up for a connection with the death of that detective, Avery Murphy. Surely, he decided, she's too nice for that.

"Did I say something wrong? You have such a strange look on your face. What's it all about?"

"Don't pay no attention to me. I was . . . uh . . . thinking about a pretty woman like you in that awful Mingo County, that is, I heerd it was not a very nice place to live, torn up by coal mines and dirty houses and such. Let's change the subject and talk about things you like to do."

"I'm with you on that. I like to read, especially mysteries and books that have happy endings. Stories by Jane Austin fill my soul with . . . with . . . tenderness. I so like to feel tender. Do you like to read?"

"I don't read very good. I hafta admit that I ain't got a education like you do. You may not want to see me again when you learn that."

"Now there you go, belittling yourself. You seem to have enough education to be successful in the mines. I like that in a man. Besides, you can always improve yourself by study, but I bet you don't have much time to read, what with all the work you do. You probably even have a wife and children to whom you devote much time."

"I do have a wife, named Kate. We had a son, but he was killed in a sledding accident. I miss him."

"How awful! I'm so sorry to hear that. How old was he?"

"Just eleven."

"It's just awful to die so young. You still have your wife."

"Yes, but we ain't hardly married no more. She

hasta take care of her mother who is bedfast in our home. Stroke, over three years ago. Cain't do a thing for herself. Like I say, I don't know if I'm married or not. You cain't know what it's like for a man to lay across the belly of a big fat woman trying to find the right wrinkle. The last time for that was many years ago."

"Oh, you poor man. No wonder you like to see me. I already knew about your wife. I appreciate your being honest about it. I've been making inquires and learned you aren't really married, because she's too fat to be a real companion. That's why I've been willing to see you again. I'm not a home wrecker, but if the home's already wrecked. . . ." She shrugged her shoulders and then brightened. "Listen! The music's started. Let's dance."

They danced, or at least they held each other and moved slowly around the floor. Both seemed lost in the ambiance of the place and each other. When the dance ended, Clyde said it was late and he had better get home.

"I understand," she said. "Maybe I'll see you next week."

"Maybe you will." He escorted her to her apartment, barely hearing her enthusiastic conversation, muttering an occasional yes or I think so. As he walked home, his mind raced. Could it be a mere coincidence that Angel had a connection with Mingo County? Is it possible that someone had connected him to the place? With all the problems he faced, why does that goon he shot in Matewan keep haunting him? Surely Angel is not attempting to trap him into saying something he shouldn't. How he ached to hold her in his arms, but was she playing a game?

Kate gave him the silent treatment all the next week, culminating in a plea for him to stay home and help her. This angered him, so he dressed in his suit and stalked out of the house. This time he intended to go to another movie. He could think there, and that's what he needed, time to think. As he approached the drug store, his resolve weakened. He had to talk with Angel one more time, not only because she was nice to be with, but so he could learn more about her, and her connection with Mingo County. He called on the phone and found her waiting.

"Oh, I'm so glad you called. I was hoping you would. Even though we've only known each other for seven months, it seems much longer, and I miss you. You're such a man, and I miss seeing a man. Come on to my apartment. I have a little surprise for you."

She opened the door dressed in a blue negligee, open to the waist, the rounded inner edges of her breasts showing. "Come in. I have a surprise. I have cooked dinner for us. Just the two of us. Don't you just love dinners for two? See, I've fixed a nice roast with potatoes and biscuits."

He hardly heard what she said. "You are the most beautiful woman I ever seen. What I want is not food, but to kiss you. Can I?"

"That's so very sweet of you, but not now. Later, after we eat. Surely you can wait till we eat? It will be even more enjoyable thinking about it. Come on and sit down. I have both beer and wine. I don't like beer, and I suspect you don't like wine. Am I right? You don't really like wine?"

"I never did drink much wine, but I'm willing to try a glass. I always say I want to try everything once."

"I like that in a man. Curious and willing to try everything once. I just knew you were that kind of man."

They ate the meal hastily, as if in anticipation.

"Now," she said, rising from the table. "You may kiss me."

Without a second thought, he kissed her deeply, and then began to probe inside the negligee. She was just as responsive, unzipping his pants and feeling for his tumescent tool. "Come on," she said. "The bed's waiting." She dropped the negligee on the floor and he tore off his own clothes.

Never had he seen a woman so beautiful as nude Angel. Her breasts were ample but not pendulous. The black pubic hair allowed only a glimpse of the cleft it covered. Her eyes laughed and she seemed as eager as he. Events leading to that moment had been sufficient foreplay and they merged quickly as nature intended.

Later, lying naked and satiated, they both went to sleep. He woke up with a start and looked at the clock. "Two o'clock! I cain't believe it. I never had nothing like that before in my life." She was also awake, smiling at him.

"You poor dear. Whatever happened to your leg that you have to wear that rubber sock?"

"A horse fell on me when I was a kid. Don't think about it, because I'm doing quite well with it."

"I'm so pleased to hear you say that. How about tonight? Were you pleased?"

"Pleased? I ain't had a woman for many years, and then I get the most wonderful one I could imagine. When you scratched my back, and screamed in my ear, I thought I was in heaven. Kate never done that. I'm not sure she ever liked sex. How did you ever learn what a man likes like that?"

"Learn? Women don't really learn that. It just comes naturally. I was screaming, because I was coming. It's easy when you're fucking a real man. I like a real man. I knew you were a real man the day I met you. I've not been with a man for over three years, and I just had to have you. I don't have any second thoughts. Do you?"

"I don't know. I really don't know, but we cain't undo what's done so let's not worry about it. You never did tell me about your first husband. Was he such a fool that he left you, too?"

"What a sweet way to put it. No. He was killed fighting unions in Mingo County. Back in 1920. I was only seventeen at the time. My daddy made me marry the man while I was only sixteen. He was a monster. He slapped me often and once knocked me down. Weighed about two hundred seventy-five pounds. Had no respect for life. I was glad when he was killed, near the railroad tracks in Matewan . . . Why, Clyde, you look startled! Was it something I said?"

His brow was furrowed, his eyes wide, and his mouth open. He had to recover quickly and act like she had misinterpreted his reaction.

"What an awful story. You say he actually hit you? He was that kind of animal? How could you marry a man like that?"

"My father was a policeman in Bluefield and met Avery at some police affair. . ."

"Avery?"

"That was his name. Avery Murphy. Daddy was impressed with the man, because he was a detective for some large agency in New York. They had a branch office in Bluefield. My daddy was a harsh man, too, and he made me marry the fiend. Avery was in charge of a group of detectives sent to Matewan to fight unions. He had two brothers in the agency, also. Avery and his brother Homer were both killed in that battle, by the chief of police. There was a lot of talk that maybe the chief, Sid Hatfield, didn't kill Avery, but nothing ever came of it."

"Why is there doubt?" Clyde watched her carefully, looking for any hint that she was setting him up for something.

"Some people swear that they heard a shot from up in the mountain, just before Avery fell. I don't really care. He deserved what he got."

"Because he was fighting and killing miners?"

"Yes, I suppose so, but mainly because he was such a mean cad. . . . Told me he had married me just to have someone to sleep with. Had no qualms about hurting me or anybody. . . . I could see my entire life being tied to him. . . . Let me continue my story." She was lying in his arm, which he curled around her so he could feel her breast.

"After Avery was killed, I came to Beckley to live with an aunt and she paid my way to Beckley Junior College. I got a job in the library in Charleston, where I met my second husband at a dance held by Pittsburgh Steel. That was in 1930. My brother in law, Dan Monroe, whom you met the night we first met, fixed me up with a date to the dance. When I met Gerald Patterson, I fell hard, and he did too.

"He was such a nice man. He inherited the Aggregated Coal Company from his father in 1932 but was determined to run it better. First off, he ordered the operators to prepare to negotiate with the union, and prohibited them from hiring any more 'detectives' to guard the mines. He said that even with the depression, he was going to improve the work conditions for miners; you know, supply their tools and improve their houses. I was heartbroken when he left me, all because I couldn't have any children. I was able to get a divorce on the grounds of desertion.

"I come to Beckley often to visit my aunt who is in a nursing home. That's why I rent an apartment. I know that sounds sad, but my philosophy is that after you've had your cry, then it's time to enjoy life again. You've made me feel like a woman again. I just don't understand how your wife could deny you all those years. Was she afraid she might get pregnant? That frightens many women. I just wish I could get pregnant. If any man can make me pregnant, it's you."

Chapter Thirteen

Clyde was troubled in ways he had never experienced before. *I should have gone to a whore, where I wouldn't be so involved, but Angel, my God, I cain't get her out of my mind. She satisfied every manly desire I ever had. Still, I mustn't forget that she had a connection with, of all people, Avery Murphy! If I told her that I shot Avery, would she be as pleased as she seemed to be, or would that be the kind of confession she's seeking? Then again, how could she or anyone else connect me with the shot from the mountain?* The thoughts possessed him.

Angel, on the other hand, had plans that included Clyde, although he was unaware of them. After they had seen each other intimately more or less regularly for a year, she went to Charleston to see her ex-husband, Gerald Patterson. "Gerry," she said, as they sat in his walnut-paneled office in comfortable chairs, sipping coffee, "I've fallen in love with a man that I want you to give a general foreman's job to in one of your mines."

"Now, Angel," he said, tilting his head, "you know how I still feel about you, but hiring a stranger just because you ask? That certainly is bold. Tell me about this man. What does he know about mining?"

"He's not well educated, but he is a certified fire

boss from the West Virginia School of Mine Extension. He's good. He quit work in Whitman and Rossmore a few years ago because he predicted they were going to explode. They did explode, killing a lot of people."

"Is that what he told you? Maybe he's lying to impress you." He lit a cigar.

"I was afraid of that possibility so I checked the newspapers for the dates he mentioned. Then I called the companies to find out when he worked there. He quit one mine one week before it exploded and the other a few months before it exploded, and that was when jobs were harder to find than now."

Gerald flicked ashes from his cigar. "A man that really knows gas, eh? Interesting. I have a superintendent in Matewan who has allowed two small explosions and led me to question his ability. Good men are hard to find. I'll have one of my investigators check out your friend. If he has the certificates you mentioned and is recommended by the foreman where he works now, I'll make him a superintendent. What's his name?"

"It's Clyde Fuller," she said flashing a beautiful smile at her former husband. "You must promise me that you will never let him know that I talked with you about him. He's a very proud man. I want you to offer him a job just as if your own investigation had unearthed him. Will you do it?"

"You obviously think a lot of this man. Yes, I'll agree to keep your name out of any contact we make with him, assuming we make a contact with him."

"I'm sure you'll contact him when you realize that he is not only talented, but is highly motivated to succeed."

"My goodness. Do you think he'll go after my job,

too?"

"That's not an impossibility. Thanks, Gerry. I owe
you a lot." She kissed his cheek.

When Angel arrived back in Beckley, she found an
envelope under her door with her name written in pencil. Inside were these words, unaddressed and
unsigned: "My wifes mother died. Be gone a few
days."

Mildred died at age eighty-four in March 1941.
Clyde supported Kate as much as he could. He had
saved a few dollars (one hundred five, to be exact) and
was able to send the corpse to Morgantown for burial,
and then accompany Kate there in his old Pontiac.
They stayed at one of Kate's cousins. After the service,
Kate took Clyde to the bedroom to talk.

"You've treated me horribly for the last few years,
and I find it hard to forgive you, even if you ask. I'm
certain that you've been seeing a woman and probably
sleeping with her. I don't know who it is yet, but I
intend to find out. When I do, I will not have mercy on
a woman who destroyed my family. You know I will
never give you a divorce, and if you are an adulterer the
law won't allow you to get a divorce. So you're stuck
with me." She was standing in front of the dresser, her
arms crossed over her ample bosom.

Clyde's face twisted into a snarl.

"I don't care what you believe. All I've been trying to do is better myself. Besides, what's wrong with
sleepin' with a woman? You ain't no wife. A wife meets
the needs of her husband. We ain't really married no
more. Why do you act as if we are?"

"Because a marriage lasts until death do us part,
that's why. All you can think about is sex, but after two

miscarriages, I got tired of sex. Don't I have something to say about when to have sex? Well, it doesn't matter. I'm not going back to Beckley with you right now. Maybe later. My cousin has asked me to stay with her for a few months. You go on back to whatever it is you find interesting in the Wolves' Club. When you're ready to apologize and say you're sorry, then maybe we can talk. I don't expect you to do it. I never once heard you say 'I'm sorry.' I think it's impossible for you. It's simply not a word you use. You just can't say you're sorry when you're not."

She did not tell him that she had inherited some ten thousand dollars from her mother (who kept it in a safe deposit box with Kate's name on it and a note saying it was hers). "I want you to know," she added with conviction, "that I have every intention of finding out if there is a tryst between you and some woman."

Somehow Kate's separation gave Clyde a sense that she no longer objected to whomever he might be seeing. He rushed to Angel the moment he returned to Beckley and both seemed overjoyed at the reunion. She soon had him laughing as he had not laughed in years.

He learned to fix his own breakfast and lunch, and he and Angel often ate supper together, usually at the Wolves' Den, but occasionally at her apartment. They managed to see each other every week and sometimes more often.

In June, 1941, he was told by his mine foreman that a man had been inquiring about him, asking about his mine record. "I recommended you very highly to this man," the foreman added, "although I told him I hoped we wouldn't lose you."

A week later, a man approached Clyde, showed

him papers representing the Aggregated Coal Company, and offered him a job as superintendent of mines at Matewan, in Mingo County. Clyde's startled look prompted the man to ask what was wrong. *Mingo County again. What is going on?*

"Why would you make me an offer like that?" Clyde said, trying to be calm about a position he had dreamed of. "You don't know nothing about me, so how can you say you want me as a super?"

"I know a lot about you. I know that you've worked in about every position in the mines. I know that you've worked in Logan County, which has the same coal seam as in Mingo. I know that you correctly predicted that a couple of mines would explode if the company didn't provide rock dust. I know the company refused the rock dust and you quit before the explosions. I know that you have certificates not only for fire bossing and mine foreman, but also for mine safety. I know you're a careful man and would not endanger the miners. I know that you helped save some miners when there was an explosion in Whitman."

Clyde wondered if the man knew that he had also been in Mingo County once. He decided to head off the discussion. "Do you know that I was in the Battle of Blair Mountain in Logan County, fighting on the side of the miners?"

"Yes, I know that. And that you'd worked also near Oak Hill, and later near Charleston, and even later near Morgantown. I know that you were charged but acquitted for your involvement in Blair Mountain. I know just about where you were during most of your life."

"If you know I fought for the miners, why would

you want me to be a superintendent?"

"Surely you realize that things have changed a lot since those days. The Wagner Act gave miners rights and we now recognize them. You don't have to be anti-miner to work at that level. It's just a few steps above the level you've been working as fire boss, and you know that bosses can't belong to a union. You'll just continue being the same man you are now, observant of people and committed to see that the job gets done for which you were hired, while protecting the lives of miners."

Clyde thought of the union card he carried in his wallet. He had been a secret member for many years and knew he would be fired if it were ever known. Was the man probing to find out such things? Why Matewan, of all places? A town with stinking hovels for miners to live in? Still, isn't a superintendency what he had always sought? Imagine, finally a very important place in the mining business. Furthermore, superintendents were provided the best house in the mining camp. Tempting as the offer was, he had to be careful about what he said and did.

"I'm right pleased with your offer," he said, "but I'd like to go over there and look at the mine, maybe go down in different sections, talk to the section bosses, before I decide."

"We wouldn't have it any other way. I hoped that would be your reaction. I have already reserved a car and driver that will take you to Matewan whenever you say. You can stay as long as you like. There's a little hotel there now, only three years old."

Clyde was more and more convinced that the offer was genuine. Still, he wished there was someone he could talk to about his apprehensions. He had not told Angel that he had ever been in Matewan, and caution warned him not to do so now. Instead, he accepted the offer of a car and driver to visit the scene of his vengeance. On arriving, he noted that the company houses were in better condition than he remembered them, the company store had been rebuilt, a small hotel had a flashing welcome sign, and there was now a movie theater, a book and card store, a funeral home, a neat restaurant, a real-estate office, a bar, and paved roads. The Tug River was still black from coal dust, but the stench was gone. Near the tipple, there was a bath-house.

"I'm surprised that there's a bath house. An' I hear that the miners are permitted to buy the houses they live in for very little money. What do you plan to do about the script?" He was talking with the man who had offered him the job.

"We plan to phase it out shortly," his guide said.

"Can I meet with the mine foreman and some of the section bosses?"

"Yes. We asked them to meet here today at one p.m. In fact, I see them coming now."

Clyde was introduced to six men, and asked each to meet him alone in the superintendent's office. He had the same conversation with each. "Tell me about the conditions underground. What's the gas situation? Is there plenty of rock dust available? Do the miners complain a lot or do they seem to like working here?" He talked with the mine foreman first.

"Mr. Fuller, I have to say that this mine could be a good place to work, but I plan to leave as soon as I can."

By the late 1930s conditions had greatly improved in many West Virginia mining communities. (Courtesy West Virginia Coal Association)

"Why?"

"Because it has become dangerous to work here. The previous super had no knowledge about gas and let conditions deteriorate. Timbers were not always delivered in time, and many miners worked under dangerous tops. I've heard about your knowledge of gas, and I'd be pleased to be working with a man like you."

Although Clyde at first suspected brown-nosing, when each man said basically the same thing, he came around to accepting the fact that he was not only needed there but welcome also.

He said he wanted to visit underground and was given the equipment to do so. He fastened a battery to his belt, ran the wire up to the back of the steel helmet and to the lamp on the front. Within three days, he visited every section and measured for gas. He told himself that he would be good for the mine, and agreed to accept the position.

On the drive back to Beckley, he passed near Blair. "Stoney," he said to the driver, "I want to go to the top of Blair Mountain. There's a dirt road right in front of you, rocky, steep, and water creased, but other cars make it so I suppose you can."

"If others can do it, I can."

"Good for you. I heerd that there's a sign of some kind at the top of the mountain describing the battle I fought in back in 1921. I want to see if it's true."

The driver took the car up a steep, winding dirt road to the fire tower on top. Clyde saw the sign he was hoping for, under the imprimatur of the West Virginia Department of Culture and History. He read the sign slowly: "In August of 1921, 7000 striking miners led by Bill Blizzard met at Marmet for a march on Logan to organize the southern coalfields for the UMWA. Reaching Blair Mt. on August 31, they were repelled by deputies and mine guards, under Sheriff Don Chafin, waiting in fortified positions. The five-day battle ended with the arrival of the U. S. Army and Air Corps. UMWA organizing efforts in southern WV were halted until 1933."

To his driver, Clyde said, "It wasn't exactly like that, but it's close enough. Actually we were winning over the sheriff's men, until the army showed up. We

**The author photographed this sign commemorating the
Battle of Blair Mountain in 1990.**

quit then because we didn't want to fight the United States."

As the drive continued, Clyde thought of Kate and how she didn't seem to understand that he was committed, and wholeheartedly determined, to improve his lot in life, to be a real success, to make people really notice him. He was certain that Angel would understand.

He went immediately to see Angel and reveled in her pleasure at his success. "I knew you could do it," she said, "I just knew you could do it. You'll make a fine super. You have the very qualities needed for running a mine. You'll soon be hobnobbing with the mine owners and politicians and even the governor. People will be interviewing you for the newspapers and the radio. Why, it wouldn't surprise me if you become famous, like a movie star. Oh, I am thrilled, just thrilled for you."

After an hour in bed, they talked about the future. "I have told you my wife will not give me a divorce, and I cain't get one without proving she has committed adultery. We probably cain't live together, because the people around here won't allow unmarried couples to do so. How am I going to see you then? I'm willing to drive back to Beckley every weekend if I hafta. What can we do?"

"That's right. You can visit me on some weekends, and I'll visit you on some."

"Matewan is a small village and we can't hide our relationship for long, I'm afraid."

"No problem. You'll have a nice income now, and I also have some money. We'll simply visit a new hotel every weekend, say in Huntington, and Williamson, and Welch, and Bluefield . . . maybe not Bluefield. I'm well known there. But there are a lot of places we can meet. It doesn't matter. Just so I can be with you. We'll have a great time, running around together, eating in nice places, sleeping in nice hotels, and making love every time we get the chance. Oh, Clyde, how could anything be better for us? I just know we're going to be so happy. Don't you agree?"

They were naked, in her bed, leaning against pillows, sexually satiated and now caught up in the promising future.

"I agree. I cain't think of a better life. I've waited for someone like you for all my life. It just don't seem possible, does it?"

"You must say it doesn't seem possible. There, I've given away a little secret I have for you. I'm going to devote a lot of time to helping you to speak correct grammar. You can't meet the governor if you say ain't and he don't and things like that. Aren't you excited?"

"I thought I talked pretty good, but if you see something wrong with how I talk, then I guess I orta let you learn me somethin'."

"No. I teach, you learn. You should say 'I ought to let you teach me something.' That's enough lesson for one night. We'll have fun learning together. Oh, I'm so excited. We have so much ahead of us . . . That's odd. There's a knock at the door. Wonder who that could be? Don't you dare get out of bed. I'll just put this robe on and see who's there."

Chapter Fourteen

Clyde heard a woman's voice and called out from the bed, "Who's there, Angel?"

"Angel! So he calls you Angel. The dirty, rotten deserter. Let me see him."

"Wait a minute! You can't go in there," Angel said.

"Oh, yes I can. That's Clyde's voice, so I can go where my husband is."

Angel, white with fear, walked in front of the waddling Kate, who had pulled a pistol from her purse. As they appeared in the doorway of the bedroom, Clyde said, "My God, Kate. What are you doing here?" He could not see the pistol.

"No, the question is what are you doing here? I hired a detective and found out whom you've been seeing, and I'm going to stop that. I've come here to do what has to be done."

"What the hell are you doing, Kate?" Clyde said, when Angel ran to a corner and he saw the pistol in Kate's hand. "Put that gun down before you hurt somebody." He was crawling out of bed.

"Shut up, you adulterer, and don't you move another inch. I want to see you in bed, naked and with this woman's lipstick on your face. I have half a notion to shoot off that . . . that thing that runs your life. You just stay where you are, while I look at the woman who broke up my family." She turned toward Angel, who, horrified, stared wide-eyed at the gun. "You're cute, but I wonder how long you'll be cute when this evil man can no longer support you. I'm going to ruin both of you."

"My God, Kate, don't," he screamed. "Angel's the woman I love. Please don't shoot her. She's all I got. Look, I finally got a good job as super over in Mingo County. Maybe we can start over. Please, don't shoot her."

"Shoot her? No, of course not. I'm no murderer. I'm going to make you useless to her and to Mingo, too." She turned the gun toward him, and he flinched, then watched in disbelief as she aimed it downward and shot him through the tibia of his crippled leg, shattering the bone.

"Oh, my God, what did you do? Are you gonna kill me piece by piece? You're mad! Please don't go on. Don't shoot me no more."

"I hope I destroyed that leg. You'll be an even worse cripple. You'll wish you never left me."

"If you murder me, you'll get the electric chair. Please, don't shoot me no more. My leg is shattered. Is that what you want? How could you be so mean? I bet someone in this building has called the police. They'll be here soon. I hear the sirens now. Don't shoot me no more, and please don't hurt Angel."

"One more shot will do it, and you'll get what you deserve." She put the gun under her three chins and pulled the trigger, and her great bulk fell across the bed, her head on Clyde's crippled, bloody leg.

Police, who had been called when the first shot was fired, rushed into the apartment and saw the body of Kate, her head in the blood spurting out of Clyde's right leg onto the sheets and her face, and Angel standing motionless and traumatized in the corner.

"What happened?" the sergeant said, feeling fruitlessly for a pulse on Kate.

Although going into shock, Clyde said, "This woman on the bed shot me in my bad leg, and then shot herself. She's still got the gun in her hand."

"What's your relationship to these women?"

"The woman with the gun is my wife. We separated a few months ago. The other woman is my friend. Oh, my God, just when things was going so good."

"Looks like a shut case to me," the officer said. "Suicide and maiming. Call ambulances. Looks like this man is going into shock."

Kate was taken to the morgue and Clyde and Angel were taken to the Beckley General Hospital. There, he was anesthetized and his leg amputated below the knee. After thirty-six hours, he recovered from the intensive care treatment, and became aware that his lower leg was missing. In a raging voice that reverberated throughout the hallways, he cursed the physicians and nurses. "What kind of animals are you butchers that you'd cut off a man's leg, without even asking him? What do I do now, stand on a corner with a cup in my hand? You're all bastards and thieves, who stole my leg and my only means of making a living. If there's a hell, I hope you burn forever. You sons of bitches have ruined my life. Oh God, oh God. What do I do now?"

For hours he kept groaning, "Everything is lost. There cain't be a God who'll allow this to happen. Ain't life hard enough without this kind of suffering? I ask you, ain't life hard enough?" He buried his face in his hands and cried, something he had done only once before in twenty-five years, and that was when his son died. He started to get out of bed and then realized he couldn't walk. A nurse came in and gave him a sedative.

"You bitch. What are you doing now? Are you going to kill me? Don't you think you've done enough to me?"

"This will help you to sleep. You'll feel better tomorrow."

Angel was sedated for two days before recovering from her shock. She went immediately to see Clyde. "Oh, Clyde," she said. "We're so lucky to be alive. I thought sure she was going to kill you, maybe one piece at a time. I even thought she might kill me, too. I can't imagine what would make a woman hate so much. Can you explain it? What would create so much hatred for a man?"

"No. I cain't explain it," he said in a weak voice. Physicians had given him another powerful sedative to quiet him. "She never seemed like that kind of woman to me. Of all things, why would she destroy my bad leg? Don't she know it would stop me from working in the mines?"

"Yes. Yes. Don't you see? That's what she wanted. For you to be helpless the rest of your life. She killed herself so she wouldn't be sent to prison. She never recognized your good qualities, and probably even thought you would prefer to be dead than crippled. That's really a sick person. Shooting your leg instead of killing you."

"She was right. I would rather be dead than crippled this way. I always swore that I'd have this leg on me when I died. Now I've been proved wrong, an' now, I'll lose you. You surely don't want no one-legged man."

"Don't be silly. Do you really want me?"

"Want you? I have lusted for you since I first laid eyes on you."

"How sweet. A woman likes to know that a man lusts for her. I like to hear you say it. We have so much to look forward to."

"Then you're gonna stay with me for a while?" His voice was hopeful but barely audible at times.

"Stay with you? How long do you want me to stay with you?"

"Forever. No man without a leg could really expect a woman to marry him. Could you just stay with me for a while till I get back on my . . . uh . . . foot?"

"Don't be silly. I'm not the kind of woman who would abandon a man just because he's been hurt badly. Of course, I'll stay with you, but if you're asking me to marry you, the answer is yes. One good thing that's come out of all this is we can get married. Had you thought about that?"

"You're right. We can get married. Do I hear you right, that you'd still marry me? You'd actually marry a man with one leg?" He smiled weakly for the first time since the shooting.

"Of course. Is that what you're asking me? Do you want me to marry you.?"

"I do. I'm in love with you."

"Oh yes, yes. I'm in love with you, too. . . . It probably won't look good for us to get married too soon. We'll have to wait a few weeks, maybe five or six months, just for appearances. We certainly can see each other, in other towns if you think we should. We can date openly, just like regular people. I must warn you, we've already been put through a meat grinder by the newspapers. Kate comes out of this looking like the aggrieved wife who lost her precious husband to a whore, and who lashed back the only way she could, by wounding you and taking her own life."

"I'm . . . I'm sorry . . . to hear that the papers have called you a whore. What does that make me? How can someone be unfaithful to a wife who failed for years to be a bed-partner to her husband? Ain't sex a part of marriage? Was I supposed to rely on wet dreams? Angel, what we done was not wrong, especially when love was also a part of it."

"Oh, you're wonderful! You see our relationship for what it is. Pure love can erase all possibility of coarseness. Life is so short, and people must find love where it is. Once it has died in one person, the other one must seek it elsewhere. I'm just so happy that after I divorced Gerald I waited three years until I met you. It was simply time for you to move on, and I was lucky enough to be there."

Two days later, still hospitalized, Clyde was alert enough to call the mine foreman at Matewan and tell him he would not be able to work, since the doctors had cut off his leg.

"Yes. I know," the foreman said. "The papers have been filled with your ordeal. I'll notify the general manager for Mingo County. I'm sure he will get in touch with you."

To Clyde's surprise, the general manager did call. "Mr. Fuller, I can't tell you how sorry I am to hear of your misfortune. I was looking forward to your working with us, and I know that Mr. Patterson was, too."

"Who?"

"Gerald Patterson, the mine owner. He's the one Angel talked to about getting you a better job."

Clyde dropped the phone and sat immobilized. A nurse heard the buzzing of the phone and replaced it in its cradle. Still Clyde did not move. He sat in the bed and stared straight ahead. The success he thought he had earned by himself drained from his consciousness. Anger swelled in him, and he cursed the doctors and nurses again, and then Angel. "How could she do this to me?" he screamed. "Is she trying to get me into Mingo County for a purpose? Does she think I'll break if I go there? She probably loved Avery Murphy and simply wants to punish me some way. Well, I ain't admitted nothin' for over twenty years, and I'm not about to begin now."

The medical staff tried to calm him and finally gave him a sedative, which put him to sleep.

Angel came to see him that evening as he awakened. "Damn you," he yelled. "You _are_ a whore. How could you do this to me? How could you pretend to love me and do this to me? As much as I loved you, I now hate you. You've ruined my life."

"Oh God," she said. "You're delirious. How could you possibly talk to me this way? What has happened to make you talk like that? Please tell me what's wrong?"

"You got me that job in Matewan! That's like cutting off a man's dick. You do have teeth in your damn pussy. You've mutilated me. You and Kate have destroyed everything that makes one a man, a whole body and a job he earned hisself. You're evil. What did you expect to get out of it?"

"Oh Clyde, I'm so sorry you found out, but you would have succeeded if you had been the superintendent. How does it matter how you got it? You were investigated thoroughly and Gerald Patterson decided you were qualified. He would not have put a man in such a high position, if he had any doubts. I see a side of you I never saw before, cruel and vindictive. You even called me names, and that I won't tolerate. I'm leaving. Good-bye." She walked through the doorway into the hall.

"Good bye," he yelled. "You think I'm going to confess to killing Avery Murphy, but you're damn wrong. I wasn't ever in Mingo County before. So how do you like that?"

Angel stopped cold, and slowly turned back in the doorway. "What did you say about Avery? Something about killing him? What are you talking about? I told you, he was killed by Sid Hatfield."

"Sure, sure. You make it sound so innocent. Like all you want is to get me into Mingo County. Get on out of here, you bitch! I don't want nothing to do with a woman who gets me a job and then pretends she didn't have no motive behind it."

Angel turned and walked down the hallway, crying. "What did I do," she said to no one in particular. "I just don't understand. Why would he turn on me like that?" She left the hospital, called a cab, and returned to her apartment.

Clyde sat in his bed, totally befuddled. *It don't make no sense. It seems like she was tryin' to get me into Mingo County for a purpose, but she seemed so*

*sincere when she said she knowed that Sid Hatfield
shot Avery. Have I been a fool? Am I making more out
of this than I should? I never loved someone so much in
my life, but I can't do nothing about nothing as long as
I'm bound to this bed.* He cried, his shoulders shaking,
the sheet on his chest gradually becoming wet.

He became aware that someone was entering the
room, and said "Angel?"

"Oh, Clyde. We didn't know about you till this
morning. We came as fast as we could. You poor boy.
Are you going to be all right?" Aunt Nell hugged him
so tight it hurt.

"Aunt Nell! Where'd you come from? How did
you know? Hello, Uncle Charlie. Here, let me shake
your hand. I'm totally surprised to see you. It's been so
long." Aunt Nell was wearing glasses and had put on
weight and had gray hair.

Uncle Charlie looked unchanged, except for a very
high forehead. "I guess it's been fifteen or sixteen
years," he said, "since before you got married. We
heerd about you marryin' someone named Kate. We
found out about you when our neighbor was in Beckley a few days ago and picked up a newspaper and read
about what happened to you. He brought it over to us
this mornin' and we had to come."

"Well, it's good to see you but not in this condition. I ain't a man no more. I can't work. Still I 'preciate you coming to see me. Did you bring the Old Man
Jack?"

"No. Your daddy is doin' poorly," Nell said.
"Maybe you can come see him soon."

"What's wrong with him?"

"It's his heart, we think. Also, his arms ache a lot.

He asks about you whenever we see him, which ain't often. I bet the last time you saw him was over twenty years ago, before you got involved in the Battle of Blair Mountain. Then you went north and disappeared from us. We didn't know where you were till we read about the shootin'. Don't you ever want to see your daddy again?"

"I been pretty busy tryin' to make a success of the mines. Travelin' costs money and I just let things slip by."

"We saw in the paper that you are a fire boss," Charlie said. "That's pretty successful, if you ask me. I been in the mines forty years, and nobody ever asked me to be a fire boss."

"You hafta go to school for that, Uncle Charlie. I went to the West Virginia University School of Mines Extension, where I got papers for bossing."

"We're so pleased for your success," Nell said. "What will you do now?"

"That's just it. I don't know. Who would hire a man with one leg? I ain't no good to nobody."

"I remember when that horse fell on you," Charlie said, "and I didn't think you'd ever walk again, but you were stubborn and you did walk again. Now I bet you'll get a wooden leg and walk as good as me before long."

"The doctor says I gotta learn to walk on crutches first, for at least three months till the stump heals, then he'll fit me with a artificial leg. How do I make a living walkin' on crutches? Am I supposed to fast for the next couple months?"

"Why don't you come back with us until your leg heals?" Nell asked. "We got a used Ford now, and can take you home, and then take you to see your daddy."

"That's right kind of you, but I don't aim to live off nobody else. I'm gonna do this my way. I always said that any man who wants to work can find a job, and I'm gonna do it."

"I bet you just don't want to leave that woman, Angel, that the paper mentioned," Charlie said, with a grin. "Are we gonna get to meet her?"

Clyde sat silent for an uncomfortably long time. "I reckon you won't get to meet her. I got angry with her and told her not to come back. Maybe the most stupid thing I ever done."

"Just tell her you're sorry," Nell said. "Women always like that. I'm sure she'll come back if you do."

"Maybe she will, but that's why I cain't go home with you. I got to see if we're gonna make it. Besides, I want to be alone for a few days and see if I can work some things out in my mind."

Chapter Fifteen

After the disappointed couple left, Clyde yelled for a nurse to bring him some crutches. A white-capped nurse came into the room with crutches, and said, "Here they are, Mister Fuller. I'll show you how to use them."

"I don't need no help. You cut off my leg and then think you can be kind to me. Just get out of my way. I'll show you that I've used these damn things before." He eased out of bed onto his one foot and slipped the crutches under his arms, stepped forward with a smirk on his face, and fell flat on the floor, slinging one crutch against the wall and the other toward the nurse who dodged it. He tried to get up and couldn't. He got up on his hands and left knee, but could not put any pressure on the stub of the sore right leg. He stayed in that helpless position for many seconds, scowling at the situation. "God dammit," he screamed, "dont stand there. Get me some help."

An orderly was called and he and the nurse lifted Clyde back into his bed.

"Now you listen to me," the nurse said. "You've abused the doctors who saved your life, you've shout-ed at the nurses, and you've felt sorry for your self. There are men here with no legs at all, and some even have no arms. So I've put up with all this self-pity I

intend to take. Now you do what I tell you to and leave
your pity to yourself, or I'll leave you to learn how to
get around all alone. Only a damn stubborn fool would
think he can do everything himself. Is that clear? I said,
is that clear?"

"Yeah. I hear you. I guess I don't have no choice.
I'll do what you say."

"That's more like it. We've had many people here
who have lost a leg, even above the knee, who learn to
live full lives. You still got a knee, so you'll be doing
well in two or three months. Now let's try this again."

Clyde learned to walk on the crutches and was dismissed from the hospital a few days later. At the business office, he was presented with a bill for two hundred fifty dollars. Since he had managed to save three
hundred dollars living alone while Kate was away, he
paid the bill. Not paying the bill never occurred to him.
*Now, how do I live on fifty dollars for eight or ten
weeks?* he wondered.

He got a taxi that took him to his rented house for
two dollars, but realized that he would owe another
month's rent of twenty dollars in a week. He paid the
rent when due, and spent six dollars on bread, milk,
eggs, and hamburger. He stretched the food out to a
week and duplicated the purchase for another six dollars. He spent another four dollars to get a taxi to take
him to the doctor to re-bandage his leg, and a dollar for
aspirin. By the end of the month, after six more dollars
for food, he had seven dollars left. While he spent the
month practicing walking on his crutches, most of the
time he sat at home and thought about Angel.

Another visit to the doctor took four more dollars
for a taxi there and back. His house rent was due in two

days. He walked out of the house to the sidewalk that took him to the drug store, where he paid a nickel and called Angel.

"Hello," Angel said.

"My God, Angel, I've got to talk with you. Please give me a chance."

"No. I want nothing more to do with you." She hung up.

As he walked back to his house, he thought of ways he might kill himself. *The pistol! That's it. I'll use the pistol.*

When he got home, he went to the bedroom chest, back in the bottom drawer and retrieved the gun. He broke it down and cursed. *I'll be damned. No shells. I'll hafta go back to the store and see if I can buy a couple of bullets.*

Slowly, he made his way back to the store and bought two bullets for a nickel. He was on the way back home when one crutch hit a stone that rolled away and he fell headlong into a stone wall. He regained consciousness in the hospital.

"Where am I? What am I doing here? How'd I get in a hospital bed again?"

"You were found unconscious by a wall, bleeding from the head," a nurse said. "An ambulance brought you here and we sewed you up. We kept you overnight. How do you feel?"

"I got a headache."

"That's not surprising. The doctor says you don't have a concussion, so you are free to leave when you want to."

"What about my crutches?"

"We have them right here. Be more careful next

time."

"I shore will."

The business office presented him a bill for thirty-eight dollars and thirty-five cents. He took his wallet from his pocket.

"I only got three dollars and a few cents."

"Why don't you write us a check, then?"

"I cain't 'cause I don't have no checkin' account."

"Are you saying that three dollars is all you have? There's no more money anywhere you can get your hands on?"

"Yes, ma'am. I don't know when I'll be able to work again, or whether I'll ever work again. Can I leave this little bit with you?"

"No. We won't take your last dollar. I'm going to mark you down as an indigent and let you go on your way."

"What does indigent mean?"

"It means you're poor, so you are treated free."

Clyde blushed and, thoroughly embarrassed and humiliated, left the hospital, carefully placing each crutch solidly on the ground. Unwilling to spend the last money he had on a taxi, he walked the mile and a half to his house, which took him an hour, and made his armpits and hands ache. As he approached the house, he saw the landlord awaiting him.

"Hello, Clyde," he said. "I was over this way, so I thought I'd pick up the rent now."

"I hate to say it," Clyde said, "but I only got three dollars to my name. Can you hold me over till I can get back on my . . . till I can get work again?"

"I can't hardly do that. This house and another one I own provide me the only income I have to live on. I

got another couple wanting this house, and they're
ready to move in next week."

"You got a place you can store my goods till I can
pick them up?"

"I got a shed back of my house you can use for two
dollars for six months. Do you want it?"

"I don't have no choice. Here's the two dollars. Do
you know anybody who might move the stuff to your
shed for a dollar?"

"Yeah, I think my boy would do it. Gimme another dollar and I'll see it's moved."

Clyde handed the man his last dollar. "Can I sleep
here tonight?"

"No. I'll have my boy move that stuff in an hour,
so it'll be an empty house."

Clyde went into the house and stuffed a pillowcase
with his shirts and socks, underwear, work clothes, and
shaving materials. He put the pistol among the clothing
and then remembered to get his mining certificates,
which he slid down into the sack. He tied a rope around
the bag and slipped the end of it in his belt and tied it,
letting it swing against his right leg. Although it was
clumsy, he was able to walk with both crutches, and
headed back toward town, although he was not sure
why. An hour later, on a side street, he came to the location of the Salvation Army and entered.

"Welcome to our humble place," a uniformed man
behind a desk said. "What can I do for you?"

"I ain't got no money, maybe thirty-five or forty
cents, and I'm hungry. Can you help me? I'll pay you
back as soon as I can."

"Whether you pay us back or not is up to you. Our
calling is to help those in need. We have a soup kitchen

in the next room and a cot nearby you can have for the night. By the way, I'm Captain Wallace."

"I'm Clyde . . . Clyde . . . Smith, and I never been like this before. Takin' charity ain't no goal of mine."

"No problem, Clyde. The depression has brought many men like you to us. So come on in and get a bite and a place to sleep."

Clyde did not say thank you. Instead he followed the captain into an adjoining room, where he ate the soup greedily since it was the best food he had had in days. At dusk, he was shown a large room with twelve cots in it, eight already occupied. He placed his sack of clothing on the floor beside his crutches, undressed to his underwear, and laid down on a cot that sank in the middle with his weight.

An hour later, almost asleep, he suddenly yelled, "My God. Somethin's bitin' me all over."

"What'chu grousing about?" a man on the next cot said. "Shut up and go to sleep."

"No. Somethin's bitin' me. I'm gonna find a light and see what it is."

"You ain't never been in a flop house before, have you? It's just bed bugs. You'll get used to them."

"Bed bugs! I'll be damned if I sleep with bed bugs. I gotta get out of here." He dressed, got his crutches and bag, and walked carefully to the door, through the office and out on to the street, his small bag of clothes bouncing against his leg with each step. He was itching terribly, and began to slap himself. Even in the dim light on the street, he could see little wet spots appear on his pants and shirt as he swatted the vermin under his clothes. He saw the Greyhound Bus sign a block away and went there. He laid down and eventually went to sleep on one of the benches, but was aroused regularly by the arrival of busses through the night.

At daybreak, a police officer awakened him. "Where're you going, buddy? This ain't no hotel, you know."

"Thank you, officer. I see that it's getting light out there, so I'll get on my way."

"Okay. Take it easy on those crutches."

"Yeah."

He tied the bag to his belt, positioned his crutches, and went out on the street, where he saw a diner. He got a cup of coffee and two donuts for fifteen cents, and noted that he had thirty-four cents left. As he left the diner, he saw in the distance the bank owner he had met at the Wolves' Den, and, to avoid the man, turned and walked as fast as he could down a side street. He sat down to rest on a bench under a tree at a park. A man was coming toward him, dressed shabbily in bib-over-alls, with a dirty face and beard stubble, and shoes with the heels completely worn off on the outside.

"Praise God," the man said, as sat down beside Clyde.

"What did you say?" Clyde asked.

"Praise God! Don't it make you feel good to be alive and to praise God for all he's done for you? Why, brother, I can look at you and see that you know God."

"Then you've made a big mistake. What do I have to praise God about? Cain't you see I don't have a right leg? God sure ain't lookin' after me."

"That's no way to look at it. You're still alive. Ain't that important?"

"Not to me, it ain't. Right now I don't care whether I live or die. An' talkin' to you ain't no help."

"Why? What's wrong with me?"

"You're filthy. I bet you haven't had a bath in weeks. I know you're after something, so out with it. What do you want?"

"I guess I can't hide it. You're right, I ain't had nothing to eat for three days. I saw you come out of that diner, so I thought you might have a few cents left over. Can you help me? Please."

Clyde stared at the pitiful looking man and sensed that he was telling the truth. He reached in his pocket and pulled out a dime and a nickel. "Here. You can get two donuts and a cup of coffee with this, or three donuts if you don't drink coffee. Maybe that'll help you through the day. Then you ought'a go to the Salvation Army. They got some food. But don't sleep there. I got to go now."

As he got up, the man said, "God bless you, sir. I hope you have a good day. I'm heading for the diner."

Clyde walked back to the bus terminal and asked the price of a ticket to Oak Hill.

"A dollar and a quarter," the ticket agent said. "Do you want a ticket?"

Clyde pulled all of his change out of his pocket and stared at it. "All I have is nineteen cents. You got any work around here I could do to earn at least a dollar and six cents? That'll get me to Oak Hill."

"Don't think so . . . wait a minute. Can you sweep when using those crutches?"

"Sure, I can sweep."

"Tell you what. If you'll sweep this entire station floor and wash that big window there, I'll give you a dollar and six cents. Normally, that kind of work only pays a quarter an hour, and that's only two hour's work.

I like to help a man that's down and out when I can."

"I'll do it. You got a squeegee for that window?"

"Yes. And I'll get you a broom, too."

It took Clyde two hours to wash the window and sweep half the floor. He watched a tall, grossly obese man with one eye enter and sit down. The man had on bib overalls, and a wrinkled hat. The blind eye was sunk back in his head, and a scar ran from it across his cheek down to his neck. His lips were twisted into a snarl. "Hey, cripple," he said, "don't bring that dust over to me. I ain't no dust bin."

"What did you call me?" Clyde asked.

"Cripple. Ain't it obvious you ain't a whole man? If you was a man, you wouldn't be sweeping a floor like a woman."

"You god-damn fat slob. What gives you the right to make fun of me?"

"Fat slob! You called me a fat slob! I'm gonna knock your block off," the man said, as he arose from the bench and waddled toward Clyde with doubled fists.

Leaning on his left crutch and left foot, Clyde flipped his right crutch up, caught it in mid air, and jabbed it into the man's face. As the man's hands grabbed his face, Clyde rammed the crutch into the man's crotch, causing him to bend over, allowing Clyde to strike him on the back of the head.

As the man crumpled to the floor, the ticket agent ran up, yelling, "What's going on here? Why'd you hit that man like that?"

"Because he said he was gonna knock my head off. I defended myself the only way I can."

The agent helped the huge man get up and led him

back to his seat, then turned to Clyde; "You're fired. I won't have any crazy man here hitting people with his crutches. Get out of here."

Clyde glared at the agent, and said in as firm a voice as he could muster, "Not till I get at least half what you promised me. I ain't leaving till you pay me, and I hope you understand me, 'cause if you don't, you ain't seen the damage I can do here."

The policeman who had awakened Clyde earlier walked in the door, and the agent yelled, "Jerry, arrest this man. He attacked that man with a crutch. Tried to kill him."

"Is that so?" the policeman said. "What's you name, fella? And why were you fighting?"

"My name is Clyde Fuller, and this fat slob said he was gonna knock my head off. So I stopped him the only way I know how, since I don't have two legs."

"Clyde Fuller? Where've I heard that name before? Oh, yes. You're the man whose wife shot him in his bad leg, forcing the doctors to amputate. That was a couple of months ago. You were a fire boss at Sprague, weren't you?"

"Yeah."

"Why are you here? Are you going somewhere?"

"I was sweepin' the floor to earn some money to get to Oak Hill, when this poor excuse for a man threatened to hit me. I stopped him before he could."

"What's a fire boss doing sweeping a floor? Are you that broke?"

"Yeah. I spent all the money I had on the hospital and doctors. My leg is still healing, so I can't get a false one yet and try to get back to work."

"Well, I didn't see the fight, so I'm not going to

arrest you. Why don't you just collect your pay and get on over to Oak Hill?"

"I'm only half finished with what I agreed to do."

"You're done here, as far as I'm concerned," the agent said. "Get on out of here."

"Not till you pay me at least half what you promised."

"What did you promise this man, Chet?" the policeman asked the agent.

"I promised him a dollar and six cents, but since he didn't do the job, I ain't paying him a cent."

"Like hell, you won't," Clyde said. "I ain't working two hours for nothing."

"Look, Chet," the officer said, "Mister Fuller isn't a bad man. He's just had bad luck. Why don't you pay him at least fifty-three cents, and let him get on his way."

"Well . . . okay, but I sure don't like fighting in my station." He went to the cash register, retrieved the money, and handed it to Clyde, who put it in his pants pocket.

"You better watch your back, old woman, 'cause I'm gonna get even for what you done," the fat man said as Clyde walked out the door.

He heard the policeman say, "Shut up, you trouble-maker."

Clyde walked to the Wolves' Den and asked if he could take a bath and shave. "Sure, Mister Fuller," the manager said. "Any member can use our facilities for something like that. Go on back."

Clyde walked back to the bathroom, which had three stalls, three sinks, two urinals, and an old bathtub with claw-feet. He looked at the tub and realized that if he ever got in it, he would be unable to get out, since there were no handicap-bars around it. He looked in vain for a chair. There were no wash cloths or cloth towels, only paper. "Damn, damn, damn," he said out loud, "I cain't take no more of this," as he searched in his bag for the pistol, just as the manager entered.

"I just happened to remember that there are no cloth towels here, so I brought a couple. Can't take a bath with paper towels, now, can one?"

"Much obliged," Clyde said. "Would you mind bringing me a chair, too. I can do better that way."

"No problem at all. I read about your bad luck and knew that's why we haven't seen you here for a while. It's good to have you back. Sorry that none of the other members are here, but most are at work this time of day."

"Thanks."

The chair was brought and Clyde was left alone. He sat down and pulled the pistol from his bag, and looked at it for many minutes. *No, now's not the time. Not when I'm in the Wolves' Den. This is where I met Angel. I cain't shoot myself here. Besides, some of the people I met here are important in this town, and they might be embarrassed. Wonder if I'm being punished by God for what I done in Matewan, killing that son of a bitch detective? That's what got me in all this trouble. I guess I ain't ever gonna live it down.*

Sitting in the chair, he undressed himself and looked inside his underwear and pants at small spots of blood where he had slapped the bedbugs. He could not accept the fact that he had sunk so low. He took a wash cloth and washed himself at the sink, still seated, especially scrubbing every point where the bugs had bitten him. He took his shaving brush and razor out of the bag, lathered himself from the soap on the sink, and shaved the black stubble from his face. He put on clean underwear, shirt and pants, folded and pinned the pants up on his right leg, and stuffed the soiled clothes in the pillowcase.

Feeling like a man again, he walked over to North Kanawha Street and began thumbing for a ride. *I ain't never been so humiliated in my life. If I can just get to Uncle Charlie and Aunt Nell's house for a while, I'm sure they'll board me till I can get a false leg. What am I gonna do about Angel? I gotta keep trying to get her to talk with me and see if she'll come back to me. What a fool I am.*

An hour later, a man in a nineteen thirty Ford truck, hauling squealing pigs, picked him up.

"Where you going, buddy?" the driver asked. "Can you get in all right, or do you want me to help you?"

"No, I think I can make it, but I might be a little slow."

"Take your time. Where you heading?"

"To Oak Hill."

"I ain't going that far, but I can get you to Mount Hope."

"Much obliged. That's half-way there."

Clyde managed to get in the seat of the truck, struggling with the crutches, which were almost too long to fit between the floor boards and the top of the vehicle.

"What's a man with one leg doin' hitch hiking?" the farmer asked. "Wouldn't it be easier on the bus?"

Clyde's head was bowed and his eyes shut, and he

was clinching his teeth. Finally, he said, "Look, mister, I ain't never had to hitch hike in my life, but I don't have enough money to get to Oak Hill. I don't think I'll survive if I don't get there. My aunt and uncle live near there, an' I'm tryin' to reach them. I'm hopin' I can get some money some way to get a false leg. Then I might get work again."

"You musta just lost that leg recently?"

"Yeah, a couple of months ago."

"I bet it'll be hard for a man with one leg to get a job. What kind of work do you do?"

"I'm a fire boss."

"Fire boss! I bet you won't be allowed to go into the mines again. They ain't gonna take no cripple in the mines."

"Don't call me a cripple, damn it. I'll find work just as soon as I get a leg."

"Didn't mean to make you mad. Sorry. Where do you want to be let off?"

"Let me off at the bus station. Much obliged for the ride."

"Think nothin' of it," the driver said, as Clyde tossed the pillowcase bag out and struggled to get the crutches out and ease himself onto them as he slid out of the seat.

Clyde walked into the bus depot, his clothes sack bouncing against his thigh. At the counter, he asked, "How much to Oak Hill?"

"Sixty cents," a young woman said. "The next bus will be here in about two hours."

Clyde slipped the sixty cents to the agent, and then took a seat in the waiting room.

He had twelve cents left, and spent it on three large

chocolate chip cookies, the only food besides candy in the station. He tried to remember the last time he didn't have a single cent, with no prospects of getting any money. He boarded the bus, arrived in Oak Hill at three-thirty, and walked out on the street, asking questions of any one he met. "Hello. Do you know Charlie Crabtree? He's my uncle and lives about ten miles from here."

The first twenty-three people answered in the negative, but the next man said, "Yeah. I know him. I know where he lives. You say he's your uncle?"

"Yes."

"You wouldn't be Clyde Fuller, would you?"

"Why yes. How'd you know?"

"I read about you in the paper. Your wife shot your leg off for running around. Damn fool thing, I'd say. I 'speck my wife'd do the same thing, if I wasn't careful. Did you get careless?"

"Cain't say that I did. I wasn't runnin' around. We was already separated. . . . I decided to come here while my leg heals, then I can get a false one and maybe find work again."

"Glad to hear it."

"What I was hopin' was that you might be going over to where Uncle Charlie lives. I could use a ride."

"You're in luck. I'm heading that way in about an hour. Why don't you set there on the bench while I wait for my son's bus to come in from Charleston? Then we'll be off."

An hour and a half later, Clyde walked up on the porch, one step at a time, and knocked. Charlie answered the door. "Well, by golly, it's Clyde. Sure glad to see you. Come on in. Nell," he called, "it's

Clyde, come to visit us."

Clyde was welcomed as he expected, and in due course told them all that had happened to him, even about being humiliated and moneyless.

"Don't you worry none about that. You can stay here as long as you want. I can even loan you some money, if it ain't too much."

"Thanks, Uncle Charlie. I already owe you a lot for being so good to me when I was a kid. I will stay with you until my stump heals, but then I gotta find a way to raise about two hundred dollars for a false leg. I can't do any real work as long as I'm on crutches. If I can get a leg, then maybe I can get a real job. Funny, ain't it? I can't get a job and earn some money, because I'm on crutches, but I can't get a false leg until I get a job and earn some money."

"Don't give up. Maybe there is something you can do. The company's check-weigh-master over at the mine died last week and they're looking for a replacement. Since the army draft was set up, there ain't any young men around, and no older man will take the job. The mines is beginning to work every day. Some people say it's because of that war in the old country. Some people say we might get in it. Anyway, they'll pay you three dollars a day, with double on Saturday and Sunday." He grabbed a short pencil and a piece of paper and began to cipher. "You could make twenty-seven dollars in a week, and in eight weeks, if they still haven't found a permanent man for the job, you would have two hundred sixteen dollars. You can stay with us for room and board. Think you can do that job every single day for eight weeks?"

"Of course I can do it. All you do is set with the

Coal continued to be laboriously loaded by hand in some West Virginia mines well into the 1930s. (Courtesy Norfolk & Western Railway)

union weigh-master in that little shack with a big scale and weigh the coal cars as they come out of the mine and then take the coal loader's check off the hook on the car and give him credit for what he loaded. Are you sure you can get me the job?"

"I'll walk over there right now and see. You'll have to be approved by the union too, ya know."

"That don't bother me none. I'm still a union member myself, even if the company don't know it."

In an hour, Charlie returned with the good news. "I talked with Dirk Schmidt, the general foreman. He remembers you from nineteen-fifteen. Said you were a quick learner. He wanted to know why you'd take a job as weigh-master. I told him about your leg. He said you can start tomorrow. So I told the union steward about you, and he said he'd heerd of you and would not fuss about having you be a check-weighman."

Clyde took the job and had some time to think, since the loaded cars came out of the mine sporadically. *This is an awful let down for a man with my papers. Still, I feel better having something that pays a little, better'n when I went completely broke in Beckley. Beckley! I keep thinking of Angel. She wouldn't give me a second chance. I'd get down on my knees and beg her if she'd talk with me. Maybe she was thinkin' of me and not Avery Murphy when she got me that job in Matewan. She was right to point out that her former husband wouldn't of hired me if I wasn't qualified. What was that fool thing I said to her? And why did I hafta call her names? She never done me no harm.*

A coal car rolled by his shack and he weighed it and took the check off the side, recorded the weight and the check number, which the union representative agreed was correct.

Clyde worked a full ten weeks, till December 15, 1941, in order to have a little extra money. His father came to visit him and Clyde realized that the Old Man Jack had become old.

"You look pretty good, 'cept for the leg," Jack Fuller said. "As bad as you was hurt back there as a boy, I 'speck you're lucky to last till now. So a woman shot your leg off? You musta made her awful mad."

"She was my wife, but we was separated. She didn't wanta be a wife, just someone for me to feed. She caught me with my girlfriend an' shot me in the leg and then killed herself. . . . So, how're you doin'?"

"Right sprightly fer an old man. Rheumatism got me pretty bad in my arms an' my chest hurts some, but I don't have much else to complain about."

After a few minutes of light talk, Clyde said, "I was a fool not to listen to you when you tried to make me go to school. If I'd listened to you, I mighta got a better education and still have work, even without a leg."

"Wal, son, I was stubborn myself. I guess we're pretty much alike. I'm sorry it's been so long since I seen you. I think about you a lot. I wanted you to go to school so bad, but didn't have sense enough to know how to make you do it. You know I didn't want you to work like a rat in a hole in the ground. I had bigger hopes fer you, but I gotta admit that you worked your way up to bossin' an' that wasn't easy for a man without schoolin'.

"I did go to school again and got papers for bossing at the mining school at the university. I know you was right in tryin' to make be stay in school. Up to now,

I done pretty good for myself. I'm gonna get a false leg soon, and then see what kind of work I can do. Now that the war has started, there must be some openin' for work I can do."

"I hafta admit you done good fer yourself. I'm pleased fer you. I'm jest sorry we didn't get along better."

"I'm sorry, too . . . Dad."

They parted as friends. Pearl Harbor had plunged the country into war, and Clyde saw the beginnings of many changes. He went to Beckley and was pleased that he had enough money for a prosthesis, and equally pleased that he could walk on it without crutches, although he felt more comfortable with the aid of a cane.

"Look," he said to Uncle Charlie, who had accompanied him, "I can walk almost as good as the next man, even if I do limp. I know I cain't work in the mines again, but there must be something I can do."

"I'll bet there's lots of jobs you can do. Jest keep watching the want ads. Something will come along that will be better than a check-weigh-master."

Clyde found a cheap apartment and, because it was so close to Christmas, got a temporary job as a clerk in a grocery store, the same A&P that he shopped in for a month and almost got fired for it. On Christmas Eve, Clyde emboldened himself to go to Angel's apartment and seek reconciliation.

She opened the door to his knock. "What do you want? Haven't I made it clear that we're through?"

"Please, Angel, I love you and can't get you out of my mind. What I said was wrong, but I was nervous about something. Cain't you see it in your heart to forgive me?"

"I still don't know what happened," she said, "but I think your words were motivated by the wrong information. In any case, I can't stand abuse from a man, and that includes you. I lived once with an abusive man and I swore never again. If you really think I have set out to damage you some way, then we need to get that cleared up as quickly as possible. Do you want to tell me now?"

"I cain't talk about it, ever. Honestly, I want to. Cain't you forgive me without my talking about it?"

"No. Whatever is going on in your mind led you to abuse me. I've got to know what it was. Good bye." She slammed the door.

Clyde returned to his own apartment slowly, thinking about his options. Should he finally confess that he killed Avery Murphy and risk her telling the police and sending him to prison? I'd better think about it some more.

After the holidays, he was asked to stay on the job at the grocery store, and within four months was made assistant manager, because of his ability to direct the other workers in their activity. The job gave him a good opportunity to get acquainted with his prosthesis, because if he fell in the store there would be people around to help him. After two months, he allowed himself to walk throughout the store without a cane, but not on the street. "I never expected to be in this condition," he told the store manager, "but it feels good to be in control of that leg again. Still, the only reason I hold on, and work in a grocery store, is my hope that I can make up with a woman I treated wrong. First, somehow, I gotta get her to talk with me."

"We're just glad that a man with your ability is available to work for us," the manager said. "I hope you get to make up with your woman, and I hope you won't leave us when you do."

"I don't know how things will work out, but I gotta hold this job until I find a better one."

In late May of 1942, Clyde became manager of the store, succeeding his predecessor, who had been inducted into the army. It was not the sort of work he had ever thought of doing, and seemed to him more appropriate for young people and women. As a result of his promotion he called Angel again, but got no answer. He would try again in a few days.

On July 15, he was surprised by a telephone call.

"Mr. Fuller?" a male voice asked, "Clyde Fuller?"

"Yes. This is Clyde Fuller."

"I'm so glad I finally found you. You've been hard to track down. We've been looking for you for a couple of months. I'm Lloyd Amherst, vice president of the Aggregated Coal Company in Mingo County. We talked last year, after your awful accident. After losing a leg, there was no way you could come here as superintendent. At least, that's what we thought then. A lot has happened in the last few months, with the war on, that changes our perspective. Three section bosses, one fire boss and the general mine foreman have all gone into service. With your knowledge of mining, we think you can help us, not by going down into the mines, but by overseeing things from the top. We'd like to offer you the job of chief advisor to the superintendent of our mines in Matewan. You would keep an eye on the novices we have to hire and try to sense how well things are going underground. You will report regularly to the super. We'll pay you fifteen thousand dollars a year, provide you a brick house to live in, and give you access to a car and driver. Have I tempted you?"

Clyde stared at the phone. "Is this some kind of a joke? You really want me in Mingo County to help the super?" His mind was racing. *Could it be true? Or do they want me in Mingo so I can be accused of killing Avery? I really don't care, since I lost Angel. I'll take the chance.*

"You've really surprised me. I have to catch my breath . . . . Yes, sir, Mr. Amherst, I'd be mighty pleased to accept your offer. I'm manager of this grocery store, and it may take a while to find someone to take my place."

"I understand. We hope you can start in two weeks. Do you think that's enough time?"

"I'll make it do."

"That's what I wanted to hear. I'll send a driver and car to pick you up on August first if you'll give me the address of your apartment."

"Much obliged. That'll be a swell way to start a new life."

He gave the address, hung up the phone, and sat at his desk and pondered the turn of events. He called the regional manager of the grocery chain and told him he was resigning, effective in two weeks. He told the assistant manager that he was taking the afternoon off, and headed to Angel's apartment. Surely, with this kind of success, she would forgive him. He knocked on the door a dozen times before turning to leave.

"Can I help you?" a man who had just walked up said. "I'm the manager here."

"Yes. I'm looking for Angel Patterson."

"She moved out months ago. Another couple lives here now, and they're both at work."

"She moved! Where'd she go?"

"Don't know. She didn't say."

"Where'd she say to send her mail?"

"Didn't say. I'm holding any that comes till she returns to get it or lets me know where to send it. Sorry."

Clyde walked slowly back to the grocery store and made preparations to leave the job and move to Matewan. He sat at his desk and thought of Angel. He thought of Angel when he got up. He thought of Angel when he was eating. He thought of Angel when he went to bed. Nothing he did could take his mind off her for very long. He wondered how he could do the job in Matewan, if he didn't get some relief from his obsession. He even wondered if maybe Angel had gotten him the new job, just to get him into Mingo County. He thought of the pistol he kept loaded with two bullets. He pondered the question of how simple, careless moments can produce drastic changes that last for a lifetime. That night, sitting in front of the radio waiting for Roosevelt's fireside chat, he cried, and eventually went to bed without ever turning the radio on.

Clyde spent the next two weeks in a mental quandary. His thoughts repeated themselves. *I never told no one about shooting Avery, but then I had to blurt out some fool thing to Angel and now she's left me. I cain't even remember exactly what it was I said to her. I hoped she'd marry me and then I'd tell her everything. Instead, I drove her away. Yet, she's the prettiest thing I ever did see. I like to hear her talk. We get on so good. And in bed she's like no other woman I ever heard of. Of course, I've never slept with many women, only*

Mary Ann in Elmer's Bar, and Kate. Maybe all loving is supposed to be like it is with Angel, an' I never knowed no better. Now, she's disappeared and I don't know where to begin to try to find her again.

Chapter Sixteen

Clyde moved to Matewan and settled into a comfortable brick house. Although he was sad, in fact he seldom smiled, he felt he had earned the position and respect he had long sought. There were other rewards as well. When he was shown his office, he could hardly restrain his delight. He was given a desk as large as the one he remembered in the faculty offices at the university, as well as a swivel chair and large, wide file cabinets that held blueprints of various mining tunnels. A large window gave him a view of the tipple, and farther away a view of the hardware store, where he had encountered Avery Murphy over twenty-two years before. He soon knew as much about the mines as anyone, even though he could not go inside himself, just by following map layouts of all activities and interviewing the bosses regularly.

"Coal production is essential to the war effort," he said to the head bookkeeper, who had an office next to his. "It makes me feel good to contribute something to the defeat of Hitler and his gang."

"I agree with you there," the bookkeeper said. "We may be too old to fight, but at least we have something important to contribute." Named Hiram Boggs, he had been with the company for thirty years. He was a short, heavy-set man, with a long nose, almost no hair, and

quite sociable. Clyde found Hiram to be a good source
of information about Mingo County.

"I know you seen a lot of changes since you come
here."

"Actually, it amazes me when I think about it,"
Hiram said, leaning back in his chair. They were talking through the common doorway between their
offices. "When I came here, this was a small stinking
village. There was nothing but constant tension
between the operators and the miners. I had to work in
a small room no bigger'n a closet, without heat.
Reminds me of Bob Crachett in Dickens' 'Christmas
Carol'."

"I guess I don't know about him," Clyde said.

"It's a good story. You ought to read it." He paused
to light a cigar, and offered one to Clyde.

"No thanks. I never took up smoking," Clyde said,
"because since you can't smoke in the mines, I never
saw no advantage smoking only in the evenings."

"You were wise. It's a filthy habit. As I was saying, it wasn't pleasant working here in those days. People were getting killed all the time. There was even a
shootout over there in front of the hardware store
between the chief of police and the company detectives. Damndest thing I ever saw."

Clyde's eyes opened wide. "You mean you seen
it?"

"Not the beginning. After it was over, I saw seven
detectives and three of Hatfield's men lying in the
doorway of the hardware store or on the road or the
railroad tracks, all dead. The mayor was one of them.
The other detectives had run off into the woods. I got
there just as Sid Hatfield put both of his pistols back in

their holsters. Quite a sight."

"He killed those detectives all by hisself?"

"No. He had some miners with him with rifles and shotguns. There was quite a dispute about who killed whom. One man I talked to said he saw that big leader of the detectives fall to the floor at the entrance of the hardware store before Sid Hatfield got his guns out of his holsters. Sid said he shot the man. It never did get clear."

"Did the conflict between the miners and operators continue?"

"Oh yes. You probably heard of the Battle of Blair Mountain, in Logan County. It occurred the next year after Sid Hatfield was shot down right on the court-house steps in Welch. He was unarmed, because he had been promised protection by the law. But those damned detectives shot him down right in the open in front of police, and the prosecutor said he couldn't find enough evidence to charge them with murder. That's what made the miners so angry and led them to come to Blair Mountain to try to avenge Sid."

"Yeah, I heerd about that battle," Clyde said, watching Hiram closely. "In fact, I worked at Blair about ten years after that battle. People were still talking about it. I guess the miners had it pretty rough."

"The tension lasted until President Roosevelt got the National Recovery Act passed. Then, miners were able to form a union and bargain. The Supreme Court declared that Act unconstitutional, but President Roosevelt came right back with the Wagner Act. Things got a lot better around here then, even with the depression on. I actually like it here now. . . ."

"Talking about that shootout with Sid Hatfield,"

Hiram continued, "reminds me that people are still interested in it. Historians drop by here all the time, asking all kinds of questions. In fact, about a month ago, a very pretty woman was here looking for the man who was manager of the company store when the shooting occurred. He may not even be alive now. I don't know whether she had any luck or not. Didn't stay long, then disappeared, just like old John Kavalli."

"Who?"

"Kavalli. He was the store manager but disappeared after the shootout. No one knows what happened to him, except I heard he became a drunkard . . . ." He looked contemplative for a few seconds.

"I've heard some good things about you," Hiram continued. "You're a cracker-jack gas man. I'm glad you're here. Some of these new men don't know gas from a fart."

Two weeks after taking the job, Clyde said to his driver, "Don, I ain't had no woman for a long time. Do you know where I can get one?"

"Sure, Mister Fuller, there's a house in Logan that has some pretty good-looking broads. Wanna go there?"

"Yeah. Let's go."

They arrived in front of an old, dilapidated house, at the end of a narrow road. "Just go on up and knock on the door," Don said.

Clyde got out of the car and stared at the peeling paint, missing porch floorboards, and loose banisters, and slowly climbed the six stairs. At his knock, a heavyset woman answered and invited him in. He entered the living room and saw three women with loose robes on, revealing lingerie. "Take your pick, honey," the woman said. "That'll be fifteen dollars."

Clyde stared at the women, two bleached blondes and a redhead. "Well, make up your mind," the woman said.

Clyde stood still, his eyes flitting about the room. The wallpaper was cracked and the upholstery patched. Slowly, he took his wallet out and gave the woman the money, as she said, "Which one do you want?"

Clyde looked at the two women with frizzled blonde hair, who appeared to be no older than sixteen or seventeen. One was chewing gum; the other was holding a small mirror and putting on lipstick. Neither appeared interested in him. The redhead appeared to be in her mid-twenties and smiled at him. He pointed to her.

"Follow me," she said as she moved down a hall, taking off her robe. She entered a room with a bed and two chairs, and facing Clyde, removed her bra and panties. Her eyes were circled in gaudy black mascara, and her lips were painted red, even outside the lip-lines. She had a pug nose, average-sized breasts, thin blonde pubic hair, and stretch marks from a pregnancy. Clyde stared at her.

"Don't just stand there. Tell me what you want me to do."

"Did you ever love someone so much that you cain't think of nothing else?" Clyde said.

"Sure. I loved a guy once till the bastard run off with my best friend. Listen, you only got thirty minutes. Are you just gonna talk?"

"What would you do if someone you loved just moved away without telling you where?"

"You ought to forget her and come see me."

"I'm serious. What would you do?"

"I'd search every place she ever lived and see if anyone there knows where she is. C'mon. Lay down here with me and you'll feel better."

Clyde opened the door and said, "I guess I was lookin' for Angel."

"Angel! Well, I sure ain't no angel. You better go to church if that's what you're looking for. You won't find her here."

"Thank you, Mary Ann," Clyde said, and started down the hall.

"What do you mean, Mary Ann?" she called. "I'm Marie. Ain't you going to fuck me? What kind of man are you?"

Clyde walked into the living room where the madam, with a surprised look, said, "Well, that was fast. What did you do in there? Quick Gloria, run back there and see if Marie is all right. I don't trust dandies that come here in a suit and carrying a cane."

"Don't worry. I didn't harm her," Clyde said as he stepped out on the porch. He navigated the stairs one at a time and got in his car.

"Boy, Mister Fuller. That was sure fast. Didn't you find someone you like?"

"Take me home, Don. This ain't the right time."

***

On September first, while he was home for the evening, Clyde heard the doorbell ring. He opened the front door to stare into the beautiful face of Angel. She was smiling. His mouth dropped open. He was speechless.

"Oh, Clyde," she said, "I'm so proud of you. I'm

more in love than I've ever been." She threw herself into his arms. Her beautiful eyes danced, her perfect teeth graced her warmest smile, and her low-cut dress revealed her perfect body. "Oh, I love to feel you close, but we must talk first. You see, I know everything. I know it was you who saved me from Avery Murphy. It's been an awful misunderstanding, and there are still aspects that I don't understand, but if you still want me, I'm here."

"You don't make no sense, but I was never so happy to see no one in my life," Clyde said. "Where've you been? Why did you come back? How did you know I was here? What do you mean you know everything? You've got my head to spinning."

"Oh, Clyde, I've had a busy time playing detective, and it's changed my whole concept of you. Let's go in and sit down and I'll tell you everything. You wouldn't have a glass of wine, would you?"

"Strange that you'd ask. I bought a bottle of white wine just because it made me think of you. I intended to keep it unopened forever. I thought I'd never see you again. I'm so excited that I don't know if I can open it now. Are you really here?"

"Yes, I'm here, and for good, too. It's so wonderful to see you. I'm so pleased to see you walking so well. I've been miserable, too, because I thought you had rejected me and for reasons I could not understand. C'mon, lets get the wine. I'll help you open it and then we'll go into the living room and talk. I can see that I'm going to like this house. I love to decorate nice places. The world is beautiful again."

They got the wine, he opened a beer, and they took soft chairs in the living room. He stared at her, smiling.

"You're so beautiful, I cain't keep my hands off you. You cain't know how much I've wanted you."

"A woman likes to hear that a man wants to put his hands on her, and you'll be able to do that soon. First, let me tell you what brought me to my senses and back to you. After I was so rude to you and slammed the door in your face last Christmas Eve, I began thinking about a lot of things. I knew you were a good man, yet you screamed something at me in the hospital about Avery Murphy, a man I assumed you did not know. It just didn't make any sense. It occurred to me that you must have had some connection with Avery, but I couldn't imagine what. I struggled with my thoughts until April, when I left Beckley and moved to Charleston, so I could do research in the library I had worked in before. I read everything I could find out about the Massacre at Matewan. I read the New York Times and the Chicago Tribune. The account of the paper in Logan was especially useful. There were frequent references to a store manager who had seen Avery kill a man in cold blood and threaten a young man who was traveling with him." She sipped from her glass and smiled at the look of incredulity on his face.

"After spending over two months in research, reading every account I could find about the shoot-out, I decided to go to Matewan and see if I could learn anything about the store manager, if he was still alive. After talking with many people here, I learned his name is John Kavalli and he had become an alcoholic and lived somewhere in Huntington. I went there and visited the police department, and found out that he had been arrested for drunkenness often, and lived in a shack near the railroad yards. I found him in his shack, on a bed, drunk. He had a creased face, pure white hair, and looked emaciated. I sat down in a chair and waited for him to sober up, about six hours. When he finally sobered, he started to get another drink, but I stopped him and persuaded him to talk with me. I had to promise to buy him a fifth before he would talk." As she took another sip, Clyde swallowed hard, but sat silent.

"I said, 'I want you to tell me what you saw before the Massacre at Matewan took place, before all the shooting between Sid Hatfield and the detectives.' He said he didn't see much, but I begged him to tell me what he did see. He said he saw two men walking into the village on the railroad tracks. He saw Avery knock the older man down, and then shoot him down in cold blood when the older man fought back. 'Just shot him down like he was a polecat,' Kavalli said. He said it looked like Avery was going to shoot the young man, and kept telling him to do something. They were too far away for him to hear exactly. Then the boy raised his pants legs, and there was some kind of bandage running from his ankle to his knee on his right leg. Kavalli said Avery then said something to the young man and walked away." She stopped talking, wiped tears from her eyes, and, almost to herself, said, "How awful, but how like him. He had no respect for anybody, but to shoot a man down like that! It's so frightening."

Clyde sat stunned, and wordless.

"Kavalli said the young man picked up his dead friend and asked if there was a cemetery nearby. He said he helped the lad bury his friend. He said the young man then went up the mountain and he never saw him again.

"Something about the way he said he never saw

the man again made me think he was lying, so I accused him of it. He looked startled, and trapped. I said, please tell me the rest. He sat looking at the floor a long time. I promised him two fifths. Finally he said, 'I've kept that secret for over twenty-two years, what that young man did, and I don't want to get him in any trouble, because what he did was right.' I begged him to tell me, and promised that I would not say anything to get the young man in trouble. Reluctantly, he said that the matter had been preying on his mind for a long time, but he believed what the young man did was the right thing. He said he thought about it every day, and only drink could get it out of his mind. For awhile, I was afraid he wouldn't tell me what he saw." She sipped her wine, and Clyde sat motionless.

"Finally, he said that because the young man seemed to be so angry he followed him up the mountain. He hid in the woods, and saw the young man meet some miners at the top of the mountain, and after some talk, a miner gave the man a high-powered rifle. The young man then walked out the ridge. He said he followed him, and saw him climb a big oak tree. Then he saw the young man shoot Avery Murphy, and saw Avery fall just as some more shooting started in the valley. He said he then returned to the valley to see what was happening."

She looked at Clyde with a smile, and he said, "Now you know."

"I knew it was you as soon as I heard about the crippled leg. I couldn't figure out how you pulled it off without anyone ever knowing."

"I had no idea that Kavalli was following me, although once or twice I thought I heard something as

I walked out the ridge, but even he didn't know my name or what happened to me after that."

"There's still one thing I don't understand. Why did you yell at me in the hospital that I wanted you to confess to killing Avery? I had no reason to think that. I just don't understand."

Clyde straightened up and looked directly at Angel. He was apprehensive but at last the truth was coming out. "Because every time someone has mentioned Mingo County or Matewan to me I had a fear that they was trying to trick me into saying something that would show my guilt in . . . a cold blooded murder. All my life I heard there was never a perfect murder. I didn't set out to do a perfect murder, but up until right now, I thought I was the only one who knowed of it. Can you understand that every time anyone mentioned Mingo County, I was suspicious that maybe someone else did know? I been looking over my shoulders for over twenty years now."

"Now I see it. Every time anything came up where I mentioned that area, you would become suspicious of me. I remember the first time I said that my first husband had been killed in a fight in Mingo. You looked startled. Then each time I mentioned something related, you would get moody."

"There. You have the whole story, but how did you find me here?"

"I went to the Wolves' Den and found a man who knew that you were the manager of a grocery store. I went to each store until I found the right one. There I learned you had moved to Matewan, but no one knew why. So I called Gerry Patterson and he told me you had been hired as an advisor to the superintendent. I threw my things together and came here as quickly as possible."

"I'm still stunned about the sudden change in my life," Clyde said. "Here I thought God was punishin' me for killing Avery, and yet he has brought you back to me. What now?"

"Oh, Clyde. I love you more than ever. I told you I was pleased when Avery was killed because he was a cruel, vicious, insensitive man. You saw what he could do when he killed your friend. I feared for my life with him. He even hit me in the face with his fist, and knocked me out once. Now I learn that he killed a man in cold blood and you were the one who freed me from him. Can you believe it? I'm going to marry the man who saved me from Avery Murphy. Let's marry right away. Are you willing?"

"More than willing. I'm simply red hot for you, and not jest your body, but as a companion. You have no idea how much I love you and miss you. I couldn't get you off my mind. Jest when I thought there was no hope, suddenly you return with the full truth. We'll go to the Justice of the Peace tomorra."

"I tried at first to forget you," she said, "but couldn't. You can't know how lucky I feel. This is a fairy tale come true. My knight in shining armor, my savior, my good friend. Oh, I love you, I love you." She threw herself on him, sitting on his lap, and they kissed deeply.

When they stopped to breathe, he said, "But you have saved my life, too. When I learned that they'd cut my leg off, I planned to commit suicide. Loving you stopped me, but after I thought I drove you away forever, I thought about it again . . . . Now I wonder how I could ever think that you might be tricking me? Forgive me, please, forgive me. I'm so sorry. I never told no one that before. I'm sorry. I don't deserve your love."

"Hush. Of course I've forgiven you already. I understand your reactions now. In your place, I would have been just as cautious as you were. We'll get married and then I'm going to do something else to help you, just as I promised before Kate shot you. I'm going to help you with your grammar. In a few months you will speak as properly as any educated person, just you wait and see."

"You don't love me as I am?"

"Of course I do, but if I had a problem that you could correct, wouldn't you do it? Well, I'm going to do it for you. You'll be surprised how it can help."

264 The Shot from the Mountain

Chapter Seventeen

After their marriage, Angel forced Clyde to study
with her two hours every day. At first, he resisted it, but
gradually came to enjoy the regularity, not only of the
training, but of the use of grammar itself. He fussed a
little at the pressure Angel put on him, but also recognized that the new grammar sounded good.

"You know, it sounds funny for me to say, 'I am
not sorry,' instead of 'I ain't sorry,' and 'he doesn't'
instead of 'he don't,' and 'I knew' instead of 'I
knowed,' and 'heard' instead of 'heered.' Do you really think I can change at my age?"

"Of course. We'll keep practicing and you'll learn
to like it. It will feel like an accomplishment. After all,
in your new position, you're going to be interviewed by
the press from time to time, and I'm sure you will be
attending gala events put on by the company. As I told
you once before, you probably will even meet the governor. You'll be pleased to speak the right grammar."

"It's already made me notice how you speak, and
I can hear some of the things you're teaching me."

Within four months, Clyde dropped ain't and
cain't from his vocabulary and found the proper past
tense for his verbs. For a while, he spoke slowly so as
to be sure to use the correct word. "Thank you, my
dear," he told Angel. "Studying with you is like a game.

Even grammar is fun. And life with you is more than any man could hope for. Our past is behind us and the future looks good."

***

One snowy evening on January twelfth, 1943, Clyde answered the ring of the doorbell, and saw a man who looked vaguely familiar. "Is this where Angel lives? I'm Cedric Murphy, and she used to be my sister in law. Heard she moved here a while back, and thought I'd visit her. You must be her new husband?"

"Yes. I'm Clyde Fuller." He turned and called into the living room. "Angel, there's someone here to see you, a brother of your first husband."

Angel gasped. "Invite him in to the living room, Clyde."

The man, as big as his brother Avery, with a creased face, thick lips, and receding hairline, came into the room, stomping his feet to get most of the snow off. He was dressed in a heavy coat and, because he appeared to be drunk, was not offered a chair. "The reason I'm here, Angel, is because I heard you had married a man without a right leg. I had to get a look at him and I'm sure glad I did. I have a memory for faces, even after almost twenty-three years." To Clyde he said, "I'll be seeing you later."

"I don't know what you're talking about," Clyde said. "Have we met before?"

"Right on the railroad tracks, not a mile from here, before you ran into the woods. I believe in an eye for an eye and tooth for a tooth. So you'd better keep looking over your shoulders."

"You don't make no . . . any sense, so you'd better go."

"I'll go, but I must tell you, Angel, that you're just as pretty as ever. Aren't you supposed to get older as the years go by? Like I told Avery, he sure was lucky to get a filly like you. If he'd lived, I bet you'd have a passel of kids by now. How many children do you have?"

"None."

"Too bad he died. He was a real man. Had what it took right between his legs." He looked at Clyde and smirked. "He'd of made sure you got with child right away. He used to tell us how sexy you were in bed. Made us all drool."

Clyde's fist hit the man squarely in the face, knocking him down across a footstool, his head hitting the floor with a thud. "You goddamn son of a bitch, get out of here before I kill you." Clyde picked up the poker from the fireplace and Cedric Murphy decided not to press his luck. He got up and stalked out the door, somewhat unsteadily.

After he left, Angel grabbed Clyde, who was still holding the poker. She was crying. "Oh, Clyde. Do you think he knows? He seemed so certain."

"How could he know? You and John Kavalli are the only ones who know. Do you think Kavalli finally talked to some other people? Even if he did, there's always been an element of doubt about whether my shot killed Avery. He may have had more than one bullet in him. Even if Cedric remembered me from the scene on the railroad track when my friend Elmer was shot, how could he know where I went after that? How would he know where I got a rifle? I think it's all a bluff."

"But he's dangerous. That whole clan is dangerous. Maybe we ought to leave here and go some place else."

"I can't do that, Angel. I finally got me a position that I have sought for years, well, maybe not this exact position, but as advisor to a high mine official. That's almost as good as being superintendent. That man is bearing a twenty-three year grudge and won't be stopped by our running away. I must stay and see what he wants."

"He's filled with so much hate, I'm sure he's not rational. He might shoot you in the back and face the electric chair, just to avenge his brother. You can't deal with a crazed man. We've got to get away."

"Then I could never live with myself. I'm a man and I got to face this situation. I have a pistol I haven't used in many years. I used to be pretty good with a pistol. Think I'll get it and see if it still works. If it does, I'll carry it in my pocket."

"Men are so stubborn. Please reconsider. I'm so frightened. Doesn't that mean a thing to you?"

"You mean the world to me, and I wouldn't do anything to hurt you. Don't you see, I have no choice. A determined man can find me wherever I go. A one-legged man is not hard to find."

Clyde found his pistol and, after buying a box of bullets, did some target practice with it. He was still a good shot. He loaded the gun, and stuck it in his jacket pocket. It was small enough that it hardly made a bulge. His eyes constantly searched the area into which he was walking, and he moved the desk in his office so that he always faced the door.

To the bookkeeper, he said, "Do you know Cedric Murphy?"

"Can't say I actually know him. I know who he is. I also know he comes into Matewan usually once every year. He hangs out at the bar, and tells people that he's going to get the guy who killed his brother, Avery. People laugh at him and ask him if he intends to shoot the ghost of Sid Hatfield. He curses them and says Sid didn't do it, that some bastard on the mountain did it. People don't pay much attention to him. Think he's crazy. Why do you ask about him?"

"He came to see me and more or less threatened me. So I got to watch out for him."

In May, when the weather got warm and the trees were leafing, Clyde thought less and less about Cedric Murphy. One day, because the weather was so beautiful, he walked the half-mile to work, despite the prosthesis and the cane he always carried when not inside a building. He felt he had to use that leg as much as possible. Besides, he liked the warm greetings he got from people along the way, especially when he was walking home. "Hello, Mr. Fuller." "Good afternoon, Mr. Fuller." "Nice to see you, Mr. Fuller."

Clyde smiled and called the names of those he knew. Besides the pleasantries, Clyde was also pleased that he was able to wear a suit and tie, and shiny black shoes, to his new job. He walked upright, his head held high, and with a smile for those he met.

That evening, a man seemed to be rushing to meet him. "Please, Mr. Fuller, don't go any closer to the bar," the man said. "Cedric Murphy is there with a gun. He's crazy drunk. Says he's going to kill you because you killed his brother, Avery. He don't make no sense."

"Calm down, Carl," Clyde said, as he stopped to talk with the man. "What's this about Cedric Murphy?"

"He's in the bar looking for you to come by. He has a gun and says he's going to kill you. I tell you, he's crazy drunk. Can't hardly stand up. Please go back to your office and let me see if I can get a car to take you home. Then I'll see if I can find the police chief."

"You say he's really drunk, eh? Then I better face him. If I run now, then we'd be putting off what must happen some day. I've just got to go, Carl, but you can run over to the chief's office and see if he's in."

Clyde reached in his pocket and fingered the pistol there and began a slow cautious walk down the road toward the bar. He put the cane in his left hand and gripped the gun in his pocket with his right hand. About seventy-five feet from the saloon, the door suddenly opened and Cedric emerged, staggering unsteadily, with a pistol in his hand. Clyde dropped his cane and balanced himself as best he could, as he pulled his gun from the jacket pocket.

Swaying to brace himself, Cedric raised his gun and fired, hitting Clyde in the stomach. He aimed again, and Clyde heard the bullet whiz by his ear. He prepared to shoot again, but by now Clyde was carefully aiming his pistol and fired. Clyde's bullet hit Cedric in the chest, and Cedric's third shot tore into the pavement as the big man pitched head forward onto the road.

The chief of police, whose office was only two doors from the bar, walked out onto the porch as Cedric fired his first shot. As Cedric fell, Clyde dropped his gun and sank slowly to the ground. The chief ran toward Clyde, yelling for someone to find Amy, the only nurse in town. Clyde was barely conscious and bleeding badly under his belt on the left side. Amy, who worked in the store, came immediately and was able to slow, but not stop, the bleeding.

"Mark," she said to the chief, "I don't know what's causing the bleeding, but I know that we must get him to the hospital in Logan as quickly as possible."

"I agree. I'll run over to Whipple's place and get his ambulance and drive him myself. You can ride in back and help Mr. Fuller any way you can."

Mark ran two hundred feet to Whipple's Funeral Home and got the ambulance, placed Clyde on the gurney, placed Cedric on the floor beside him, and raced the thirty miles to Logan.

Watching Cedric fall was the last thing Clyde remembered before coming to in the hospital in Logan. Slowly he opened his eyes and said, "Angel?"

"Yes. I'm right here. The doctor said you'll be all right in a couple of weeks. I've been so worried."

"What happened?"

"You were shot by Cedric Murphy. He was drunk. Ran out of the bar and shot you in the presence of many witnesses. He fired three shots at you, but missed all vital organs. Apparently, he was too drunk to shoot straight. You shot him in the chest and he's not expected to live. The county prosecutor has said that if he lives he will be charged with attempted murder, but the prosecutor also wants to talk with you. The doctor said he could see you probably tomorrow, or the next day. How do you feel?"

"Sore, right here on my left side."

"The bullet entered beside your stomach passed through the bottom of your lung and through a rib. The doctor says you're a lucky man. If Cedric Murphy hadn't been drunk, you'd have been killed."

"It's nice to know that I've had good luck, but it

doesn't feel like it right now. Still, it's good to be alive. I wonder what the prosecutor wants to talk about?"

"I don't know, but you just rest now. The doctor said I could only see you for a few minutes today."

"How long have I been out?"

"About thirty hours. Mostly from shock, I think, but also sedation. It's in the middle of the night now, so I have to run. I've been here since you were shot, and I must go home and get some rest."

"You poor dear. Of course you must go home."

"Good bye, honey. The doctor will tell you all about it when he sees you in the morning."

At eight o'clock the next morning, Clyde recognized Doctor Milton Hedley as he walked into the room, older, and with white hair, and pleasant smile. "I remember you from over twenty years ago when you treated my leg right here in this hospital. How time flies. In case you've forgotten, I'm Clyde Fuller."

"It's not the same hospital," Doctor Hedley said. "We tore that one down and built a new one on its spot. Yes, I do remember you, but not your name. When I examined you I was certain I had seen you before. Then when I saw the missing leg, it all came back to me. I remember telling you that you might eventually lose the leg, so I guessed right on that one . . . That bullet went straight through you, did a little damage but it will heal all right. You're a lucky man . . . As I remember you worked in the mines when I saw you. What are you able to do now?"

"I'm chief advisor to the superintendent for Aggregated Coal Company in Matewan."

"Good. You've made a success of your life. Always glad to hear that . . . . We'll keep you here for at least a week and if things go well you'll be able to go home."

The following day a stranger came to see him, a short man, neatly dressed, with black wavy hair, a straight nose, and an open demeanor on a pleasant face. "Hello. I'm Bert McCoy, the district prosecutor for both Logan and Mingo counties. May I ask you a few questions?"

"Sure."

"Were you and Cedric Murphy enemies?"

"Not that I know of. I first met him a few days ago when he came to my house and sort of threatened me, but I don't know why."

"How did he threaten you?"

"He said he knew me from years ago and knew how to get an eye for an eye. That's really all I can say about it. It was weird."

"It is weird. He boasted publicly that he was going to kill you. Said you killed his brother Avery back in 1920, when there was that famous shootout in Matewan. He said that he's certain you were the young man who had a friend who hit Avery with a tree limb and Avery, in self-defense, killed him. He says that's why you ran off and got a rifle somewhere and shot his brother from up on the mountain. Says he believes a murderer always returns to the scene of the crime. That's why he comes back here regularly. It's truly weird . . ." McCoy watched Clyde closely, apparently looking for any clue that might make sense of Cedric's attack.

"I've gone over the record of that shooting," McCoy said, "and from all I can gather, it appears that Sid Hatfield killed Avery Murphy. At least he said he did, and he was the chief of police. Of course, Cedric and one other witness claimed the shot that killed Avery came from off the mountain. Other witnesses said Hatfield shot first and a couple said Avery shot first. As far as I'm concerned, Sid Hatfield killed Avery and I don't see why you have to be bothered . . ." His eyes were focused on Clyde's face.

"The only thing that would foul this case up would be if you confessed that you shot Avery from the mountain. Even so, we wouldn't be able to prove that it was your shot that killed him. If you said you killed him, we'd simply have to leave it up to a judge to decide if you did or not. . . ." Clyde remained silent.

"Regardless, that hardly justifies Cedric's attempted murder. I'm just pleased that you have said you didn't know what Cedric was talking about. Makes my case easier. We'll charge him with attempted murder, if he recovers. He must have been possessed and couldn't get the killing out of his mind and decided you fit his image of what he wanted to believe . . ." Clyde waited for him to continue.

"One other thing. You were carrying a concealed weapon without a permit. That's a misdemeanor. Still, I'm not going to charge you with it. As I see it, a judge and jury are likely to agree that you had reason to suspect your life was in danger, and you are alive simply because you decided to protect yourself. You might even argue that since Cedric was already in town, you didn't have time to get a permit. No sir, as I see it I couldn't win a case against you for carrying a gun. So I won't press charges."

"Thank you. It'll be good to get all this behind me."

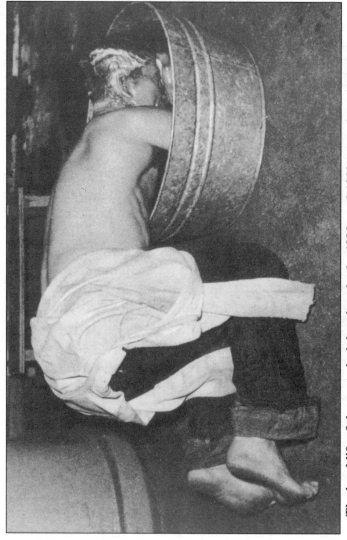

The hard life of the west virginia miner in the 1920s and 1930s sometimes included a primitive bath at the end of the work day. (Courtesy Farm Security Administration)

"I'm just glad to be able to talk with you. As I said, you've made my case easier by saying you don't even know what Cedric was raving about. Good-bye."

"Good-bye. Send my wife in if she's out there."

Angel arrived within a minute. She kissed him, being careful not to squeeze him. "I'm so happy. I talked with the prosecutor and he said that he knows that Cedric shot the wrong man. That Sid Hatfield shot Avery. He even suspects that Cedric might have been the man who shot Hatfield in the back the following year when he was entering the courthouse in Welch. In any case, I think the past is now buried. We can live without any further worry."

Bert McCoy, the prosecutor, came back into the room. "Sorry to bother you again, but I thought you ought to know that Cedric Murphy died awhile ago."

After McCoy left, Clyde turned again to Angel. "I guess it's working out for us. I will always know that I shot Avery and possibly killed him, yet the prosecutor hinted that even if I was to confess it, there are not sufficient grounds to convict me. I guess I'll have to go through the rest of my life thinking that I'm a murderer and . . . Say, what date is this?"

"Why it's May twenty-third. Why do you ask?"

"That means it was May nineteen when I shot Cedric. That was the exact day in 1920 that I shot Avery. Life sure is funny, ain't, I mean, isn't it? Twenty-three years exactly."

"That certainly is a coincidence. But you don't have to look over your shoulders any more. Your past is truly behind you, and you have become a successful man in coal mining."

"I guess you're right. But after you reach your

goal, it don't . . . I mean doesn't . . . seem that important. Makes me want to establish some new and higher goal. I guess I hafta have a goal to keep going."

"There are many goals available for you. One would be to become the advisor of all Aggregated Coal operations in Mingo County. Another would be to become the superintendent of the entire county, rather than the advisor. You once ran for political office, so maybe you'd like to try that again. With your knowledge of mining, you could aspire to move to Charleston as a vice president of Gerald Patterson's operations. And with your curiosity about so many things, I'm sure that you will not be without goals very long."

"No wonder I love you. You know how to support a man who's trying to make a success out of life. And we'll get to do it together. I do love you more than I can say."

The End

Sources Consulted with Commentary

Richard D. Lunt, 1992. <u>Law and Order vs the Miners: WV 1906 - 1933.</u> Charleston, West Virginia: Applachian Editions.

He is devastating in his descriptions. He said that in 1912, the miners in Kanawa County went on strike. "All of the operators hired Baldwin-Felts armed guards to evict striking miners from company houses" (p. 23). In 1913, the mine operators "ran an armored train called the 'Bull-Moose Special' into the miners' tent colony at Holly Grove. The train was equipped with iron-plate siding and machine guns manned by guards who fired away at the miners' tents, killing one person and injuring one other. The miners retaliated by attacking mine guards at Mucklow. The result was sixteen more dead on both sides. During the third period of martial law [Governor] Glasscock arrested eighty persons, including Mother Jones who had urged the striking miners to defy 'Crystalcock's militia.'" (p. 28).

Lunt mentioned that in 1922, the American Civil Liberties Union investigated Logan County and found it controlled by the mine operators: "In return for his handling of the situation with regard to the unions, the operators have turned over to [Sheriff] Chafin as his share of the arrangements complete political control of the County, the operators furnishing the necessary money to keep the organization going." Chafin even controlled the polling places: "Only such voters are allowed to vote as suit the organization" (pp. 155-56).

Again and again, Lunt cited occasions when the southern operators of West Virginia adamantly refused to have any dealings with organized miners, and on many occasions used the harshest violence against them. The extreme carnage aimed at miners in Mingo and Logan Counties is given in great detail in chapters Three and Four (pp. 92-144). Included are descriptions of the battle of Matewan, May 1920, in which the Chief of Police Sid Hatfield and his men killed 7 of the Baldwin-Felts detectives, while losing the mayor of Matewan and two miners. Hatfield was indicted and faced trial in McDowell County. As Hatfield and his deputy (both unarmed) and their wives, "climbed the courthouse steps, Lively and the other Baldwin-Felts detectives greeted them, drew their guns, and pumped ten rounds into each of the two men, so perforating their bodies that later they could not be embalmed" (p. 99). Also described is the battle of Blair Mountain, August-September 1921, for which the State of West Virginia now has placed an historical marker at the top of Blair Mountain, which is pictured on p. 212.

Former Attorney General of WV, Howard B. Lee, 1969. Bloodletting in Applachia: The Story of West Virginia's Four Major Mine Wars and Other Thrilling Incidents. Morgantown: West Virginia University Press.

He stated that between 1920 and 1925, "no fewer than fifty thousand men, women and children were evicted from their homes in southern West Virginia. They found shelter under cliffs, in tents, and in improvised shacks built by the union. Year after weary year, they lived and starved in these unwholesome surroundings. Malnutrition and unsanitary conditions increased the death rate to appalling figures, especially among children. But there was no relenting by the coal barons. To many of them, the hungry, protesting workers were pariahs, or outcasts, to be starved until hunger forced them to return to the service of their master. In the end, hunger won, and the workers slunk back to the mines, with hearts filled with hate and their minds embittered by the memory of the wrongs they suffered."

David Alan Corbin, 1990. The West Virginia Mine Wars: An Anthology. Charleston, WV: Applachian Editions.

He laments the fact that the coal mine wars were not even mentioned in the history classes he took in the public schools of WV, and likened those "histories" to the "Soviet encyclopedias under Stalin." "The coal company town was a complete system. In addition to owning and controlling all the institutions in the town, coal company rule in southern West Virginia included the company doctor who delivered the babies, the mines in which the children went to work, and the cemeteries where they were eventually buried." (p. 1).

He notes that housing was "slapped up, seldom repainted and allowed to go unrepaired" (p. 8). This book contains chapters detailing hearing before U. S. Senate committees, most deploring company brutality, but at least one defending the rationalization if not the cruelty of the companies. One chapter is entitled, "Private Ownership of Public Officials." Corbin cities statements made by operators admitting that the company gave over $30,000 each year to the sheriff of Logan County. One deputy sheriff said he was paid $175 a month, which put him on the company's payroll: "If a man is fired I give him a notice" (pp. 96-110). Yet another chapter details the so-called treason trials of the miners in Charles Town, WV, in which all defendants were acquitted, partly, one newspaper argued "because no government existed in West Virginia against which treason was possible." Another stated that "Government in West Virginia had broken down, and its power had passed in part to the mine operators." (p. 139). Besides hiring Baldwin-Felts detectives, the companies also supported constabularies, made up of lists provided by the companies, which jailed union men meeting in their offices, so that even the right of free assembly was violated (p. 111). When the governor declared martial law, "it was enforced only against miners' assemblies, commercial and other associations being allowed to meet freely" (p. 111).

Other evidence corroborating the foregoing can be found in the following works:

Cohen, Stan. 1984. King Coal: A pictorial History of West Virginia Coal Mining. Charleston: Pictorial Histories Publishing Company.

Corbin, Alan. 1981 Life, Work, and Rebellion in the Coal Fields; The Southern West Virginia Miners 1880 - 1922. Urbana, IL: University of Illinois Press.

Eller, Ronald D. 1982. Miners, Millhands and Mountaineers: Industrialization of the Appalachian

South. Knoxville: University of Tennessee Press.

Hume, Brit. 1971. Death in the Mines. NY: Grossman.

Jordan, Daniel P. 1977. The Mingo War: Labor Violence in the Southern West Virginia Coal Fields, 1919-1922. Westport, CT: Greenwood Press.

Laslett, John H. M. 1990. The United Mine Workers of America; A Model of Industrial Solidarity? University Park, PA: Pennsylvania State University Press.

Laurie, Clayton D. 1991. "The United States Army and the Return to Normalcy in Labor Dispute Interventions: The Case of the West Virginia Coal Mine Wars, 1920-1921." West Virginia History. Vol. 50.

Mooney, Fred. 1967. Struggle in the Coal Fields: The Autobiography of Fred Mooney, ed. By J. W. Hess. Morgantown, WV: West Virginia University Library.

Phillips, Cabell. 1974. "The West Virginia Mine War." American Heritage. Vol. 25, #5, pp. 58-61, 90-94.

Savage, Lon. 1990. Thunder in the Mountains: The West Virginia Mine War, 1920-1921. Pittsburgh: University of Pittsburgh Press.

Sullivan, Ken, ed. 1991. West Virginia Mine Wars. Charleston, WV: Goldenseal Magazine, 1977-1991.

About the Author

Claude S. Phillips attended the University of Tennessee, where he took a B. A. (1947) and M. A. (1950) in political science and philosophy. In 1954 he took a Ph.D. in political science from Duke University. He has devoted 35 years to teaching, mostly at Western Michigan University in Kalamazoo, Michigan. At that university he was the founding director of the Institute of International and Area Studies and studied at both Osmania University in India and at the University of Ibadan in Nigeria, and later was a visiting professor at the University of Ife in Nigeria. At WMU he won the Distinguished Service Award in 1984. Among his most important publications are the following:

The Development of Nigerian Foreign Policy, 1964, Northwestern University Press.

The African Political Dictionary, 1984. ABC Clio Press.

"The Bilateral Treaty Network of Non-Western States," 1970. In De lege Pactorum, ed. David R. Deener, Duke University Press.

"Nigeria's New Political Institution," 1980. The Journal of African Studies.

"Nigeria and Biafra," 1980. Ethnic Separatism and World Politics, ed. Frederick L. Shiels, University Press of America.

"The Influence of the United States Constitution on Other Countries," 1996. The American Constitution at the End of the Twentieth Century, eds. Ralph Clark Chandler and William A Ritchie. New Issues Press.

The author posed before the New River Gorge in 2002.